DV BERKOM

A LEINE BASSO THRILLER

THE BODY MARKET

The Body Market

A Leine Basso Thriller
Copyright © 2015 by D.V. Berkom
Published by

First print edition January 2015
All rights reserved.
ISBN-13: 978-0692495780
Cover art by Deranged Doctor Design

***Join my Readers' List** to be the first to find out about new releases and exclusive, subscriber-only special offers:

(See back of this book for details.)

The Body Market

A retired assassin is called in when a celebration south of the border turns into a nightmare.

Everything's for sale...

Former assassin **Leine Basso** is hired by a wealthy Beverly Hills power couple to find their missing daughter, Elise, who was last seen partying with her boyfriend at a club in Tijuana. At first, police believe the two teenagers are the victims of a carjacking. But when Leine finds their missing vehicle with the boyfriend's mutilated body inside, and the local cartel warns her away, she knows if Elise isn't already dead, she will be soon, or worse.

In the lethal world of organized crime, there's always a worse.

As Leine races to uncover the reason behind Elise Bennett's disappearance, she must also battle the powerful interests fighting to keep her from the truth.

1

LEINE BASSO CROUCHED in the shadows next to the hulking metal shipping container. The odor of oil mixed with hydraulic fluid and diesel clashed with the briny sea air. Bright spotlights pierced the darkness casting a harsh yellow hue over the container yard. Leine checked her watch: eleven o'clock. Only three hours before the *China Blue Star* was scheduled to leave port for Hong Kong.

Three hours to find one shipping container in a massive sea of identical containers.

Lou paid off the security guard, which gave Leine only a short window to find the container before he released the dogs. She adjusted the fit of the pack, tightening the straps so it molded to her body. She'd pared down the equipment as much as she could, but it was never enough.

C'mon, Lou. Give me some good news.

She closed her eyes and imagined the young face in the photograph. A lead from the trafficker's hard drive had led her to a seaport currently run by cartel thugs on the west coast of Mexico. She hoped she wasn't too late.

Three hours.

"Leine." Lou's voice came over the wireless earpiece.

"I'm here," she replied.

"Left, three aisles, number fourteen-thirty-four-twelve."

"Got it." Gun drawn and keeping to the shadows, Leine moved along first one aisle, then another, searching for shipping container 143412.

There it is.

Stacked three high, the 40 foot-long steel boxes loomed above her. The one she was looking for was stacked 40 feet in the air on top of two other boxes. She moved to the end of the bottom container and reached for a handhold. Before she could grab the next one, someone seized her pack and yanked her off, slamming her back-first into the pavement. Her nine millimeter skittered across the asphalt, disappearing in the darkness between two containers. The impact took her breath away, the pain from a recent rib injury spiking through her like a spear.

Leine rolled, narrowly missing a kick to the face. She grabbed her attacker's foot and gave it a vicious twist. The assailant corkscrewed and landed on his side with a grunt.

Ignoring the deep ache in her side and with adrenaline fueling her, she sprang to her feet and kicked the gun from his hand. The weapon pinged off the side of the container and bounced into the shadows, out of sight. Before she could get clear, he scissored his legs and caught her at the knees. She sprawled forward.

This time she couldn't ignore the pain.

Winded, she slid a knife free from the sheath attached to her leg. She pushed off the ground, rolling to a crouch as her opponent climbed to his feet, a knife in his hand. He lunged forward. Leine parried with a thrust to his throat. At the last second, he ducked.

They circled each other like roosters in a cockfight, both acutely aware of the weapon in their opponent's grip. Leine feinted left and rushed forward, scoring a direct hit on the man's shoulder, slicing through the black fabric of his shirt and drawing blood. He pivoted and came at her from the side but she rotated her torso, narrowly missing a slash to her kidney. She turned to face him as he came at her again. At the last second she stepped wide, allowing him to slip past her. Using his own momentum, she shoved him forward. He stumbled a few steps, recovered, and spun to face her.

Leine swept her arm forward in an arc and released the knife. The blade buried itself in his eye socket, a scream dying in his throat as his hand flew reflexively to his face. He collapsed to the ground as he exhaled his last breath.

"Leine. What's going on? Are you okay?" Usually unflappable, the sharpness in Lou's voice betrayed his concern, even over the radio.

"I'm fine." Her hand supporting her now-throbbing rib, she leaned over the body with a grimace and extracted the knife, wiping the blade on the dead man's shirt. The tattoos on his forearm suggested cartel affiliation. Leine doubted he was working alone. "Just some unexpected company."

"Did you find the container?"

Leine scanned the metal boxes above her.

"Got it."

"I don't have to tell you to be careful, right?"

"No, but it's nice to know you care."

Leine grabbed the man's legs and gritted her teeth as she dragged the body into the dark gap between containers. She removed his transmitter, turned off the voice activation, and slid on the earpiece. She didn't want the next gunman to come along and sound the alarm before she had a chance to subdue him. After she retrieved the weapons she checked to see that the body couldn't be observed from the aisle. Satisfied, she walked back to container 143412.

With a quick glance to be sure the fight hadn't attracted company, she latched onto a vertical handle at the end of the first container, wedged her toe onto a hinge, and began to climb.

As she was preparing to hoist herself up and over the top of the container, she heard movement below her and froze.

"Where are you?" the voice muttered in Spanish, clear enough for Leine to hear through the transmitter.

She craned her neck, trying to catch a glimpse of the man below her. Compact in bearing and dressed in black like the man she'd just killed, instead of a knife he carried a modified submachine gun.

"Answer me," he snapped into his earpiece. When he received no reply, the man stepped over the smear of blood left by his compatriot. It looked like he might continue on when he abruptly stopped. Leine held her breath. If he glanced down, he'd notice the blood. With her left foot wedged onto the barest of toeholds and gripping the top of the container with her left hand, Leine slid her gun out of its holster, ready to fire—something she was loath to do since the sound would bring others.

The man pivoted 180 degrees, scanning the area, his gun in front of him. Leine ignored the muscles screaming in her left hand as the metal cut into her flesh.

He stood still for another moment, observing his surroundings. After a few seconds, he touched his earpiece.

"He's not here." The person at the other end acknowledged the transmission. "I'll keep looking," the gunman said as he moved out of Leine's line of sight.

She released her breath in a quiet sigh and slid the gun back into her shoulder holster. With her right hand now free, she grabbed onto the top of the container, relieving her left hand. She waited a couple of beats to make sure the gunman was clear and then pulled herself up and over.

The higher vantage point worked well to monitor the yard.

When the other gunman had traveled far enough that he wouldn't hear her, Leine shrugged out of her pack and set it aside. She stretched flat onto her belly and put her ear to the container. There was no discernible movement inside.

That didn't mean much.

"I'm on the roof," she said in a low voice.

"Hear anything?" Lou asked.

"No."

Leine unzipped the main compartment of the bag and pulled out a battery pack and a mini plasma cutter and placed them on the roof beside her. Next, she reached into another compartment for a fiber optic night vision camera and a collapsible light hood.

She deployed the hood and marked the area to be cut, then flipped the plasma cutter's switch to on and adjusted the amps. Angling the tip as she cut, the small hole took only a few minutes. Turning off the cutter, she stowed it back inside the pack along with the hood.

Alert for movement on the ground below her, she activated the camera and fed the probe through the hole, watching the video feed on the small LCD monitor as she did. At first, all she could make out were the metal ribs of the container. She fed the line further into the dark interior and a moment later the camera swept past an object. Leine pulled up on the scope to get a better look. The object moved. Two tiny light circles appeared and blinked off and on.

As she angled the camera for a better view, she realized she was looking at a dark-haired girl huddled in the corner, her eyes glowing dots in the camera's lens. Leine pulled back for a wider shot. Dozens of bodies came into focus, placed side by side on the floor of the container with no room between them. Most were lying prone—except for the young girl.

"I've got something," Leine said into the mic.

Lou let out a sigh as though he'd been holding his breath.

Another girl, this one with light-colored hair, sat up and looked first at the girl in the corner and then at the camera.

Leine's heart beat faster. From what she could tell, she matched the picture.

Amy.

"Is she there?" Lou's clipped tone gave away his anxiety.

"Yeah. I think so. And she's not alone."

Leine relaxed her shoulders, relief flooding through her.

"Let's get them out of here, Lou."

2

———

ELISE WAVED A fistful of pesos at the bartender in an attempt to flag him down. She stood her ground as the press of spring-breakers surged against her, pushing her into the crowded, mile-long chrome bar. The oppressive heat from the packed club combined with the pulsating music from the nearby speakers reminded Elise of an old movie from the seventies she'd seen a few nights before, and not in a good way. The bartender raced past, his dark eyes barely registering her.

Earlier, when Josh had been with her, the bartender had gushed over them both. That was over two hours ago. The bar wasn't as busy then. With an impatient sigh, she lowered her arm. Elise was not used to being ignored when money was involved. In her world, currency was king. Both her parents ran with an elite crowd even for Angelenos—the A-Listers of the financial world. Her father was the head of a thriving biotech company about to go public, and her mother worked as a financial consultant, dealing primarily in hedge fund management. Both ultra-busy professionals, neither had time to spend with their seventeen-year-old daughter. Elise preferred it that way. If she needed an adult, which was rare, she went to the house-keeper, Teuta, a grandmotherly woman from some Eastern European country Elise had never heard of.

"I'll only be gone five minutes," Josh, her date for the evening had said, and disappeared with some guy he'd just met at the bar. That had been two hours ago. Elise was now officially bored.

And pissed.

Giving up on getting a drink within the next millennium, she shoved the money back in her Louis Vuitton clutch and squeezed past the crush of wasted partiers. Teuta would be horrified to know her little Eliseka had crossed the border from Southern California into Mexico with a boy she hardly knew, ending the evening alone at a bar in Tijuana.

Unable to locate Josh anywhere in the club, Elise made her way to the exit, pushing disgustedly at the ogling drunks who staggered up to her. Apparently they'd never seen a blonde wearing a low-cut, sparkly dress and five-inch Louboutin heels.

So juvenile, she thought.

Outside, the heat from the unseasonably hot spring day radiated off the sidewalk into the evening air and mixed with the nauseating smell of car fumes and cigarettes. Brash neon from the row of nightclubs lit the street as though it were daylight, casting everyone around her in a sickly kaleidoscopic glow. People milled past, laughing as they hurried to the next bar. Her anger growing, Elise dug her phone out of her purse and called her best friend, Brittany.

"Hey—what's up?"

Elise plugged an ear, unable to hear over the music blasting from the club behind her.

"Josh left me at the bar."

"Seriously? He is so dead."

"Yeah. Listen. Can you come and pick me up?"

"Of course, sweetie. I can be at the border in a couple of hours."

"Sorry. Didn't mean to ruin your Saturday night."

"Believe me, you didn't ruin it. I'm happy to get out of town. There's *nothing* going on."

Elise ended the call, slipped the phone back into her purse, and turned to wave down a taxi. It wasn't far to where she was going to meet her friend, but Elise didn't feel like walking and possibly breaking a heel. A cab immediately pulled to the curb and Elise walked over to the driver.

"How much to the border?" she asked.

The cab driver scanned her from head to toe and back again, his leer punctuated by a missing front tooth.

"For you, señorita, almost free."

Elise rolled her eyes. She turned and walked away, ignoring the slow crawl of the taxi behind her. She'd find another, more respectful driver.

"Come on, *chica*. I didn't mean anything by it."

Elise kept walking. The cab driver attempted to get her attention, but when he saw it wasn't working, sped past her.

"Elise! Wait."

Josh hurried toward her through the crowd, an apologetic smile on his face. She crossed her arms and glared at him.

"Babe, I'm so sorry. Please don't be mad. The guy had this killer weed, and I lost track of time and…"

"Are you kidding me? You left me alone in that club for two hours, Josh. *Two hours.* What the hell?"

Josh stepped closer to Elise, sliding his hand along her bare arm. The casual, thrown together look of his über-expensive T-shirt and jeans, along with the perfectly tousled, sun-kissed hair reminded her of a model she'd seen in a magazine advertising men's cologne.

"Aw, come on, babe. Don't be like that. I'll make it up to you."

His grin brought out the dimples in his cheeks and Elise tried hard to suppress a smile. He was still the hottest guy she knew. So what if he was a little forgetful? It was probably the weed.

"See? I made you smile. I know you love me." Josh grinned, hugging Elise with one arm as he turned them around and headed in the opposite direction.

"Wait." Elise stopped. "Brittany's supposed to pick me up."

"So text her and tell her not to come. The guy told me about a sick party near Rosarito. Some movie star rented a house outside of town and is having an all-weekend bash. There's a band."

"Like who?" Elise wasn't impressed by most celebrities. Her mother did a lot of business with A-Listers in the film world, too. She couldn't think of many she'd go out of her way to meet.

"He didn't say who the actor was, but he told me Swarm of Nihilists is going to be there all weekend!" Josh did the Nihilist Salute fist pump. Elise almost rolled her eyes again. Josh was heavy into S.O.N.

"Fine. But can we leave if it's bullshit? I mean, how do you know this guy?"

Josh's earnest expression almost made her laugh. "He's a roadie for the Nihilists. He totally knows his shit."

Elise shook her head but after a few minutes of cajoling finally relented to Josh's pleas. They walked to where he had parked the Porsche his dad had given him as an early graduation present and were soon headed out of the city center toward the beach town of Rosarito. Elise texted Brittany, telling her to cancel her plans to come and get her.

r u sure? i can b there in 2 hrs, Brittany answered. *Josh is hot, but how well do u really know him?*

i'm sure. ty 4 worrying, she replied. Elise slipped the phone back in her purse. She knew all she needed to about Josh. He came from a wealthy family, was gorgeous, and drove an awesome car. Plus, he hadn't really abandoned her at the club. So what if she had to go to some party where she didn't know anybody? If Swarm of Nihilists actually turned out to be there she'd have a great story to tell her friends Monday morning during first period.

Josh wove through the back streets as though he knew where he was going. Elise relaxed and watched as they passed darkened dentists' offices and brightly lit neighborhood groceries. Locals had gathered near a popular *taqueria* with *banda* music blaring from a loudspeaker. Drunk high school and college kids crawled the alleys for forbidden excitement, all against a backdrop of colorful billboards that screamed cheap pharmaceuticals and even cheaper attorneys. The neighborhood thinned as they drove past the turnoff to the main freeway.

"Where are you going? Isn't that the way to the toll road?" Elise asked, looking behind them.

He reached inside his pocket and pulled out a book of matches. "The guy wrote down how to get there on the back of this." He handed her the directions. Elise turned on the overhead light to read them.

"He called it the library or something."

"You mean *libre*? The free road?" Elise shook her head. "You're not seriously trying to get out of paying the toll. What is it, like two bucks?"

"No, of course not." Josh frowned in irritation. "It's just that he said it'd be easier to find the house if we went this way."

"Who was this guy again?"

Earlier in the evening, the man with the Russian accent had started a conversation with Josh while they were at the bar waiting for drinks and had offered to get both Elise and him high. Elise had declined.

"A friend."

"A friend. And you've known him how long?"

Josh gave her a look. "You sound like my mom. Don't worry. It'll be fine. We're gonna see Swarm of Nihilists!"

With a resigned sigh, Elise leaned her head back and closed her eyes. The warm night air drifting through the window felt so much better than being inside the hot, stuffy bar. Thoughts of what she was going to wear to her friend Nicole's big party the next weekend filled her mind. She wasn't sure she wanted to invite Josh. She'd have to see who else was available. They'd look good together though, she'd give him that.

A few miles later, Josh had Elise read the directions out loud. He found the street and turned right, heading west along a gravel road. The car began to climb and they left the lights of the city below them.

"You're sure you know where you're going, right?" Elise asked, wondering why there weren't any streetlights.

"Yeah. He said it would look like we were heading nowhere but to just keep going to the top of the hill."

The road grew steeper and Josh shifted into second gear to get traction. Just as Elise was going to ask him to take her back, a dramatic white arch with black lettering loomed in the darkness before them.

"What does it say?" Josh asked.

Elise glanced at the lettering on the stucco façade as they passed underneath.

"Vista del Mar."

"That's it. He said it would be a little ways past that, and we'd see the house in front of us."

They continued along the gravel road. Hulking concrete skeletons of unfinished homes stood as brooding sentries on each side.

"Must be a really new development," Josh said, by way of explanation. Elise wasn't so sure. There were no building materials lying next to the houses, and she didn't see any heavy equipment.

"Where are the streetlights? You'd think there'd be something, right?"

Josh shrugged. "Who knows? Maybe that's the reason they decided to have the party here—less people, less hassle. Look —" Josh pointed through the windshield. "You can see the lights of Rosarito."

Elise's gaze followed his outstretched arm as he pointed at the bright lights of the seaside town far below them. She rummaged inside her purse for her phone as they drove further along the darkened street. She brought up the GPS and squinted at the lit LED screen, trying to figure out where they had ended up.

They turned a corner and Josh stopped the car. "What the fuck."

Elise looked up. The Porsche's headlights spilled across the road and onto an oversized, black SUV parked in front of them, blocking the way. Two flares burned bright orange in the expanse between the two vehicles. A muscular man with blond hair leaned against the truck, arms crossed, smoking a cigarette.

Confused, she turned to Josh. "What's going on?"

"I don't know."

"That isn't the guy from the bar, is it?"

Josh shook his head. "Uh-uh." He made to get out of the car, but she grabbed his arm.

"Don't. What if he wants to rob us?" Elise had heard stories about carjackings and highway robbery near the border. From what her friends had told her, those kinds of things weren't supposed to happen between Tijuana and Rosarito.

"He won't get much. I blew most of my money at the bar."

"Yeah, but you're driving an expensive car. He could steal it, and then we'd have to wait out here until someone comes to get us or walk all the way back." Elise glanced out her window at the deserted buildings nearby and shivered.

"Shit. I never thought of that." With a quick look behind them, Josh seized the gearshift and slammed the car into reverse. Elise braced her feet against the floor and gripped the armrest as Josh backed away, the tires spitting rocks.

Elise twisted in her seat to watch through the rear window. A second SUV came out of nowhere, bounced onto the road behind them, and blocked their escape. Elise screamed. Josh braked hard and the Porsche skidded to a stop.

"What should we do?" Elise's panicked voice sounded overly loud in the small space. She raised her window and locked her door. Josh did the same.

"*Shit*. I can't give them the car. My dad just gave it to me. He's gonna be so pissed." The whites of his eyes glistened in the glow from the dash. "What should I do?"

He's scared to death, she thought. Cold dread crept its way up her spine as she recalled the horror stories she'd read online. What if they figured out they both were from wealthy families? It wouldn't be hard, not with the kind of car they were in, or with what they were wearing. She glanced at Josh's expensive wristwatch, worth enough to feed a developing nation, and then at her shoes. The diamond chips on the heels twinkled in the darkness. What if they kidnapped them both and held them for ransom?

Jesus, Elise thought, her heart racing. *My parents don't even answer their phones unless it's business. They won't know what happened to me until it's too late.*

"Did you take a wrong turn?"

Josh shook his head. "I'm sure it was the right one. Maybe they just want us to turn around."

"I don't think so, Josh." A chilling thought flitted through Elise's mind. "The guy at the bar. He did this, didn't he? He saw your watch, or maybe he even knew what you were driving and decided to make some easy money."

Josh shook his head. "No. It's not like that, Lise. He was totally cool." His voice didn't sound as confident as it had just a short time ago. A sheen of sweat formed on his forehead.

The man with the cigarette leaned down and picked something up off the ground. He flicked the butt away before he ambled over to the driver's side and tapped on the window. Josh stared straight ahead, his fingers clamped to the steering wheel.

"Get out," the man said, motioning at the door.

"Th-this isn't my car."

Josh's pleading tone grated on Elise's nerves. So not the guy she thought he was.

The man smiled benignly and stepped back. He raised his arms and something hard came crashing down across the windshield, buckling the glass. Josh jumped at the same time Elise screamed.

The man slammed the tire iron against the window again and again, methodically smashing through the safety glass. Then he moved near the front of the car and smashed the left headlight.

"Stop—!" Josh shouted, his voice a double octave higher than normal. "Not the *car*."

The man stopped and walked back to Josh's window. He leaned against the fender and stared at him through the glass.

"Open the door." His muffled voice and bemused smile didn't lessen the impact of his demand. Josh was shaking, and his hands looked like they were going to choke the life out of the steering wheel. When he didn't respond, the man went to work on the side mirror.

At that moment, a second man appeared at Elise's window and she screamed. She closed her eyes and turned away, hunching her shoulders, afraid to look directly at the man standing next to her and wincing at each blow of the tire iron.

The man outside her window tapped again, more insistently this time. Her breath now coming in short bursts, Elise opened her eyes to slits and slowly turned her head, hoping that the scene before her could be controlled by what she did or didn't allow herself to see.

Her stomach lurched at the sight of a gun against the window. She closed her eyes again and shook her head.

Tap, tap, tap. Hot tears spilled down her cheeks as Elise gripped her knees to control her shaking hands.

"Get out of the car. Now." The man's menacing tone made it clear it wasn't a request.

"We'd better do as they say, Lise." Near tears and trembling, Josh reached for the door.

"No, Josh. *Don't.*"

But it was too late. He opened the door and climbed out. The first man seized him by the arm and shoved him away from the car and onto his knees, aiming a gun at his head. With the weapon still trained on Josh, he reached inside the car and unlocked Elise's door.

"No!" Elise screamed as the second man wrenched the door open, grabbed her by the hair, and yanked her out of the car. She landed hard on the gravel beside the Porsche. A sharp pain lanced down her leg, followed by the warm, sticky-wetness of blood.

Elise didn't have time to gain her feet before the man grabbed her around the waist and lifted her off the ground. She kicked and squirmed and tried to rake his face with her nails as he dragged her away from the car, losing one of her shoes in the process, but the man never faltered. The moment before he shoved her into the back of the open SUV, Elise managed to twist around and look back at Josh.

Shoulders shaking and head bowed, his wristwatch glinted in the moonlight. A light breeze ruffled his hair.

"Take my car. I promise I won't report it if you let me go," he pleaded with the man in front of him.

"I thought you said it wasn't your car," the man replied with a smile as he moved behind him.

"I lied. I'm scared. Please don't kill me. I—I'm only eighteen." Sobbing now, Josh put his hands up as though they were playing a game and it was time to quit. Elise held her breath. Overwhelming fear tightened her chest and spread to her throat, the nausea in her stomach gaining momentum.

Before she could utter a sound, the man aimed the gun at the back of Josh's head.

And fired.

3

EINE BASSO LANDED her board with an impressive splash and moved smoothly into shore, turning to watch Santiago Jensen as he caught air and completed a 360-degree rotation. The homicide detective's red and white kite danced as he landed on a wave and then launched back into the air where he pulled out another turn before heading down-wind. Leine marveled at how quickly he caught on to kite surfing, although she shouldn't have been surprised. He'd shown an aptitude for learning whatever he put his mind to.

Especially if he found the activity a challenge. He approached everything he did the same way he attacked a new murder case: like a Rottweiler with a meaty bone, not letting go until he'd sucked out the last of the marrow.

The sun dipped low on the horizon in another perfect, golden, Southern California sunset. Leine had stripped down from her wetsuit to her bikini and put the equipment away by the time Santiago, or Santa as she referred to him, joined her. The nickname fit, as far as she was concerned. Not because he looked like the jolly old elf. Far from it. It was more that Leine thought of Santa as a gift she never thought she'd get to open.

Since she had started working for Stop Human Enslavement Now, better known as SHEN, Santa's partner, Don Putnam, had given his blessing to their relationship—with one caveat. Putz said he'd be happy to take Leine on, former assassin or not, if there was even the whisper of a chance that she'd leave Santa with a broken heart.

Fat chance, she thought. Leine was done. Stick-a-fork-in-her done. She'd be able to betray Santa about as easily as she'd be able to think without a brain.

She smiled at his intense green eyes, framed by the slicked-back, dark hair and deep tan, all blending seamlessly with the black neoprene wetsuit. The body-hugging material contoured the hard, muscular lines of his torso, and Leine briefly wondered if they might skip dinner altogether.

"Is this a perfect day or what?" Santa's rich voice carried easily over the cross-shore breeze—textbook conditions for kite surfing. He dropped his board on the sand and opened the valves on his kite, deflating the struts.

"No kidding," she said, pulling her wet hair back and securing it with a couple of bobby pins. "I saw you hot-dogging it out there. What are you trying to do, show me up?"

Santiago chuckled and shook his head, sending a shower of salt water over Leine.

"Never," he said, and pushed her onto her back, capturing her arms above her head as he leaned in for a kiss. His lips were warm and salty, and Leine couldn't get enough, especially now that they were free to be together. Being a suspect in a triple homicide tended to put a dent in your love life when the person you wanted to be with was a detective with the LAPD's Robbery-Homicide Division.

Santa deepened the kiss, proof of his affection growing obvious through the wetsuit. Leine broke the lip lock and before he could stop her, flipped him onto his back, straddled his hips, and grinned. Desire flared in his eyes and he slid his hands along her legs.

"Not so fast, cowboy." Leine stopped him before he went somewhere she'd have a hard time saying no to and climbed to her feet. "We're still in public, and I'm not interested in selling tickets." Santa grinned as he sat up and lowered his gaze, licking his lips.

"Yes, you can have some when we get back to your place. As long as you behave like a gentleman," she added, stepping back as he reached for her again. With a dramatic sigh, he got to his feet. He took a step closer and leaned in. Leine had to restrain herself from ripping off his wetsuit.

"What is it that makes me *crave* you?" His warm breath skated across her cheek.

Leine closed her eyes, reveling in the deliciously wicked sensations streaming through her, setting her skin ablaze with every nerve strung tight. He smelled of ocean and sweat and promise.

Not since Carlos had she felt this alive, this desirable. But Carlos had been an anomaly, or so she'd thought. She'd ended her career as an assassin because of a monstrous betrayal by her recently deceased boss, Eric, and had avoided caring for anyone except her daughter, April.

Not now. She couldn't break free from Santa even if she wanted to. It had been worse than torture not being able to touch him, to be with him. As soon as she was cleared of the murder charges they became inseparable.

Santa nuzzled her neck and, with a teasing smile, walked to his equipment and proceeded to put it away. Leine fanned herself and checked her watch. Barring bad traffic, they could be back at his place in about thirty minutes. Dinner could wait.

Luck was with them, and they made it back to Santa's in just under thirty-five minutes. Santa carried Leine's board to her car and stashed his in a locker provided by the building. They took the elevator from the garage to his apartment and barely made it through the front door before both shimmied out of their clothes, leaving them in a heap on the entry floor.

Leine smiled as he took her by the hand and led her into the bedroom. It always amazed her how perfectly their bodies fit together, as though each had been made for the other. It also amazed her that she was with him. Santa was a man she could respect. He was clear and levelheaded except when it came to Leine, and she was okay with that. She felt the same about him.

After they made love, they prowled the kitchen hunting for something to make for dinner. Santa was strangely quiet. Curious as to what he was thinking so hard about but respecting his pensive mood, Leine pulled fresh pasta from the fridge and grabbed a pot, which she filled with water and a little olive oil. She set the pot on the stove and lit the burner, adding a pinch of salt. Santa poured them each a measure of red wine. They touched glasses and Leine took a sip, enjoying the peppery Zinfandel as it slid down her throat.

"What?" she asked. She knew his moods. Admittedly, he didn't have many. He was straight-forward and direct, and she was rarely in doubt about his feelings. It was such a refreshing change from her ex-husband, Frank, who kept most things to himself. She'd had enough subterfuge and deception from both him and her old life to last an eternity.

Santa watched her intently, as though deciding whether to cop to what he was thinking. Leine waited patiently, swirling the wine in her glass.

He cleared his throat and set his glass on the counter. "I'm a little rusty at this..." he began.

The water began to boil in the pot and Leine moved to the stove and opened the package of pasta. She dropped the fettuccine in and turned to face him.

Oh shit. Is he going to propose? Leine's heart rate kicked up and she had to fight the urge to run. *Please, oh please don't. You're going to wreck a great thing, Santa.* Marriage hadn't worked out well for her the one time she'd tried it, and she had no desire to repeat the nightmare. People changed when things were legally binding. She'd sworn to herself she'd never attempt it again.

With increasing dread, she sucked it up and pasted a smile on her face, hoping against hope she was wrong.

"We've barely spent a free minute apart these past couple of months." He picked up his glass, took a sip of wine, set it down. "If you're not staying here, we're at your place."

Oh, no. Don't, Santa. Please. What the hell do I say?

He held her eyes, his gaze intense. She couldn't have looked away if she tried.

"I've never felt this way about anyone, Leine. Not my ex-wife, not any of the badge bunnies I dated before I met you—no one. What I'm trying to say is," He took another drink, this one quite a bit larger than the last.

Leine couldn't stand it any longer. "Santa, if you're about to do what I think you are, don't. Just don't. We've got such a great thing going here, why muck it up with legalities? We've both tried it before and came out different people on the other end. Do you really want to risk all that happening again?"

Santa's puzzled expression morphed into one of disbelief. He cocked his head to the side and the corner of his mouth quirked up in a half-smile. "Did you think I was going to ask you to marry me?"

"I—uh, well, weren't you?" Leine's cheeks burned. *Shit, Leine. You'll never hear the end of this.*

Santa's half smile turned into a full-on grin. Leine debated whether to leave while she was still behind.

"Not exactly, although that was an interesting response."

"Hold on." She set her wine on the counter and opened the

oven door. "I'm just going to stick my head in here for a minute..."

Chuckling, he reached past her and fished for something in a drawer. He found what he was looking for and held it up. "I was going to ask if you'd like to move some of your things in here," he said, and placed a key in her hand.

Leine looked at the key, the embarrassment of the misunderstanding momentarily forgotten. "You do know I don't need a key to get into the apartment, right? The locks on your door aren't much of a deterrent."

Santa rolled his eyes.

"Yes, of course I know that." He crossed his arms. "Consider it symbolic. Instead of breaking and entering, from now on you get to come and go legally."

"Don't you think this is a little soon?" She reached for his hand and placed the key on his palm, closing his fingers over it. "I mean, the next thing you're going to do is ask me to move in."

Santa laid the key on the counter and reached for his glass. "Would that be so bad?"

"Not bad. Just premature. We've talked about this already. Like I said when I thought you were going for the M word—why muck up a good thing?" Leine was determined not to rush into serious with him. Things had been gliding along smoothly, and she was reluctant to change anything. For the first time in a long time Leine was happy. Besides, she hadn't been the best judge of men in her life.

Santa sighed. "Okay, but I'm going to keep coming at you until you can no longer resist my superior charms."

Leine smiled and moved closer, trailing her hand down his stomach and coming to rest at a sensitive point.

"Promises, promises..."

4

———

T HE SUV RACED along the gravel road, jarring Elise's head into her spine. She braced herself against the rear wheel well to keep from being bounced into the ceiling. The driver whistled while he drove as though he were out for a leisurely road trip, not kidnapping somebody.

And that was what Elise told herself was happening. She refused to think about Josh, concentrating instead on her remaining shoe. She'd have to see if the store would be able to match the one she lost. Her dress was ruined, too. There was a six-inch rip up the side, and a whole section of tiny, pear-shaped crystal beads was missing. Tears of frustration brimmed in her eyes. She'd only wanted to have fun like everyone else.

Monday morning she was so going to ream Josh's ass for wanting to go to that party.

Josh is dead, Elise.

The thought jolted her at the same time the SUV hit a pothole, throwing her against the side of the cargo area.

She squeezed her eyes shut, trying to force away the image of Josh's head exploding in a mass of blood, bone, and brain.

He couldn't really be dead. That only happened in the

movies.

Or the news.

Why didn't they keep him alive? His father was worth at least as much as her parents combined. And, both his mother and father loved their son, so they'd willingly pay a huge ransom. She didn't know how her parents would respond when the kidnappers issued their demands. Sure, they'd probably pay, but what if they kept asking for more? Her father was a hard-assed negotiator. He'd boasted on countless occasions that he never gave in to extortion or unreasonable demands. Her mother wasn't much different.

What if he was going to rape her? Elise curled her hands into fists; her throat squeezed tight in terror. Maybe that was why he hadn't killed her yet. Her hands started to shake and she dug her fingernails into her palms.

Calm down, Elise.

She tried to do the breathing exercises she learned in yoga class, but it only worked for a minute. Soon, she found herself sucking in short breaths as she fought the panic building in her chest.

She risked a glance at the driver, staying low in case she caught his attention. He appeared to be younger than she'd first thought, giving Elise a brief flicker of hope. Maybe she could bribe him, promise him that if he let her go, she could get him a reward. Just as she was working up the courage to speak, the SUV slowed to a stop.

Elise looked out the window to see why they stopped, but they were in the middle of nowhere and it was pitch dark. He'd pulled over for some kind of animal sitting in the road, illuminated by the headlights. No longer whistling, the driver shifted into park, turned off the ignition, and got out, leaving the door open.

He walked slowly with his hand out, palm up, and speaking

in a low voice, toward what Elise realized was a dog. The animal bared its teeth and flattened its ears, emitting a low growl.

Galvanized into action, Elise used the diversion to find a way to escape. With one eye on the man and the dog, Elise tore at the rubber mat beneath her, searching for something she could use either as a weapon or a tool to break out of the vehicle.

Nothing.

She'd already combed through the small space for a door handle or a release on the wire cage that separated her from the rest of the SUV, but the rolling prison was solid. She removed her remaining shoe and lay on her back with her feet angled toward the seat, and kicked as hard as she could. The seat back didn't budge.

She glanced through the windshield to make sure the driver's attention was still on the dog before trying to kick out a small side window. The power of her five-foot-three-inch frame was no match for the safety glass, and she gave up when she saw the driver turn back toward the vehicle with a dark expression on his face.

The dog hesitated a moment as though trying to decide whether to follow. The man reached into his pocket and tossed something. The canine dipped its head down, sniffed the object warily, and ate whatever he'd thrown. Nose sniffing the air, the animal watched him intently, waiting for more. The man patted his leg, motioning for it to come.

"Don't come back. Not yet..." Elise whispered as she ran her hands along the edges of the back window, hoping to find a gap in the weather stripping, or something else she had missed in her earlier search.

"*Vamanos,*" he said to the animal and threw something onto the front seat. The dog's nails clicked against the running boards as it scrambled into the SUV and wolfed down the treat on the console. The man got in and shut the door. The mongrel stayed on the passenger side, watching the driver, a low-decibel growl resonating from its throat.

The brief glimpse Elise got of the dun-colored animal revealed short hair and a stocky body like a pit bull, but with a narrow head, similar to a Doberman. Angry scars ran along its face and neck, as though it had been whipped or beaten, or used in a dogfight.

"Aren't you afraid he might bite?" Elise stammered in Spanish, hoping to at least have the man acknowledge her. Three years of Advanced Placement language classes were finally coming in handy.

Without a word, he shifted into gear and continued driving.

Elise wiped the perspiration from her forehead and leaned against the cage, threading her fingers through the wire to stay upright.

"Looks like he has a collar. Does he belong to someone you know?" The dog cocked its head toward her. She still held out hope that the driver would at least talk to her. Anything was better than being ignored.

Instead of replying, the driver held another treat out to the dog. The dog sniffed at his hand and then snatched the food, chewing as though it hadn't eaten anything in a week.

Hot tears brimmed in her eyes and spilled onto Elise's cheeks. She slumped back against the side of her cage and buried her face in her hands.

Why didn't I just have Brittany pick me up at the border? Despair descended on her like a thick, soggy blanket, and she found it difficult to breathe. Elise's imagination latched onto a recent article she'd read about unsuspecting women being abducted and tortured by serial killers, never to be seen again.

Don't think like that, Elise. He didn't kill you. There's something he wants that you have.

She didn't want to think about what that might be.

5
___

L OU STOKES GREETED Leine at the front door of SHEN. An operative for Leine's former employer, when Lou reached retirement age, he'd decided to end his association with the secret government agency and created the anti-trafficking organization. She'd been working for SHEN ever since she'd rescued Mara, a twelve-year-old girl who'd been abducted and sold to the highest bidder by a now-disbanded trafficking network. The bidder happened to be a well-known Hollywood producer who was currently doing time in a federal penitentiary. The sentence wasn't nearly harsh enough in Leine's opinion, mainly because it didn't include castration.

The relief of having rescued the shipment of human cargo at the port in Mexico the week before was short lived. Leine knew only too well it was just a drop in a massive sea of trafficked victims. On a positive note, she'd had the satisfaction of reuniting Amy with her older sister, Selena, a woman who had been abducted by the same group. The rescue had been a victory for SHEN and anti-traffickers everywhere. Still, Leine tried to remain realistic about the cases Lou assigned her. Most victims of trafficking were never found.

"The girl's parents are in room one," Lou said as they walked past reception and through a set of glass doors. "Their housekeeper, Teuta Vercuni, is with them. Apparently, the Bennetts didn't have any idea their daughter was in Mexico until the girl's best friend called them."

"Have they notified police?" Leine asked.

Lou nodded. "And the FBI. Since the parents believe the abduction occurred in Mexico, ICE is reaching out to the authorities there, but until there's a ransom demand or some other evidence of a kidnapping, there's only so much they can do." He paused at the door to the hallway leading to the interview room. "There's a possibility the daughter ran away."

"Why do you say that?"

Lou opened the door, allowing Leine to walk through first. "I'll let the parents tell you."

They continued down the hall to interview room one and walked in. A woman in her late thirties sat at one end of a rectangular table while an older woman, presumably the housekeeper, sat across from her. A man closer in age to the younger woman stood at the other end of the room, his pacing interrupted by their entrance.

"Dick and Belinda Bennett, Leine Basso," Lou said as he closed the door behind them. He nodded at the older woman seated at the table. "Teuta Vercuni works as the Bennett's housekeeper."

Leine stepped forward, her hand extended. Belinda Bennett's fingers were cold and smooth and her handshake brittle. Dark circles ringed her eyes, as though she hadn't slept the night before. With her platinum blonde hair styled in a long, inverted bob and a no-nonsense expression on her tanned, Botoxed face, she gave Leine the impression of a woman used to being the boss. The ice-white designer suit and expensive, avant-garde jewelry added to her refined air.

In contrast, the callouses on Teuta Vercuni's fingertips belied the soft, grandmotherly feel of her palm. The housekeeper had pulled her steel-gray hair back in a conservative bun and wore nondescript tan slacks paired with a blue and white knit shirt. Worry etched her face, and a deep frown line separated her gray-blue eyes.

Dick Bennett ignored Leine's hand and came to an abrupt halt.

"Is she qualified?" he asked Lou. Tan and fit with classic good looks, Dick Bennett commanded the room. He wore an untucked designer polo shirt with a pair of fitted trousers and expensive loafers. Hands in his pockets and leaning forward he looked as though he was standing at the bow of a ship, heading into the wind.

"One of our best," Lou offered by way of explanation.

"Your best what?" Belinda Bennett's crisp tone serrated the room. Leine turned to face the ice queen.

"I get results."

"Her recovery rate is the highest of our agents," Lou added.

Belinda Bennett inclined her head in acknowledgement.

"What makes you believe your daughter's been abducted?" Leine asked.

Belinda glanced at Dick who was now on the other side of the room, his arms crossed. He nodded.

"We're here at the recommendation of our attorney," she said. "He suggested we try all avenues in case Elise was..." Belinda's voice faltered and her eyes grew moist. "She's a straight A student. Very popular, of course." Lou grabbed a box of tissues from a filing cabinet and held it out to her. She took one and used it to dab her eyes.

"Of course," Leine said.

"Teuta believes she ran away with Josh," Belinda said with a dismissive wave toward the housekeeper. "Elise would never do that. She was too grounded."

The housekeeper seemed to want to say something but instead looked down and kneaded her hands. Leine turned her attention to the older woman.

"And you believe otherwise?" she asked.

"Eliseka run away with handsome boy in nice car," Teuta said, her lower lip extended. "She tell me everything in heart." She touched her chest, a knowing expression on her face.

Belinda Bennett gave a derisive snort. "I sincerely doubt that, Teuta. Elise had plans beyond marrying the first boy who caught her eye." She turned to Leine. "You see, Ms. Basso, Elise has always been focused on attending college and eventually earning an MBA from either Harvard or Stanford." She gave Teuta a withering stare. The housekeeper's jaw was set in a stubborn line.

Interesting dynamic, Leine thought.

"Mrs. Bennett," Leine said, "did Elise ever mention Josh? Did it appear that their relationship was getting serious?"

A slight frown crossed her features for an instant. She shook her head. "She mentioned him in passing. Hardly the stuff of a heady, 'I'm going to elope to Mexico' kind of thing."

Leine looked at Lou. "Has anyone spoken to the boy's parents?"

"They've filed a missing persons report, but that's all I know at the moment. For what it's worth, they don't believe the two of them ran off together."

Belinda Bennett crossed her arms and glanced at Teuta with an *I told you so* look. Dick Bennett came around behind Belinda and put his hands on her shoulders. Belinda glanced up at him with a grateful look and touched his hand.

"Josh received an expensive car for a graduation present. Teuta mentioned that he was driving it when he picked her up for their date," Dick said as he kneaded Belinda's shoulders. "The police said it's possible they were victims of a carjacking." At that, Belinda began to cry softly. Dick bent down and murmured soothingly into her ear.

"Do you have a picture of your daughter?" Lou asked.

Belinda nodded and reached inside her bag. She pulled out a five-by-seven photograph in an elaborate frame, which she handed to him. He looked at it and gave it to Leine.

It was a portrait by a well-known photographer and showed a pretty platinum blonde with brown eyes smiling into the camera, wearing lip gloss and light makeup. She wore strapless ensemble and a set of tasteful diamond earrings with a matching necklace.

"Do you remember what she was wearing when she left the house?" Leine asked Teuta.

She nodded. "Her favorite dress." She turned to Belinda. "You know the one. White with crystals, yes?"

Belinda nodded. Fresh tears threatened to fall. "We bought it on a mother-daughter shopping trip to Singapore."

Pain raking his face, Dick stopped rubbing Belinda's shoulders and bowed his head. Belinda took a deep breath and dabbed at her eyes again.

"I'm sorry. It's just that the trip was one of the last happy memories we have of Elise."

"Were you and she having trouble?" Leine asked.

Belinda took a deep breath. "Elise is...difficult."

"How so?"

"Oh, you know, typical teenager angst," Dick quickly cut in. Belinda didn't offer additional comment.

"May I keep this?" Leine asked, indicating the photograph.

Belinda and Dick Bennett both nodded. "Yes, of course."

"So what's next?" Dick asked.

"We'll circulate Elise's picture and description to our

contacts worldwide," Lou replied. "Leine has several sources she uses when searching for missing children, as well. If anything at all comes to our attention, we'll be in contact with you immediately. In the same vein, if the law enforcement agencies you've contacted find out anything, we'd appreciate you letting us know."

"Of course. Thank you." Dick turned toward Leine, this time offering his hand. "And thank you, Leine. I appreciate your help in finding our daughter."

Lou opened the door to the hallway, and the three of them got up to leave. As Teuta filed out behind the Bennetts, she grabbed Leine's hand and clutched it to her chest.

"You must find my Eliseka, Mrs. Basso," she said. "She is much too young to marry. Besides," she glanced at Mrs. Bennett's retreating back, "Mrs. Bennett could not live with herself."

6

ELISE OPENED HER eyes and stared into the dark room. She tried to lick her lips but her mouth felt like it had been stuffed with dryer lint. Her shoulder throbbed and she closed her eyes in concentration as she tried to remember what had happened to her.

All she could think of was Josh. And blood.

So much blood.

She'd seen him crumple at the gunman's feet. Shortly afterward, the man who had dragged her out of the car threw her into the caged cargo area of the SUV.

What had happened to the driver and the dog? And where was she now?

The room was cool and damp, and smelled of mildew and something far more dank. She shifted her body and the springs underneath her screeched in protest. Elise sat up on the mattress, her movement cut short by a chain attached to her wrist. Her head spinning, she pulled at the cold metal handcuff. There was no give.

Fear pooled in her stomach and slid slowly upward, clamping her throat shut as panic turned to dread. She remembered now why her shoulder ached. After hours of driving, they'd stopped at what looked like an abandoned warehouse. The driver had dragged her out of the back of the SUV by the arm and stuck her with a needle. The last thing she remembered before she blacked out was the world tilting sideways and the deadweight of her arms and legs making it impossible to move.

How long had she been out?

Elise inhaled sharply as she probed where she'd hit the ground after being dragged from the Porsche. Her right hip and leg were both tender. Her shoes were missing, and her feet felt like blocks of ice. She rolled onto her side and tucked her legs close, the hot sting of tears forming in her eyes.

Whatever these men wanted, it wasn't good. Elise now wished that she had listened to her father's security guy when he warned her not to wear expensive jewelry or designer accessories when she went out, as well as to choose a lower heel and more comfortable clothing in case she had to get anywhere fast. She'd scoffed and waved him off, thinking he was being overly cautious. Elise felt safe in her exclusive Beverly Hills neighborhood and never gave security a second thought. Partying in Mexico on a Saturday night was usually no big deal. She and her friends would often cross the border to go drinking on the weekends, especially when there wasn't much happening in town.

Elise hugged her knees and buried her face in her arms. Tears coursed down her cheeks as panic rose to the surface. She wished Josh were there. At least he would have been someone to talk to. He might have tried to calm her frayed nerves.

But he's dead, remember?

The reality of her situation came crashing down, bringing a fresh round of tears. She'd never known anyone who had died, much less someone who was *murdered*. She agonized over why the man had shot him but not her. Although, if she really thought about it she wasn't certain they'd actually *killed* Josh—just hurt him to make him do what they wanted. Just because there was all that blood didn't mean anything. She'd read that head wounds bled a lot. Besides, it was so dark and she'd been so scared she wasn't sure she'd even seen what she thought she had.

Elise didn't think her parents would believe she'd been abducted, if the kidnappers could even reach them. Dick and Belinda Bennett certainly didn't act like they wanted her around. Her mother usually rolled her eyes and admonished her to "stop the drama" whenever Elise tried to get her attention. To Elise, family was highly overrated.

Even though Brittany grumbled about having to be home for dinner every night, Elise noticed her friend didn't skip out of a lot of meals with her parents and usually didn't talk smack about her family. Sometimes, when Elise was bored, she wondered what it would be like to actually have parents who cared.

The sound of a key rattling the lock echoed through the darkness and Elise froze, all thoughts of home and family supplanted by a jolt of fear. She clamped her jaws together to keep her teeth from chattering and tensed as the door opened. Light spilled from the doorway, outlining the silhouette of a man.

The overhead light clicked on, and Elise squeezed her eyes shut against the glare. The man moved next to the bed and set a glass of cloudy water on the nightstand. Then he squatted, a small digital camera in his hands.

She didn't recognize him. Older than Elise by at least ten years, he wore his light brown hair cropped close, had a generous mouth and full lips, and his left eye was much larger than the other. Elise shivered involuntarily as he aimed the camera at her.

"Say chiss," he demanded, his accent thick. With a click, the shutter released and he lowered the camera. He frowned and motioned for her to sit up. "You must sit."

Not wanting to anger him, Elise complied and sat up as far as the chain would allow.

The man nodded. "Better." He took another picture and stood, sliding the camera into his front pocket. He turned, preparing to leave.

"Wait."

The man waited, his face expressionless.

"Where am I? Why am I here?"

"No," he answered and reached for the light switch.

"Do you *know* who I am?" Outraged that the man would ignore a direct request, she overcame her fear and gave him a haughty stare. "My father knows people. People who will find me and hunt you down." All she got was a blank stare. Either he didn't understand English or he didn't respond to threats.

"I can't drink that—it's gross," she said, switching gears and eyeing the murky liquid on the table beside her. "Bring me bottled water, like Gloss." Just because they kidnapped her didn't mean they could mistreat her this way.

The man tipped his head and smiled as if amused, fueling her anger.

"It's not funny. There could be bacteria in there that might make me sick. And if I get sick, my father won't pay. He'll send the military to find me, and then you guys will be dead." Elise had no idea if getting the army involved was even possible, but if she didn't know, then he probably didn't either.

Her threats were met with silence. She tried a different tactic. "I have to go to the bathroom."

The man pointed underneath the bed. Elise leaned over the mattress. Her moral outrage withered at the sight of a plastic bucket and a dirty roll of toilet paper. Did he really expect her to use an open bucket to go to the bathroom? She stared at him in shock. The man just grinned. Then he stepped through the door and closed it behind him. The key rattled in the lock, followed by the echo of his fading footsteps.

With a wail, Elise collapsed backward onto the bed and curled in a ball, burying her face in the lumpy pillow. When she'd cried herself out, she rolled over to her back and stared at the grungy ceiling. Crying wouldn't help. She needed to do something. Her father's face appeared in her mind. She closed her eyes and tried to imagine what he'd do in this situation.

That's stupid, Elise. He would never be in this situation. She resolved to be more like him and try to negotiate the next time someone came into the room. What was it he always said? As long as you have something the other party wants or needs, you can win.

And she obviously had something they needed.

At least the man had left the light on. Ignoring the glass of foul-looking water, Elise took stock of her surroundings. A dirty concrete floor with gray block walls made up the majority of the small room. Her bed and the table beside it were the sole pieces of furniture, not including the bucket. Emotion welled inside of her at the thought of her beautiful canopied bed with the 800-thread count sheets in her well-appointed bedroom back home.

Stop it. Crying will only mess up what makeup you have left. You have to do what you can to look your best or the kidnappers won't take you seriously. She longed for her iPhone so she could text her feelings to the world. First thing she'd do was take a selfie and show these horrid surroundings. Surely someone in her feed would be able to help her.

Eventually, thirst won out. She brought the glass to her nose and sniffed the turbid water, gagging at the faint but unmistakable odor of diesel. Repulsed, she set the glass back on the table with a grimace.

Brace yourself. You may have to drink tap. Disdain shoved fear out of the way when she realized her captors couldn't possibly be refined enough to know the difference.

Elise's limited life experience was a detriment to her now. Just because she'd traveled extensively didn't mean she'd seen anything of the world except for five-star hotels and the pretty parts. Oh, sure, she'd been aware of how the poor lived in the Caribbean, and she'd seen pictures of the shitty sections of Los Angeles, but that was as far as it went. Her parents shielded her from anything unpleasant, and Elise had gone along. Daddy's plane took her and her friends wherever they wanted to go, and she didn't want to go anywhere that had anything less than luxury bedding and a full-service spa.

She shuddered when she thought about her blog followers' reaction to finding out she'd had to put her lips to something other than the fifty-dollar-a-bottle, crystal-studded Gloss H2O. *Beverly Hills Blonde, Rich and Loving It!* was renowned for its trendsetting style—in clothing and accessories as well as what to eat and drink. Her loyal fans could never know.

Oh my God. What will happen to my Alexa ranking? A jolt of fear spiked through her at the thought of her blog's über-high position in the popular rating system sinking into oblivion, matching that of someone who rarely posted. All the work that went into achieving the rank—the daily blog posts, the selfies wearing her #ootn (outfit of the night), the artfully constructed foodie photos—gone because she wasn't able to post to her lifestyle blog. And, cha-ching—because of *Beverly Hills Blonde's* popularity certain companies had begun to contact her about advertising on the site.

Kiss that revenue stream goodbye.

Confidence began to return to Elise in increments, partially replacing the fear she'd felt when Josh had been shot. The kidnappers hadn't hurt her and gave her water, so they needed her alive.

And, the man took her picture. She figured it would only be a matter of time before they sent the photograph to Dick and Belinda Bennett. She should have told him to upload it to Instagram or Snapchat. They'd get a much better response than sending it to her parents. Although when she thought about it, she was relieved she hadn't suggested it. The photo of her was probably horrible and she'd never live it down.

Soon, reality reached its invasive little tentacles into her brain, and she realized none of it mattered. It wouldn't be long before her kidnappers figured out the Bennetts didn't respond well to blackmail. Elise had already tried that. She closed her eyes at the thought of her mother telling her father that she was just "doing it for the attention."

Elise took a deep breath. Daddy wasn't going to send the plane this time. She'd played the drama card once too often. Her parents would think she was bluffing to get more money. They would never pay the ransom, assuming she was staging another abduction.

Despair replaced confidence and burrowed in for the long haul as she settled back on the mildewed bedspread, and hoped her parents would realize the truth before it was too late.

7

S SOON AS her tablet picked up the signal from her neighbor's wireless account, Leine signed into FindMe with one of the aliases she'd set up for interacting online. If she had her way, she wouldn't use the social media site at all, preferring to communicate via secure chat. But that wasn't something her daughter, April, was interested in doing, and April was in Europe. Leine used whichever site her daughter posted on.

Leine hated the digital footprint her online activity left behind and always used a program to shield her identity, but given enough time and resources a talented hacker could find out who and where you were.

With Leine's past, that could get her killed.

As she scrolled through her daughter's photos of Amsterdam and Paris, Leine thought back to one of her last trips to Europe with Carlos. True, they'd both been there for a job but had taken a few days afterward to enjoy a romantic vacation on the Italian Riviera. At the time, Leine hadn't analyzed her ability to compartmentalize work and pleasure, and now she realized how protective the skill had been. Apparently, that ability was seeking expression in other ways.

Case in point: her relationship with Santa.

Even though back at the apartment Santiago hadn't asked her to marry him, she could see the inevitable march toward cohabitation and, knowing Santa, matrimony. The idea had a certain appeal—waking up with Santa every morning would be heavenly—but Leine wanted to keep things on an even keel for as long as possible and not rush into anything. She viewed their romance as a delicately woven tapestry with only the first few rows complete. Not yet strong enough to withstand the pressure of daily wear and tear.

With a sigh, Leine read her daughter's latest post detailing how awesome the impressionist paintings in the Musée d'Orsay had been. April went on to describe their meal at a Parisian restaurant followed by drinks at a club in the Latin Quarter. Leine stopped herself from posting a warning about pickpockets in the Quarter and instead wrote, "Glad you and Cory are having a good time."

When her daughter, April, had been abducted by a serial killer, Cory had helped Leine locate her. That had earned him a special and permanent place in Leine's heart. Although her daughter traveled extensively, Leine worried like only a mother could and was relieved Cory went with her. In a way, the fact that she worried was comforting. Leine had assumed she was a shitty mother without the ability to nurture, warped by the nature of her past profession as an assassin, but it turned out the mothering instinct trumped assassin all day long.

She signed off and did a search for Richard and Belinda Bennett, finding the usual entries for a well-known power couple: *Entrepreneur* magazine profiles, interviews in *Forbes* and *Fortune*, an article in *Bloomberg Businessweek* about the biotech firm Dick Bennett founded. But it was an essay in the *Economist* that captured Leine's attention. The piece mentioned that five years ago Dick Bennett had received startup money for his company from an investment firm run by an Albanian national named Z. Ristani. The name rang a bell. Leine did a search, but the *Economist* article was the only result with any relevance.

Leine closed her eyes, trying to remember why she knew the name Ristani. Images of a hit she did in Paris of a Bulgarian arms dealer who was about to sell a long-range missile to a visiting North Korean general played through her mind. But the name didn't fit. She found a short news item in a French publication reporting on the unusual manner in which her Bulgarian target had died. Investigators deemed it an accident, and the death hadn't received a lot of coverage. A grainy photograph of the target and two other men accompanied the article.

Leine isolated the photo and enlarged the image to see if she recognized either of them. The two men stood next to the Bulgarian she'd been sent to kill: one was stocky with a thick neck and a shaved head. Tattoos crept up the side of his face and onto his skull, giving him a fierce, tribal appearance. Leine tried but couldn't quite make out what the tats signified, hoping to see which criminal affiliations he had. Since he appeared to be an acquaintance of the target she was pretty sure he had several.

The other man had partially turned away from the camera. He was tall and lean with broad shoulders, an aquiline nose and a shock of white hair. Unlike the other two, he wore an expensive-looking suit and sunglasses. The caption only identified the Bulgarian. Nothing about either of the two men triggered her memory.

Giving up on the Bennetts and Ristani for the moment, she checked public records for both Elise and Josh to see if there might be anything the Bennetts neglected to tell her. Then she ran a general search of their names.

Josh turned out to be the grandson of a wealthy financier but was only mentioned in passing. Elise's blog, *Beverly Hills Blonde, Rich and Loving It!* appeared at the top of search results for her name.

Photographs of 'artistic' menu items and expensive clothes and shoes littered the pages—most included Elise modeling and/or mugging for the camera near easily identifiable landmarks like the Coliseum and Abbey Road. Comments on the posts ranged from the erudite *OMG, this is the best blog evah,* to *squee!* Leine skimmed recent entries, but she didn't find anything helpful.

Josh and Elise appeared to be just two of thousands of kids partying in Mexico for spring break.

The carjacking theory was beginning to look like the most plausible explanation. Usually, the occupants of the car being stolen were left alive in a rural area and had to find their way back to civilization. By the time that happened, the carjackers would have already stripped the car or delivered it to a prearranged buyer after changing the VIN and plates. But no one had heard from Josh or Elise, and there had been plenty of time for a couple of healthy teenagers to find their way back.

Unless the robbery had gone bad. It was possible that Josh made the mistake of being a hero and tried to stop the hijackers from stealing the vehicle, which could have easily gotten him killed. Still, Mexican authorities hadn't found the car or even a hint of foul play. Leine doubted the carjackers would have taken the time to bury the bodies and Tijuana was a highly populated area. Dead bodies would be noticed.

Leine rummaged in her pocket and found the note with Elise's friend's name and number, and punched it into her cell phone.

"This is Brittany," a chipper female voice said.

"Brittany, my name is Leine Basso and I work for SHEN."

"The human trafficking agency?"

"That's the one." *Interesting that she's heard of SHEN,* Leine thought. Then again, the organization was all over the news when they'd located Mara. "I've been asked by Elise's parents to try to find her, and I was wondering if we could meet somewhere and talk?"

"Sure." Brittany paused before continuing, a hint of fear seeping into her voice. "Do you think she was sold...as a sex slave?" The last two words came out in a whisper, as though speaking them aloud would make it true.

"There's no way of knowing, at this point."

"I will absolutely meet with you. I'm on my way to Yvette's French Café on Beverly Drive. Would that work?"

"Is that in Beverly Hills?"

"Yes."

"I can be there in thirty minutes."

YVETTE'S WAS BUSY. FILLED WITH CHIC, REED-THIN WOMEN WITH long hair, big sunglasses, and even bigger pocketbooks, they kissed the air in greeting and chatted animatedly with each other, all the while preening at themselves in the glass behind the counter. They reminded Leine of a colony of squawking flamingos she'd seen years ago in the Florida Everglades.

Leine walked to the counter to wait in line as the customer ahead of her ordered a half-decaf, two-pump, no foam, sugar-free praline and vanilla latte to be delivered at precisely one hundred and seventy degrees. The coffee bar's air conditioner wasn't working very well and Leine pulled her hair up off her neck and secured it with a couple of bobby pins as the cashier scanned the woman's phone for payment. The young clerk looked at Leine expectantly, fingers poised above the register, ready to capture her instructions.

"Black coffee. Large," Leine said.

The clerk stood in flustered silence for a moment before replying. "Would you like room for cream?" she asked, her fingers quivering over the keys.

"Black coffee. Large," Leine repeated, wondering what the hell was so difficult about the order.

"Oh, okay. Sure. Coming right up." The clerk jotted the drink on the side of a cup as though she might forget what Leine had just ordered in the next two seconds and turned back to the hulking coffee urns behind her. As she filled the eco-friendly paper cup with steaming hot coffee, Leine scanned the café for Brittany.

She'd described herself as a Rhianna look-alike, but several of the café's patrons could have fit that description. In the end, it was Brittany who found Leine.

"Leine Basso?" a feminine voice said behind her.

Leine accepted the coffee from the cashier and dropped the change into the tip box sitting on the counter before she turned around.

"You must be Brittany."

Diminutive with jet-black hair, deep brown, almond-shaped eyes, and dressed in a form-fitting pale yellow top and pencil Capris, Brittany could have easily passed for the pop star. Upon closer inspection, Leine revised her age downward after realizing that underneath the artfully applied makeup Brittany wouldn't pass for more than seventeen.

They had a seat at a table by a window in the corner, the nearest customer far enough away that they wouldn't be overheard.

"Tell me about Josh and Elise," Leine began.

Brittany took a sip of her coffee. "They'd just started hanging out together. I think this was the third time Lise went out with him."

"Third time? So they weren't serious?"

Brittany shook her head. "Not even. In fact, the last time I talked to her, she'd been pissed at him because he left her at the club."

"The bar in Tijuana, right?"

"Right. The Blue Manatee."

"And you were supposed to drive down to the border to pick her up?"

Brittany nodded, her eyes tearing. "Yes. But then she texted me not to bother, that she was going to some party on the beach with Josh and that she'd text me later." She looked at Leine, the worry she felt for her friend evident in her eyes. "I never got another text."

"The Bennetts' housekeeper believes Elise ran away with him. That they were going to be married."

Brittany rolled her eyes. "Teuta's nice and all, but she's just the maid. She doesn't know anything. She's convinced Lise is pure as the driven snow and would never sleep with a boy, much less go out drinking in Tijuana with one." She picked up her phone, scanned the screen for messages, and set it back on the table. "Elise is definitely not a virgin. And she isn't going to get married before she graduates. Believe me."

"That's what her mother said."

Brittany smirked.

"What?" Leine asked.

"Like she'd know."

"Why do you say that?"

"Because Belinda Bennett only looks out for Belinda Bennett. Personally, I don't get why she even had a kid. She doesn't care about her." She crossed her arms. "The only thing the Bennetts care about is money."

"They seemed pretty shaken up when I met them."

She shrugged. "Maybe they finally figured out that they had a daughter. Believe me, it'd be a first."

Leine asked Brittany a couple of other questions about Elise's relationship with her parents and then handed her a business card.

"In case you hear from Elise or remember anything else that might be helpful."

Brittany took the card and slid it into her purse. "Thanks." She paused and looked at Leine. "There's something I didn't tell you."

Leine waited.

"Elise has disappeared before."

Leine glanced at her sharply. "What do you mean, disappeared?"

"She ran away a couple of times, trying to get her parents' attention, but it backfired. The last time she did it, they didn't even bother to notify police." She leaned forward. "This time is different, though, I know it."

A brief flicker of anger surged through Leine. If Elise had staged her abduction in order to get her parents' attention then the kid was wasting everyone's time. Leine could be much more effective elsewhere, searching for actual missing children. And why hadn't the Bennetts mentioned it in the interview? The previous times Elise ran away would be easy enough to check if the Bennetts had reported her missing.

"Why is this different?" Leine asked.

"She always texted me before, let me know where she was so I wouldn't worry about her. One time," Brittany lowered her gaze to the floor, "she was at my house while the cops were looking for her."

"Good to know." Leine got up to leave.

"Like I said, she hasn't texted me so I know something

happened. And Josh never came back either, which worries me even more."

"He wouldn't help make her parents believe she wasn't lying this time?"

"No. I don't think so. Josh wasn't—isn't that into her. I doubt he'd want to lie about something that serious. Besides, he's graduating this year. If he screws up he won't get to keep the new car his dad gave him."

"Thanks for the information, Brittany." Leine made a mental note to contact the officer who took the missing persons report.

"Thank you for taking this seriously. Please find her." Brittany looked close to tears. "I know she's still alive. She has to be."

"I'll do what I can." Leine threw her cup into the garbage as she walked out the door, and wondered whether she was chasing a ghost, or a lying, spoiled brat.

8

———

As Leine pulled into the parking lot at SHEN, her phone beeped, alerting her to a text message. She grabbed her cell out of her purse and squinted at the screen. The text from Santa read, *Putz @ ER. Talk later.*

That can't be good, Leine thought. A trip to the emergency room could be either work- or lifestyle-related. In addition to being a detective who sat behind a desk for hours at a time, Santa's erstwhile partner eschewed anything resembling exercise and had a weakness for all things fried.

Keep me posted, Leine texted back. She hoped it was a false alarm or at least nothing major. Santa and Putz had been partners for a long time and worked well together. Leine trusted him to always have Santa's back.

As she got out of her car, the theme from *The Godfather* erupted from her phone. It was Lou.

"Hey, Lou. I'm in the parking lot. I'll be inside in a minute," she said.

"Good. You're going to want to hear this." Lou's voice had weary written all over it.

She locked her car and made her way up the sidewalk,

wondering what could make her old friend sound so drained. Leine marveled at his capacity to ignore the seeming insurmountable hopelessness of their mission while staying upbeat and positive. Whatever happened must have something to do with one of the cases she'd been working. Leine braced herself for a setback.

Lou was leaning against his desk when she walked into his office. The lines on his face seemed deeper than usual, giving him the appearance of a man much older than his sixty-odd years. He was joined by two men, both cradling a paper cup of office coffee. Leine recognized them from Immigration and Customs Enforcement, or ICE, having worked on several trafficking cases with them before. Wondering whether they were there with good news or bad, she greeted them and sat on the edge of Lou's desk.

"Leine, Nabokov and Gunderson here have some news about Josh and Elise." He turned to the ICE agents, giving them the floor.

Nabokov shifted forward and set his coffee cup on the desk in front of him.

"Naturally, what I'm about to tell you isn't general knowledge and goes nowhere," he said.

"Naturally," Lou answered.

Nabokov nodded. "We traced Josh Rider's iPhone to a place a few miles outside of Tijuana. Mexican authorities found it in the weeds alongside the road in an unfinished housing development."

"Did they find the car?"

Gunderson shook his head. "No. And there was no sign of either Miss Bennett or Josh Rider. There was, however, a large amount of dried blood on the ground along with several sets of footprints and broken glass. We sent samples to the lab."

"So, either it's a carjacking gone bad, or somebody wanted to make it look like one," Leine said.

"Looks like it. We've asked our Mexican counterparts to distribute photos of the two of them throughout their networks and keep us apprised of any related information, but—" Nabokov raised his hands, palms up. "The car's gone, there aren't any bodies, and no one's made contact with either set of parents. Not a lot to go on."

"That's where you come in," Lou said to Leine. "Obviously, evidence is pointing to the probability that something happened beyond them running away together, but Nabokov and Gunderson here have hit a wall with the local police. They're resisting the idea that two kids from wealthy families were abducted in their fair city. Someone higher up is afraid if the information gets out it might curtail the influx of spring break-ers." Lou crossed his arms. "I need you to go down to Tijuana and check things out."

Leine nodded. "And stay under the radar."

"You got it."

"I'd send my own people, except they're known commodities in TJ. The authorities down there tend to get a little peevish when we come around sticking our noses into things. You know, not having jurisdiction and all," Nabokov added. "Not to mention the agency's stretched so thin you can hear the screams."

"No problem. I can leave tonight."

"The sooner the better." Gunderson handed Leine a thin manila envelope. "This is what we've got so far. I'll call Lou as soon as the lab report comes back."

Leine took the envelope and looked inside. Along with a copy of the police reports of the two teenagers' disappearance, there were recent photos of Elise and Josh, a picture of the Porsche, and a satellite map marking where Josh's phone had been found.

"Thanks. This is helpful." Leine turned to Lou. "Can you make a reservation for a car and a hotel?"

Lou nodded.

Gunderson reached for his briefcase. "We've got footage of them crossing the border into Mexico, but nothing coming back." He pulled out a tablet, powered it on, and turned the screen toward Leine. The surveillance video showed a late-model Porsche with two occupants entering Mexico at 7:30 p.m. the previous Saturday evening. The passenger had long, blonde hair and resembled the photograph of Elise Mrs. Bennett had given to Lou the day before. The driver easily fit Josh's description.

"Border agents didn't record their passports, but we're sure it's them. The plates match the car in question. I doubt the kid would let anyone else drive that car."

"Unbelievable that he even drove it across," Nabokov added, shaking his head. "He was asking for trouble."

"So what's your gut tell you?" Leine asked, looking at the two agents.

Nabokov spoke first. "Pretty sure there's been at least one murder. Depending on whose blood was at the scene, I'd say the two were targeted straight off the bat because of either the car or the girl or both. If we go with a crime of opportunity and it really was a vanilla-type carjacking, it's possible they realized she would net them a bigger payoff than the car when they saw her."

"I lean toward the latter explanation, myself," Gunderson said.

Leine tucked the envelope with the report into her bag and stood to leave.

"Thank you, gentlemen," she said. "I appreciate your help."

"No problem, Leine. I hope you find something," Gunderson said. "We'll continue to follow any leads we come across. We'd appreciate it if you'd keep us informed."

"Of course."

"I'll follow you out." Lou accompanied Leine from the office, leaving Nabokov and Gunderson to finish their coffee.

"What's your feeling on this, Lou?" Leine asked as they walked through the door to the parking lot. Lou had a sixth sense when it came to the criminal mind.

"I think the first scenario makes the most sense. Why were they in an abandoned development in the first place?" Lou shook his head. "And, according to the housekeeper, Elise was wearing an expensive dress with a lot of bling. They would have gotten more than their share of attention no matter what because of the car he was driving, but adding it all together makes it an even more attractive proposition."

Leine unlocked her car and put her bag on the passenger seat. "I'll keep in touch. Let me know if anything comes up. Depending on what I find, I may need a gun." Leine refused to take a chance crossing the border with a firearm. Mexican authorities tended to frown on tourists with weapons. Jail time wasn't pleasant anywhere, but especially not in Mexico.

"No problem. I've got just the guy. Be safe." Lou walked back into the building. Leine climbed inside her car and checked her phone. Santa had sent another text: *Putz ok. c u @ home.*

Relieved, she put her cell back into her purse and started the car.

Home. He meant his apartment, of course. Leine waited for the familiar claustrophobic feeling to make its presence known, but it didn't even rear its head. She looked at her watch. There was just enough time to grab some takeout and have dinner with Santa before she left for Tijuana.

The thought gave her pause. She marveled at how easily she had slipped into relationship mode. A smile playing at the edges of her lips, she shifted the car into gear and drove out of the parking lot, headed for home.

9

───────

LEINE HAD JUST lit two tapered candles on the dining room table when Santa walked in the door.

"How's Don?" she called out.

She heard him drop his keys on the table in the entryway and move into the living room.

"He's stable. The hospital's going to monitor him overnight. He's scheduled for more tests in the morning." Santa walked over and planted a kiss on her neck. "You should have heard the words that came out of his mouth when he found out he had to stay."

"What happened?"

"Chest pains, shortness of breath," Santa said, heading for the couch. "The guy's been in denial too long. He's gonna have to wake up. Change some things."

"You look beat," Leine said as she came around behind him and gave his shoulders a squeeze. "He's a fighter. He'll be fine."

Santa gave her a tired smile and reached for her hand. "Yeah. I know. He'll be out on a medical for a few weeks."

"Which means you get a new partner."

"Yep."

"Well, maybe this one will be a quick study. It's only tempo-rary, right? Until Putz is allowed to resume his duties?"

"He'll probably have to pull light duty for a while when he comes back." He sighed. "When you've been partners as long as we have you develop a kind of shorthand when you work together. Makes things easier. It's always a crap shoot whether a replacement is workable."

"You'll still be able to talk to Putz about your cases. It's not like he'll be completely out of commission. You know he's gonna call you all day long while he's recuperating. He won't be able to stand it."

Santa smiled, brightening. "You're right." He took her hand and guided her to sit next to him on the couch. "I noticed your bag next to the door. Are you going somewhere?"

Leine allowed herself to be led and sat down. "I'm leaving tonight. Josh's phone was traced to an abandoned housing project outside of Tijuana."

"Any leads on the car?"

"No. Some safety glass, but that's it. There was blood on the ground, but results from the lab aren't back yet so there's not much to go on at the moment. The ICE agents who told us what happened said some higher-up in the local police department wasn't too interested in pursuing the idea that a couple of rich kids from LA had been kidnapped and possibly murdered. They're afraid it'll slow the tsunami of partiers into the city."

"So you get to go to TJ during spring break. Lucky you."

"Yeah. Not so much. I figure I'll check out the area where they found the kid's phone, talk to the bartenders that were on staff that night, see if anyone recognizes them."

"I know a DEA field agent who works out of there, if you want his information. He'll be able to give you some tips or maybe a contact or two."

"Sure. The more the merrier." Leine stroked his cheek and

leaned in for a kiss. "You hungry?" she asked. "I picked up some Pad Thai from the Green Onion."

"Perfect." With a smile, Santa slipped his hand behind her head and pulled her to him. The scent of citrus and cedar aftershave enveloped Leine. She closed her eyes and inhaled, giving herself over to the sensory overload that always accompanied a kiss from the smoldering detective. After a few moments, she put her hand on his chest and drew back with an apologetic smile.

"Much as I'd love to stay and play, I need to eat dinner and get on the road." She took both of his hands in hers and stood up, pulling him to his feet. "The faster I go, the faster I can come back."

Brief disappointment skated across his features but was soon replaced by a wicked smile. He leaned in close and whispered, "Fast is good, but only when it's you coming back."

THE BORDER CROSSING WAS BUSY BUT NOT AS CROWDED AS DURING daylight hours. To make things easier, Leine walked across and picked up her nondescript SUV from the rental agency, drove downtown, and parked at a secure parking lot near the Blue Manatee. It was still early by Tijuana standards—only eight thirty—and the party atmosphere hadn't yet kicked into high gear. Bouncers stood outside of bar entrances shilling for early arrivals, hoping to entice them with promises of scantily clad women, cheap booze, and pulsing laser light shows.

Leine knew if she walked into any one of the "Gentlemen's" clubs in the border town she'd have a good chance of finding several women who had been trafficked in some form or another. Security was tight in these places, and unless she wanted to stir up a hornet's nest of pissed-off cartel members and protection racketeers, Leine would have to avoid them. The women themselves were often drugged or beaten or both, with their identification confiscated by their handlers to ensure compliance. Many refused to accept offers of help for fear their families would be targeted, or they'd be hunted down and dragged back to work, or even killed for their trouble. Others believed their lifestyle was the best they could hope for, or were too addicted to see beyond the syringe or pipe in their hand.

The problem didn't have an easy, one-size-fits-all solution.

Leine admired the agencies that worked tirelessly to win over the women, to convince them they were worth more than what they'd been brainwashed to believe by the ruthless men and women who controlled their destinies. Diplomacy and patience were not words Leine would use for her approach to the scum-sucking parasites who ruled the sex trafficking underworld. Hand grenades and a flamethrower made more sense.

The sights and smells of downtown Tijuana brought back deeply buried memories: the seared meat juices soaking the drip pan at the ever-present food stands accompanied by the familiar smell of refried beans and handmade tortillas; overripe melons and strawberries and pineapples piled high on top of fruit carts; spilled *cerveza* and tequila mixed with the faint (and not-so-faint) odor of exhaust and urine.

The garishness of the city at night with its blatant neon and blaring music blended seamlessly with the hive-like drone of hundreds of hustlers and entrepreneurs, all working the system and tourists to make a buck. This was not the place to come for a quiet siesta or to find quality time alone with your sweetheart. Tijuana after dark existed for the fast and reckless, for the alcohol-fueled folly of thousands of daily visitors hell-bent on experiencing something different from their privileged American lives—addictive entertainment that smacked of the vaguely dangerous.

Elise and Josh found dangerous all right, Leine thought.

She located the Blue Manatee down a side street, the door unmanned and wide open to the balmy night. She walked into the cool, dark club, empty of customers except for a man sitting at the far end of the Lucite-and-chrome bar nursing a beer. Disheveled and probably hung over, he acted as though it was too much effort to acknowledge anything other than the cigarette in his hand. He had the look of someone who had become disillusioned with life, moved to Mexico, and now found himself drinking alone in Tijuana. He could have been thirty. Or sixty.

A large screen at the other end played a music video of the pop star du jour. Blue laser lights flickered at random intervals, attempting to give the impression of an electrified, high energy interior. The club's namesake—an enormous, plush blue manatee—hung above the bar.

A dark-haired man who Leine estimated to be in his early twenties was stocking bottles on the shelves behind the bar. She approached him and sat on one of the padded Lucite stools. He turned to her with a smile and wiped his forehead with the back of his arm. A tattoo of a rattlesnake devouring a scorpion was visible on his neck.

"What can I get for you, señora?" he asked. His name tag read Jorge.

"I'm looking for some information, Jorge," Leine said in Spanish. "By any chance did you work the bar last Saturday night?"

"Sí—I always work," Jorge answered with a practiced grin.

Leine reached into her pocket and pulled out the photographs of Elise and Josh that Gunderson had included in the report. "These two were in here last Saturday evening. Do you remember them?"

Jorge leaned over the bar and squinted at the pictures. He cocked his head to one side and frowned.

"She looks familiar to me, but I can't be sure," he said. He stepped back and shook his head. "He does not. I see so many people each night. They all begin to look alike after a few hours."

Leine contemplated offering him money to jog his memory but rejected the thought. The possibility was too great that he would just tell her what she wanted to hear. "Did anyone else work the bar that night?"

Jorge nodded. "Guillermo is here every Saturday." He glanced at his watch. "Tonight he is at another club one street over. The Gypsy."

"Thank you, Jorge." Leine slid a business card with the name Lana Turner and her cell phone number across the bar. "If you remember anything, would you give me a call?"

"Of course. May I ask why you are looking for them?"

"They never came home." She rose to leave and held out her hand. Jorge shook it.

"I appreciate your time," she said.

"No problems. I hope that you find them."

Leine left the Blue Manatee and headed for the Gypsy. Tucked in the back of a small outdoor mall with several shops surrounding it, the place appeared to be less nightclub than restaurant, serving food at low prices to the locals. There was a bigger crowd than the Blue Manatee, with several tables full of diners.

She walked over to a man standing behind the counter wearing a white linen guayabera and a pair of khakis. Tortoise-shell glasses perched on top of his head.

"Is Guillermo working tonight?"

"Who wants to know?" the man asked with a disarming

smile. He reminded Leine of a younger version of an actor she'd seen in movies from the 80s named Raul Julia.

"My name is Lana Turner. Jorge at the Blue Manatee told me that I would be able to find him here."

The man's smile widened into a grin, revealing even white teeth. "I am Guillermo. What can I do for you, Lana Turner?"

Leine returned the smile and pulled out the photos.

"I'm looking for someone who remembers either of these two people. They were at the Blue Manatee last Saturday night."

Guillermo slid his glasses down and leaned in to take a closer look at the photographs. His cologne had a deep, exotic scent.

After a minute he nodded, tapping the picture of Elise with a well-manicured fingernail. "Yes, I remember her." He leaned back and smiled. "She was a vision in a white beaded dress and fabulous shoes. Christian Louboutin, if I'm not mistaken. He wasn't so bad, either," he added with a wicked grin.

Bingo. "Do you remember if they were with anyone?"

Guillermo nodded. "I do, because he was so striking. A big man with an accent—maybe Russian? Tall and muscular with white hair and light blue eyes. He looked kind of like an actor I've seen before." He paused for a moment, frowning in concentration. Frustrated, he shook his head. "I can't remember who, now. He and the boyfriend took off and left her alone at the bar." He made a *tsking* sound with his tongue. "Poor thing. She waited a long time. When he didn't come back, she became angry and walked out."

"So she didn't leave with him?" That complicated things.

Guillermo shrugged. "I don't know. The boyfriend returned to the bar not long after she left and asked me if I knew where she'd gone. I told him no, but that she looked angry and had only left a few minutes before. After that he disappeared into the crowd."

"Was the Russian man still with him?"

He shook his head. "I didn't see him." Guillermo watched Leine for a moment, an unreadable expression on his face. "They are missing, yes?"

"Yes."

"Then I hope you find them."

Leine reached into her pocket and pulled out a folded fifty-dollar bill and a business card. She placed them on the counter, covering the money with the card. "Thank you, Guillermo. If you see them or hear anything, would you give me a call?"

Guillermo smiled and nodded as he pocketed the cash. "My pleasure, Lana Turner."

Leine walked out of the Gypsy and into the warm evening air, thinking about what Guillermo had said. Obviously, Josh had caught up with Elise and talked her into going with him to the party. What Leine didn't know was the part the Russian played in their disappearances. It was possible he had nothing to do with it. It could have been a cartel kidnapping.

The noise on the street had increased and the growing energy was palpable. Leine stood on the busy sidewalk watching the human carnival drift by, absorbing the place. Normally, she would have changed her appearance in order to blend with her surroundings, but the trip had been unexpected and she hadn't felt the need. She would have liked to have been a bit more anonymous. As it was, people glanced at her as they passed but didn't engage.

Worked for her.

Not wanting to attract attention, she headed back to the secure parking lot and her rental. Lou had made hotel reservations a few miles out of town at a place called the Vista Inn, which wasn't far from the abandoned housing development where they'd found Josh's phone. An early night followed by an early start meant better odds of being home in time for dinner.

But first she wanted to connect with the DEA agent Santa had told her about, Bob Herrera. If the Russian had been hanging out for any period of time, he'd more than likely heard of him.

She kept to the shadows and moved along the back streets before cutting between buildings to reach the parking lot. No guard greeted her at the entrance. As she approached her rental a prickle of awareness tracked up her spine.

Someone was watching her.

10

ADRENALINE SPIKING, LEINE slowed down and took stock of her surroundings. The absence of the guard gave her pause. The parking lot, though touted as secure, held several dark spaces from which a person could attack. She stopped mid-stride and reached for the switchblade secured to her calf, acting as though she were adjusting something on her shoe. She straightened, careful to conceal the weapon in her hand.

Without appearing to, Leine scanned the area as she skirted her vehicle, alert for anything out of the ordinary. She turned left as she exited the lot and jogged to the end of the street. She checked behind her and, seeing no one, slipped around the corner. As she continued along the dark boulevard, she pulled out her phone and hit speed dial.

"Herrera," a man's voice answered.

"Agent Hererra, my name is Leine Basso. We have a mutual friend—Detective Santiago Jensen?"

"I've been expecting your call. Santa contacted me earlier, letting me know you were going to be in town. What can I do for you?"

"Did he fill you in on why I'm here?"

"It's about the two missing teenagers, right?"

"Right. Can you think of any reason I might be followed?"

"Not unless the police were given advance notice. Have you spoken with anyone in town regarding the case?"

"Yes. Two bartenders. One from the Blue Manatee, one from the Gypsy. But I haven't been in town long. Less than an hour."

"A local businessman named Felix Otero is majority owner of the Blue Manatee so he'll know you're here, eventually. He'll probably have his guys keep an eye on you. Anybody asking questions about something as potentially explosive as a murder and kidnapping in this city is going to be subject to intense scrutiny. An hour's pretty fast for them, though." Herrera paused. "We should meet. There's a *carne asada* place about two miles outside of town on the free road. Has a big white sign with the picture of a happy cow on it. Meet me there in half an hour."

"I'll be there." Leine disconnected the call and continued along the sidewalk. She reached the end of the block, crossed the street, turned right, and then continued to the corner. There, she turned right again and entered an alley. She stepped behind a dilapidated pickup parked next to the building and waited. Sirens wailed in the distance. Somewhere a dog joined in with a low howl.

Several minutes ticked by before a shadowy figure with an unsteady gait walked past the entrance to the alley. A few moments later the same figure reappeared and stopped on the sidewalk, hesitating as he peered into the darkness. Leine waited patiently, willing him to step under the lone streetlamp so she could get a better look at him.

The man glanced both ways before proceeding slowly into the alley. Something about him seemed familiar. She took a step back into the shadows as he approached. He passed the pickup, unaware she waited nearby.

Leine grabbed both of his arms from behind. He stiffened and struggled to break free of her grip as she wrenched one hand up between his shoulder blades.

"Hey—what are you doing?" he said in English, his voice ratcheting up an octave as he continued to resist.

"I might ask you the same question," Leine replied through her teeth. She forced him behind the truck and shoved him face first against the alley wall, pinning his free arm with her body. She gripped his elbow, letting him feel the tip of her knife next to his left kidney.

An American accent, she thought. *Probably not cartel.* Realizing her captive was overweight with virtually no muscle tone, Leine relaxed slightly, allowing the adrenaline in her body to ebb. He probably wasn't somebody's enforcer. The smell of cigarettes and stale beer mixed with sweat and body odor wafted between them. Not a pleasant combination.

"Why are you following me?" she asked as her gaze cut to the alley entrance and back again.

"Let me go and I'll tell you," he said, panting. He inched away from the knife, attempting to become one with the wall. "I have information."

"How about you tell me, and if I like your answer you live," she replied. "And stop moving. This knife is hella sharp."

He stopped moving.

Leine sighed and glanced at her watch. *I haven't got time for this.* "Let's try something simple. What's your name?"

"Willy. Willy Flint. You may have heard of my blog—Flint's Stones?"

"Doesn't ring a bell." She pushed his arm a few inches higher, eliciting a grunt of pain. "Why are you following me, Willy Flint?" she repeated, watching the entrance.

He turned his head so his cheek rested flat against the wall.

"I heard you asking the bartender in the Manatee about those two kids."

"You were the one drinking a beer at the bar."

WILLY NODDED, HIS BREATH COMING OUT IN A WHEEZE. LEINE LET up on the pressure slightly.

"How long have you been following me?" she asked. How did she not notice him?

"Jorge told me he sent you to the Gypsy."

"Why would Jorge tell you anything?"

Willy hesitated. Leine gave his arm a twist.

"I told him I wanted to ask you for a date."

Is this guy for real?

"Why not tell him you had information?" she asked.

"I can't just tell everybody what I know. It's very sensitive."

"Such as?"

"Let me go and I'll tell you."

She gave his arm another push. Willy gasped in pain.

"Okay, okay. I have a friend," he said, between breaths. "In the police department. He told me everything."

"And?"

"I know about the cell phone and the blood." Willy closed his eyes and tried to swallow.

Leine backed off a little more, releasing some of the pressure. "And you want to help me, why exactly?"

"Why else?" he replied. When she didn't respond, he continued. "Money. I saw you slip some to the guy in the Gypsy and figured there was more where that came from."

"I take it Flint's Stones isn't cutting it on the affiliate links."

"Ha ha. Very funny."

"What makes you think I gave him money?"

"What else would you slide across the counter that would give somebody a shit-eating grin?"

"He's an old friend."

"Right. An old friend who just happens to be a bartender who works Saturdays at the Blue Manatee."

Leine released her hold. He started to turn but she stopped him. "Stay where you are and put your hands on your head."

Willy slowly raised his hands. Holding the knife in her right hand Leine frisked him with her left. When she didn't find any weapons, she stepped back.

"You can turn around," she said.

Willy faced her and leaned against the wall, his gaze riveted on the knife as he wiped the sweat from his forehead with the back of his arm.

"What're you going to do with that?" His voice cracked and he cleared his throat.

Leine glanced at the knife and back at him.

"That depends on you," she answered.

He visibly swallowed. "I suppose you want me to tell you what information I was referring to earlier?"

Leine blinked. *How drunk is this guy?* "You're wasting my time."

He hesitated.

What the hell is he waiting for?

Money. This idiot still thinks I'm going to pay him. Wow. She shook her head.

"Listen, Willy. *You* made the mistake of following *me*," she said, making sure she enunciated the words slowly. "Now, I know you aren't familiar with the way I work, but that isn't how I do things. You'll be lucky to walk away from this encounter with your appendages intact, so I'd advise you to tell me what you know and be on your way. No hard feelings."

Willy gave her a blank look.

"No *dinero*. Get it?"

Understanding lit his face, followed by consternation. He met her gaze.

"But I—"

Leine rolled her eyes and stepped back. "You need to leave." She nodded at the street beyond the alley. "Now."

"Wait. What if I tell you what I know, and if you think it's worthwhile, you pay me for the information?"

"Fine." Leine glanced at her watch again.

He cleared his throat. "About a week ago, I overheard some guy talking on his cell phone outside of the little market near my apartment. He mentioned that he was expecting a special delivery from LA in a couple of days and that he'd be able to complete the transaction soon. I didn't think anything of it at the time, but two days would have made it Saturday. It seems kind of strange in light of the missing kids, don't you think?"

"Or, it could have been that the guy was actually expecting a delivery. Did you notice an accent? Was he speaking English?"

Willy shook his head. "Definitely Spanish. Why?"

"No reason." Leine narrowed her eyes. "How did you know the kids were from LA?"

"Like I said, my friend at the police station. Anyway," he continued. "I told him what I'd heard, but he said that I should keep quiet and not talk about the case or he'd be in deep shit for telling me."

"How would his superiors find out?"

"They might have been watching him or something." Willy shrugged. "My blog gets a lot of local traffic. It's possible he was worried I'd write a post." His chest seemed to expand a bit. "I'm known for writing a headline that gets noticed."

"Ah," Leine said. "Well, thanks, but what you've told me isn't worth anything." She stepped back and pointed at the alley entrance. "And now you need to go."

His eyes widened. "You're not going to pay me?"

She shook her head. "Nope."

Willy looked at the ground. He puffed out his cheeks and sucked them back in.

"What?" Leine asked, exasperated. *Why won't this guy leave?* She glanced toward the entrance again in case he was stalling, waiting for someone else to show up.

He looked up and down the alley before speaking in a low voice. "I know what happened to the car."

Leine looked at him sharply. "What car?"

"The kid's Porsche."

"I'm listening."

Willy crossed his arms. "Uh-uh. No more info without the *dinero.*"

Shaking her head, she dug into her pocket and held up a fifty. Willy made a grab for it, but Leine put it back in her pocket. "Not until you give me something I can use."

Willy sighed and pulled out a wrinkled handkerchief from his back pocket to mop his face.

"I could get into some serious shit for telling you this." He glanced behind him. "My friend knows the guy who got rid of it," he whispered.

"Go on."

Willy closed the distance between them, a conspiratorial look on his face. Leine stepped away, trying to get upwind.

"According to my friend, a guy who does side jobs for some, uh, businessmen here in town got a call to go up to Vista del Mar and get rid of a vehicle that was parked there. So this guy gets what he thinks is a brilliant idea and decides he's going to take this fearsome Porsche and hide it in his garage, intending to sell it in a couple of weeks when things die down."

"And?"

"When he went out to file off the VIN he noticed a bunch of

flies buzzing around the trunk so he opened it. What do you think he found?"

"I'm guessing a dead body."

Disappointed, Willy appeared to deflate from Leine's non-reaction. "How did you know?"

Leine ignored his question. "Male or female?"

"My friend didn't say, but he found this." Willy dug in his front pocket and showed her a man's wristwatch. Leine reached for it, but he pulled it away before she could see the make.

"That could be anyone's watch," she said, annoyance creeping into her voice.

"Yeah, anyone's *expensive* watch, with *To Josh from Mom and Dad* engraved on the back."

"Show me." Leine nodded at the timepiece. Willy held it up so she could read the back.

"What did this guy end up doing with the car?"

"He took it out of town and pushed it into a ravine with the body still inside."

"And your friend knows this, how?"

"He helped him do it."

"Where?"

Willy frowned. "I want a guarantee that you'll pay. How do I know I can trust you?"

"You don't."

By the look on his face, he wasn't going to budge.

Leine shrugged. "Yeah. I figured you were bluffing." She turned toward the alley entrance and made a sweeping gesture. "After you."

Willy's expression morphed from belligerent to panicked. "Hold on a minute."

Leine crossed her arms and waited.

"If I tell you where the car is and the wrong people find out, my friend could get into a lot of trouble. The circle is small, if you get my drift."

She watched him in silence, her arms still crossed.

A fine sheen of sweat appeared above Willy's upper lip. He puffed out his cheeks and sucked them back in again as his gaze darted from Leine to the alley entrance and back again.

Leine took a step toward him. "If you're waiting for someone, you'd better tell me now, or you're going to be in a world of hurt. And so will they."

Willy shook his head. "No, no. There's nobody else."

"Then why do you keep looking at the street?"

"Like I said, if anyone sees me talking to you, my friend could get hurt. *I* could get hurt."

Leine rolled her eyes. "Listen, Willy. It's dark. No one's going to recognize you. Or me. Okay?"

"Not until I get the money."

She ripped the fifty in half and handed him a piece. Willy gave her a look. She smiled. "You get the other half when I find the car."

"That plus at least another hundred," he said, and pressed his lips together.

"We'll see."

"Okay." He pulled a small, wire-bound notebook and pen out of his back pocket and flipped to a clean page. He glanced at the street lamp at the other end of the alley. "I need light."

Leine reached into the side pocket of her pants and produced a small flashlight, which she turned on, shining the beam on his notebook.

"It's off the Rosarito Highway, just past the goat farm," he said, drawing a crude map. "Look for a white house on your left with a fenced yard. Go six kilometers past the house and the drop point will be on your right. My friend said it was a pretty steep ravine, so no guarantees you can see the car from the road." He added a phone number, ripped the sheet out, and handed it to Leine.

"I wrote my cell on there so you can call when you find it." He pointed at the number as though she might miss it. "It's worth a hell of a lot more than whatever that bartender told you."

"Who asked him to get rid of the car and why didn't they just dispose of the body? That Porsche was worth over a hundred K."

"My friend didn't say, exactly." He shrugged. "My guess is it was cartel business."

Willy's story sounded more and more like a load of bullshit. Leine hadn't had many dealings with Mexican drug cartels, but she suspected they wouldn't let a dead body in the trunk slow them down when it came to money. And Willy hadn't offered to go with her to make sure he got paid if she found the car.

"What color is the Porsche?" she asked.

"Red."

She nodded. The fact that he got the color right was something, although red would have been a safe guess. Her enthusiasm had cooled when he mentioned that the car might not be visible from the road. Leine folded the paper and slid it into her pocket. She checked her watch again, giving Willy a pointed look.

"Oh. Right," he said. He shifted his weight from one foot to another but made no attempt to leave. Leine folded her arms and glared at him.

Shift, pause. Shift, pause.

"What?" Leine didn't try to conceal the exasperation in her voice. *I should have dropped his ass when I first saw him,* she thought in irritation.

"How much do you think the information is worth?" Willy's facial expression would have put a newborn puppy to shame.

Leine emitted a disgusted sigh as she brushed past him. "You're pushing it, Willy. How about nothing? *Nada*. Got it?"

"Whoa. Take it easy. I'm sorry." He grabbed for her arm but pulled back when he saw the look on her face. "How about I just wait for your call?" He cleared his throat and nodded. "Yeah. I'll just wait."

"Leave now, Willy," Leine said, her voice weary. "I'll call you when and if I find the Porsche."

He gave her a wan smile before he took off at a brisk pace toward the alley entrance. Halfway to the street Willy stopped and turned back. "Promise you won't tell anyone?"

"The ice is getting pretty thin, Willy."

"Okay. Got it. Don't forget," he stage whispered as he walked away, hand to his ear like a telephone. Leine exhaled with relief when he finally turned the corner and disappeared.

Glad to have Willy Flint gone, Leine thought about what he'd said. Why would someone damage a car worth that much, essentially leaving money on the table? It couldn't have been a carjacking gone wrong. It didn't make sense. The possibility that Elise might have been the intended target was beginning to sound a lot more plausible. Even though she figured Willy was full of shit, she'd still check his story. He'd known too many details—the phone, the Porsche, Vista del Mar—for her to completely discount him. If his story checked out, she was pretty sure she knew who the guy doing the driving had been.

At least now she had something to work with. Herrera's input regarding the local police would help her to determine whether there might be a larger cover-up to consider.

Leine retracted the blade and slipped the knife into her pocket. She made a mental note to call Lou and see if he'd found her a semiautomatic.

She had the feeling she was going to need it.

11

———

LEINE WAITED A few moments before exiting the alley. Once she'd made sure no one else was following her, she returned to her rental. She paid the attendant, who had reappeared and was eating his dinner out of a tinfoil wrapper, and drove out of the parking lot, through town to the free road.

The sign with the happy cow was lit from below and easy to see. Leine pulled into the outdoor restaurant's dirt lot and parked. Besides the man behind the grill and an older woman making tortillas, there were three other customers. A young couple sat at one of the tables eating tacos and drinking beer. A man with a cowboy hat resting on the table in front of him occupied another. Leine walked over to the man with the hat.

"Bob Herrera?"

"Yes, ma'am," Herrera said, standing. "You must be Leine."

Leine shook his hand and had a seat. "Thank you for meeting with me."

"A pleasure. Thirsty?" he asked.

"I'd take a beer."

Herrera signaled the woman behind the counter preparing

tortillas. She nodded and a few minutes later came by their table with two ice-cold *Dos Equis.*

Bob Herrera had the look of a man comfortable in his own skin, although his relaxed expression had a wariness that matched the sardonic tilt of his mouth. Dark hair shot with gray and cut short framed the beginnings of a five o'clock shadow. Along with the cowboy hat, he wore a faded yellow golf shirt, black jeans, and scuffed cowboy boots. A slight paunch had made itself at home around his midsection, but he otherwise appeared fit.

"How is ol' Santa, anyway?" He smiled, his teeth gleaming in the soft glow of the string lights hanging across the seating area. The smell of fresh lime and seared beef drifted over from the cooking area.

"He's doing well. Says to tell you it's your turn to pay."

He chuckled. "Last time I saw him we closed down a little cantina just this side of the border. As I recall he ended up footing the bill."

"Good as it was of you to meet with me, Agent Herrera, I assume there's another reason you wanted to talk. Am I right?"

"Call me Bob, and yes, there is." He shifted in his seat and took a drink of his beer. "Santa explained that you're working for SHEN but that the missing girl's parents believe she may have been targeted because they're wealthy."

"That's it in a nutshell."

"And they came to SHEN on the advice of their attorney?"

Leine nodded. "There's been no ransom demand, which leaves the possibility she may have been targeted by traffickers."

"We've been seeing an increase in criminal activity around TJ—carjackings, kidnappings, extortion. According to my sources, it doesn't have anything to do with the local criminal element."

"Outside talent?"

Bob nodded. "I've heard rumors the Eastern Europeans are in town."

"The bartender I talked to said he saw the missing owner of the Porsche with a guy who sounded Russian."

"That jibes with the rumors." Herrera let out a long sigh. "That won't sit well with the local boys."

"Earlier on the phone you said the owner of the Blue Manatee might have me followed. Why would he care about me being here? I'm no threat."

"Otero's good friends with the mayor, who is particular about controlling information regarding his town. The disappearance of two wealthy kids, an expensive car, and a possible murder could derail his marketing efforts." Agent Herrera's gaze met hers. "I would tell you not to worry about it except Otero is known to be connected to organized crime. Even though he considers himself a religious man, he operates a whorehouse outside the city that caters to his 'messengers of Christ,' that's what he calls his employees. Hell, a lot of people in town think he's a great man, do side jobs for him for extra cash. Some of the local police are on his payroll, although that's slowly changing. The police force has gone through a cleansing in the last few years. That being said, I'd recommend you tread lightly. That is one pot you don't want to stir."

"Sounds like the mayor's going to have a marketing nightmare on his hands whether he wants one or not." Leine watched the cars passing by on the highway. "A lot of innocent people could get caught in the crossfire."

"Yeah."

"What do you know about a guy by the name of Willy Flint?" Leine asked.

Herrera snorted. "Flint's Stones? Jesus, talk about a royal pain in my ass. What did he want?"

"Nothing, really. He was having a beer at the Blue Manatee."

"Willy's been hanging around TJ for a long time. Your typical shyster, always on the lookout for easy money. He popped up on my radar a year after I was transferred, sure he had inside information I could use." Herrera shook his head with a wry smile. "Ninety-eight percent of the time he makes shit up, hoping to get a payout before I check his stories."

"What about the other two percent?"

"Problem with Willy is, every once in a while he'll have something worthwhile. But the bogus information outweighs the truth, by far."

"Thanks for confirming my impression." Leine rested her beer on the table. "If your mayor is so sensitive about his town, why did the police tell ICE about the phone? Seems to me if he'd wanted to keep things quiet, he would have tried to bury the evidence."

"The mayor didn't know about the phone until it was too late. The Chief of Police was on vacation in Cabo and found out when he got back two days ago. At that point, the department had shared their findings and the guys from ICE had already taken samples of the blood."

"Where's the phone now?"

"I assume the police have it."

"We still don't know for sure if Elise was in the car with Josh. If not, then we've got a couple of different possibilities. Tell me what your gut says." Leine proceeded to give him the information she had on the disappearances, avoiding any mention of what Willy Flint told her about the car. If things shook out the way Willy had intimated, and that was a big if, she'd let him know.

"Would you say it sounds like the work of local organized crime or outsiders?"

Herrera shrugged. "Hard to say. Both kids were a prime target. Could've been either." He paused for a moment, thinking.

"You say the girl told her friend they were headed for a party at some actor's house on the beach. The housing project where they found the phone may have a water view, but it's a far cry from an oceanfront mansion."

"So Josh was tricked into driving to the abandoned development where no one would see him."

"Sounds like it. I'll lay five to one it's the boy's blood, not hers."

"Does that fit the MO of your locals?"

"Possibly. One thing bugs me, though. The kidnappers could have found a way to force Josh out of the car without damaging the vehicle. That was one valuable Porsche. That they didn't tells me whoever did this cared more about the occupant or occupants than the car."

"Replacing a windshield isn't hard, especially with all the body shops in town."

"Yeah, but they found part of a side mirror and headlight glass. I know the local guys. They're lazy as hell. Most of them are interested in easy pickings. No muss, no fuss." Herrera glanced at his watch. "I assume you're going up to the housing project tomorrow?"

"I'm sure it's been gone over with a fine-tooth comb, but I still want to get a feel for the place."

"I'm happy to drive you there, if you want."

Leine nodded. "I figured I'd get an early start. Meet me here around sunrise?"

"See you then."

12

———

ARLY THE NEXT morning, Leine took a quick shower and then checked her phone. Lou had sent her a text with a name, telephone number, and the word *baitbox*. Baitbox referred to a job she'd done in Italy with Lou acting as logistical support. Whenever he'd set something up that she needed to physically retrieve, he would give both Leine and the supplier a specific pass phrase to act as an identifier. He knew she'd remember which one they'd used in Italy because their weapons contact worked a fish market in Naples as a front and, inexplicably, had offered Leine a box of free fish bait with the merchandise. She texted Lou to thank him and called the number.

"*¿Bueno?*" the voice on the other end said.

"I'd like to order some bait," she said in Spanish.

"Of course, señora. What kind would you like?"

"Minnows, please," she said, indicating a semiautomatic handgun.

"What size container do you need?" the voice asked.

"A number nine should do it," Leine replied, denoting a nine millimeter. "And could I also get a box of night crawlers?" One box of ammunition would be more than enough.

"No problem. Your order will be ready for you to pick up within the hour. Do you need this bait on ice?" On ice meant a suppressor.

"No, thank you. However it comes will be fine."

The man on the phone gave her directions to the pickup location and ended the call. He didn't ask for payment. Lou would have already taken care of that. Leine left immediately to make it to the drop before the delivery happened.

It was still dark, which suited Leine. She preferred darkness when dealing with activities the local authorities tended to frown upon. After a quick reconnaissance of the abandoned gas station parking lot, she continued behind the building and up a rise with a good visual of the drop site, and cut the lights.

Fifteen minutes went by before a late-model pickup pulled into the gas station and continued around to the back. Leine reached into her bag for a pair of night vision binoculars and trained them on the new arrival. A man carrying a package exited the truck and walked to a large metal barrel next to a tree. He looked behind him before placing the package inside and returning to the truck. A few minutes later, the pickup's taillights blinked on, and the man drove out of the parking lot and back onto the highway, heading south.

Leine remained where she was another ten minutes, waiting to see if anyone else showed up. Once she was satisfied no one lurked in the shadows, she drove around and pulled into the gas station, continuing behind the hollowed-out structure to the rusty blue barrel. She parked and got out, scanning the area as she walked over to the drop.

The package was sitting on top of a cardboard box, a foot below the rim of the barrel. Leine picked it up and returned to her vehicle. The gun and a full magazine wrapped in dirty flannel had been stuffed inside a plastic grocery bag, along with a box of ammunition. Leine worked the slide and snapped the magazine into the grip. Everything worked the way it should. She looked at her watch. There was time before her meeting with Herrera to head out into the desert for target practice. She hated not having firsthand experience with a firearm that she might need to use.

After an hour of shooting an old beer can and satisfied with the accuracy of the gun, Leine pulled up next to Agent Herrera's pickup in the parking lot of the Happy Cow restaurant. The place was closed up tight. She rolled her window down and he did the same.

"Good morning," he said.

"Morning," Leine replied. "Yours or mine?"

"I know the roads. How about you ride with me?"

Fifteen minutes later, they drove through the white arch and proceeded into the abandoned Vista del Mar housing project. The absence of streetlights and sidewalks and the crumbling shells of houses with weed-filled front yards should have been enough of a deterrent to anyone looking for a party.

They continued to the location shown on the map given to her by the ICE agents. Herrera shifted into park and killed the engine. They both got out and scanned the area. There was no indication that the police had even been there.

"This doesn't look like a crime scene," Leine said.

"No body, no car, no crime," Herrera replied. "The guys from ICE already took photos and went over the area." He looked around and shook his head. "Man, I got two teenagers at home in San Diego. I hope they'd know enough to turn around and get their asses back to a well-lit, populated place if they saw this instead of what they were expecting."

"Promises of going to a party hosted by a celebrity tend to trump a lot of people's common sense," Leine said. "And it's not just teenagers. I've seen adults go off the charts when it came to associating with the rich and famous." Leine thought back to when she worked security for an A-list movie star in LA the previous summer. She'd balked at the sycophantic hangers-on surrounding him like so much confetti after a parade. She didn't understand the allure.

"They found the phone over there, in the weeds." Herrera pointed to the right side of the road.

"Then that's where I'll start." Following a grid pattern, she methodically walked back and forth across the area, scanning the ground for anything the local police or ICE agents might have missed. Herrera did the same on the opposite side.

"The blood's over here," he called. Leine made a mental note of the section where she'd stopped and walked over to join Herrera. The dark patch was about two feet in diameter with a distinct footprint to the right of center. Herrera squatted to take a closer look.

"Whose footprint do you think that is?" Leine asked.

"My guess would be police."

Leine gave him a sharp look. He glanced up at her, squinting against the sun. "Evidence gathering is kind of hit or miss in these parts."

It didn't matter. They'd have the results back from the lab soon, telling them whose blood it was. The suspects had likely covered their tracks by now. Leine hadn't expected to find much.

They resumed searching on opposite sides of the road. They'd been at it for the better part of an hour when the sound of a car approaching brought them up short. They both turned as a dark blue Suburban with tinted windows and a shiny gold grill appeared, heading toward them.

"Who is it?" Leine asked, her voice low.

"Locals," came Herrera's clipped reply.

Leine wondered if the DEA agent was armed. By the way he

was acting, this wasn't a social visit. The semiautomatic resting at the small of her back eased her mind slightly.

The SUV slowed to a stop but continued to idle. Both the driver and passenger wore dark sunglasses. Leine couldn't make out more than that through the windshield. Herrera stood next to his pickup, waiting for whoever was inside to make their presence known.

The driver cut the engine and the front doors slowly opened.

13

THE MAN IN the passenger seat emerged first. Dressed head to toe in black, his Fu Manchu mustache and goatee gave him a mildly evil appearance, although a beer belly the size of the Bronx somewhat ruined the look.

Herrera turned toward him, hands at his sides where both men could see them. The driver hopped out of the jacked-up truck and stood near the golden front grill, leaving the door open. Several inches shorter and just as heavy as the other man, he wore a Hawaiian shirt, black jeans with spit-shined cowboy boots, a flashy watch, and a major attitude. Leine deepened her breathing in order to slow the adrenaline dump into her veins.

"Ignacio," Herrera said, acknowledging Fu Manchu. Ignacio inclined his head but didn't smile.

"Who's your friend?" Ignacio asked, nodding at Leine. The driver leaned against the fender, silent.

"The parents of a missing girl hired her to investigate her disappearance."

Ignacio's lips curled into a smile. "An investigator, eh? Maybe she'll want to investigate this." He grabbed his crotch and leered.

Leine cocked her head but didn't say anything, gauging the

distance between them. The guy would be easy. Herrera could take out the driver. Plausible scenario, but she wasn't excited about the fallout. When Ignacio didn't get the reaction he was expecting, his mouth curved down into what could only be described as a pout.

"Our mutual friend is not happy," he said, speaking to Herrera but still looking at Leine. "Just this morning he said to me, 'Ignacio, you must be sure that this woman is escorted safely from our city. We wouldn't want something terrible to happen to her while she is here.'" Ignacio removed his sunglasses and stared at Leine. His gaze held the hint of menace.

"Tell our mutual friend that he has nothing to worry about," Herrera replied. "As I said, she is here at the request of the parents of a missing teenager. Nothing more."

"Why doesn't she speak?" Ignacio asked, irritation apparent in his voice. "Doesn't she understand Spanish?"

"I understand Spanish very well," Leine answered. "I just didn't feel the need to add to what he said." *Or antagonize an asshole who clearly doesn't respect women*, she thought.

"You are wise, señora." Ignacio brushed his hand against his hip and briefly lifted his shirt, flashing the butt of a pistol.

"I hear the lines are very long at the border," he said, watching her intently. "You may want to get there early so that you have no problems returning home." He turned to Herrera with a smile and saluted. "Have a good day, my friend."

Ignacio returned to the Suburban and climbed inside. His silent sidekick did the same. The driver revved the engine, turned the SUV around, and slowly drove away. Leine and Herrera watched them leave.

"Well, that was enjoyable," Herrera said.

"I assume the mutual friend he referred to is Otero?"

Herrera nodded. "Yep."

"You did say he'd have me watched. I'm surprised he sent someone to warn me away."

"Me too." Herrera frowned. "In fact, I'm more than surprised. Otero isn't usually so ham-fisted." He glanced at Leine. "Santa never did give me your background."

Leine shrugged. "I worked security for a low-level diplomat for a few years, but that shouldn't have raised any flags." There was no way that Otero could have found any information about her previous profession. She'd had a friend in her old agency do a series of high-level background checks on her. Nothing had come up. At least that was one thing Eric hadn't lied about. Her old boss had promised to scrub her past when she left the business. Apparently, he'd kept his promise.

"Obviously, Otero feels threatened by my presence. How far do you think I can push things without turning this into an international incident?"

"His sending Ignacio and his BFF tells me there's more to the story. I'd watch your back from this point on." Herrera scanned the development. "I think we've done all we can do here."

Leine sighed. "I really hate it when someone threatens me."

Herrera squinted at her. "Santa told me you had a rebellious streak. I'd be remiss if I didn't strongly advise against antagonizing Felix Otero or Ignacio. But, you gotta do what you gotta do. Just don't make my job harder, okay?"

"I'll do my best."

HERRERA DROPPED LEINE OFF AT HER VEHICLE WITH ANOTHER admonishment that she take Ignacio's warning seriously. She was taking it seriously, all right. But first, she had one more errand before she left Mexico.

She ordered two tacos from the now open restaurant and

asked the woman making tortillas where she could find a hardware store. The woman gave her directions to one a few kilometers away. Leine thanked her and drove there as soon as she finished eating.

She picked out several meters of heavy rope, a pulley, some clips, a machete, and a pair of leather gloves, and paid at the front counter. Then, following the crude map Willy gave her, she drove to the place where his "friend" had purportedly driven the car over the cliff.

Six kilometers past the white house with the fence, Leine slowed as she came to an area missing several meters of metal barrier. The spot was remote, with no visible homes or businesses. She pulled over just beyond the break and parked. Grabbing the binoculars from her bag, she got out and walked to the edge of the road.

Steep and composed of heavily eroded soil with sparse vegetation sprinkled near the top of the cliff, the slope grew less severe approximately halfway down. A mixed palette of desert trees and shrubs partially obscured the bottom of the ravine. Leine scanned the slope for pieces of Porsche, but nothing stood out. She was about to chalk Willy's story up to a lame attempt at a payoff when something far below in the dry brush caught her eye. She trained the binoculars on a small red patch of color between two straggly mesquites and zoomed in. In between the branches, she picked out a slim, metallic letter R resting against a red background.

Well, what do you know? Leine lowered the glasses and studied the area surrounding the ravine. A sturdy mesquite grew by the edge of the road near the terminus of the old, rusty barrier, half of its roots gripping the shoulder, the other half weaving their way into and out of the cliff face, seeking a stronger hold.

Leine walked back to the rental and stowed the binoculars in her bag, which she took with her to the rear of the SUV and placed in the cargo area. She grabbed the equipment she'd purchased, slid her phone into her back pocket, and shut and locked the door.

After looping the rope around the tree trunk, she threaded the other end through the pulley, making sure it was secure. Using the clips, she rigged a harness with the remaining line and tested the combination. Then she tied the machete to her back and slid on the leather gloves. She gripped the rope and stepped backward down the steep slope, allowing the line to slide through her gloves as she went.

Halfway into her descent, she stopped, gagging at the putrid stench filling the air. Leine pulled her T-shirt over her nose and took shallow breaths through her mouth. It didn't do much to mask the nauseating odor.

Memories from a time in Morocco years before came flooding back. In search of a target she'd been sent to kill, Leine walked into an abandoned building and was greeted by the sickly sweet smell of a decomposing body. An unlucky associate of the intended target had been shot twice and left to die in the stifling room as a message to potential traitors. She never forgot the smell, like a month-old chicken carcass doused in maple syrup and left to rot in the sun, only worse.

Regretting the tacos she'd eaten earlier, she continued to pick her way down the cliff. A few yards further, the cliff face began to level out and she found the going easier. The closer she got to the Porsche, the thicker the brush and the stronger the smell.

The car had wedged itself at its widest point between two trees about a third of the way up from the bottom of the ravine. Shrubby vegetation blocked both doors. The windshield on the driver's side had been smashed and the side mirror was missing. The front end, where the trunk was located, had buckled from the impact of the car's journey down the cliff. Dozens of flies droned at the opening.

Leine untied the machete and brought it to the front. With one hand on the rope, she hacked at the brush near the passenger side with the other, clearing a path to the front of the car. The temperature in the canyon had spiked with the climbing sun. Leine wiped the perspiration from her forehead with the back of her arm between swipes with the machete. Due to the heat, the stench emanating from the trunk took on a more robust aroma and Leine finally gave in to her gag reflex. The tacos quickly became lunch for the local coyotes.

After several passes with the sharp blade, Leine cut through enough to allow her access to the trunk. She slid the machete behind her back and secured it before she let out more line, permitting her to climb onto the roof and slide over the right fender to the front of the car.

Leine gagged again from the intense odor, but she had nothing left to offer and dry heaved into a nearby jojoba bush. She wiped her mouth with the back of her hand and repositioned the T-shirt over her nose as she peered into the trunk. Unable to see into the shadowy recesses, she wound the rope around her leg, gripped the hood with both hands, and pushed. With a metallic screech, the trunk opened the rest of the way. Excited by the interruption, dozens of flies scattered and regrouped, buzzing her face and shoulders.

Oh, shit. Almost too late, she clamped her lips shut in case one flew into her mouth. Santa said it happened to him once, during an investigation, and she didn't want the same experience. Breathing shallowly with her lips barely apart, Leine swatted the insects away and peered into the trunk.

The bloodied corpse laid on its side, missing a shirt, the skin dark and mottled. The body had ballooned from its decomposing gasses, resembling a freakish piñata. Maggots crawled around what was left of the face, making efficient work of cleaning flesh from bone, and something had gnawed at an arm. By the looks of the shoes and pants, hair, and body composition, the deceased was a male. Something else caught her eye, and she held her breath as she peered closer.

Blood had congealed along a jagged, six-inch gash on the corpse's back, near where the right kidney would have been. She moved the body to get a better look at the rest of the back. A similar gash could be seen on the left.

Leine slipped her phone out of her back pocket and held it in front of her. Focusing on the body, she took several pictures from different angles, zeroing in on the gashes and the expensive clothing. Next she took a couple of wide shots of the car and the VIN tag on the dash. Gunderson or Nabokov could run the number to confirm the car's registration.

She put her phone back in her pocket and closed the trunk as far as it would go to prevent access by the larger scavengers in the area. Then she made her way back to the passenger side.

The door initially wouldn't open more than a few inches, having sustained damage during its trip down the cliff, but with dedicated effort she was able to widen the gap enough to squeeze inside. Still breathing shallowly, she rummaged through the console and dug behind the seats and under them, but came up with nothing. Leine sat in the passenger seat and studied the interior.

Her gaze drifted lower. Her foot rested on a bump in the floor, near the dash. Leine slid out of the seat and onto her knees outside the car and peeled the carpeting back. On the floor lay a hot pink iPhone. Leine picked it up and held it to the light. She hit the button to turn it on, but the battery was dead. The words *Elise's phone* were prominently displayed in gold on the back.

Elise had been inside the car. Brittany's story was beginning to look a lot more likely.

14

LEINE BEGAN THE long, slow climb up the face of the cliff. When she reached the top, she took a moment to rest before unhooking the rope from the tree. The area around her rib throbbed with each breath, like someone was jabbing her lungs with a hot poker and enjoying it. Pissed off, she ignored the pain and untied the harness, removed the pulley and clips, and coiled the rope.

When she walked to the back of the SUV she noticed a rank odor waft toward her from somewhere nearby. Unable to locate anything in the surrounding area, she sniffed her shirt, grimacing at the cloying scent of the dead.

She'd have to change. She refused to smell like a corpse all the way back to LA. She slipped her phone out of her back pocket and called Lou, but got voicemail.

"Hi, Lou. It's Leine. I found the car—somebody drove it off a cliff into a ravine. I think we can rule out carjacking on this one. Looks like Josh was murdered—a white male matching his description was inside the trunk with his face blown off. I have photos for Gunderson and Nabokov. I haven't located Elise, but I found her phone. She was more than likely in the car when Josh drove up to Vista del Mar."

She paused, thinking. "You should probably know I've had a run-in with a couple of local heavies but the situation's under control. I'm planning to be at the border in the next couple of hours and should be home by tonight. I'll give you a call when I get back."

She disconnected and opened the door to the cargo area where she began to stow the equipment. The sound of an approaching vehicle caught her attention, and she covered the rope with the floor mat before turning to see who it was.

The dark blue Suburban slowed, coming to a stop several yards away. Leine pulled the door to the cargo bay closed, the machete still in her hand and concealed behind her leg. This time Ignacio and his driver immediately exited the vehicle. Neither looked happy.

"You're pretty stupid for a *gringa*." His eyes glittered as he walked toward her. "Didn't you get my message?"

The driver stayed a step behind Ignacio. His look mirrored his companion's. Ignacio stopped abruptly and waved at his nose.

"What the fuck?" He glanced over his shoulder, searching for the source of the rank odor. Sidekick mimicked him, looking left and right. Unable to pinpoint where it was coming from, Ignacio took a step toward Leine and stopped. Comprehension lit his face. Clearly, he recognized the smell of a decaying corpse. His eyes narrowed, and he slowly shook his head, making a *tsking* sound with his tongue. "You've been a bad *gringa*."

"I was just leaving." Leine kept her expression neutral but her body was strung tight, thrumming in anticipation of his next move.

"Too late. You should have left when I told you to." He

stepped back and nodded at Sidekick. "Teach her how things are done in Tijuana."

Sidekick lifted his shirt and went for his gun. Events slowed in the haze of adrenaline as Leine swung the machete. The blade sliced into Sidekick's right arm, blocked from severing it when metal hit bone. Eyes bulging, he screamed and gripped the gaping wound. The gold-plated nine millimeter clattered to the ground as the first spurt of blood from an artery soaked Ignacio's expensive black boots. Leine flipped the machete and swept it back, carving into the soft flesh of Sidekick's belly.

The shocked look on Sidekick's face as he collapsed to the ground paled in comparison to Ignacio's. His eyes wide, he fumbled for his gun while Leine pivoted forward, bringing the blade with her. Unable to get a grip on his weapon, he threw himself backward with a cry as the machete bit air.

Ignacio recovered and pulled his gun free, but Leine kept coming, throwing him off balance, not giving him time to set up, sweeping the machete in wide arcs as she advanced. He managed to squeeze off a round, but the shot went wide.

Leine ignored the pulsing ache from her recent rib injury and kept the blade moving, advancing toward Ignacio with laser-like focus. He stumbled backward, regained his footing, and raised his gun. Leine heard the gun fire several times, felt an acid-like burn in her left arm and ignored that, too, the adrenaline spurring her on as she brought the blade across and down.

He'd apparently miscalculated the length of time it would take her to cover the distance between them, and Leine scored a direct hit, slicing through tendon and muscle and the smaller bones in his wrist. Ignacio cried out as the gun fell from his now useless hand.

Clutching his forearm, Ignacio backed away but pulled up short, his way blocked by the mesquite. He leaned against the tree, raising his arm in order to slow the bleeding. Leine stepped over the gun and walked toward him, her gaze never leaving his sweat-soaked face.

"Who the fuck *are* you?" he choked out the words and doubled over, gasping from the pain.

"The woman your mother warned you about." Leine brought the machete back and took aim.

A smirk flashed across Ignacio's face. "She never warned me about women." His good hand snaked toward his ankle, but he was too late. Leine let the machete fly.

Ignacio's eyes bulged as the blade cleaved through his skull. Blood spurted from the rupture, arcing through the air. He stood for a moment, wavering. A river of red coursed down the center of his face before his eyes dulled and he tumbled backward into the ravine.

"Maybe she should have," Leine said.

The caustic pain in her upper arm roared back and she glanced down. Blood flowed from a gunshot wound. The force of the adrenaline evaporated and she started to shake. She applied pressure to slow the bleeding as she made herself walk to the edge of the cliff. A large shrub had blocked Ignacio's descent. He'd landed face up, his leg bent at an unnatural angle beneath him, the machete no longer attached to his skull. Leine scanned the cliff face and found it, several yards up and to his left. She briefly considered what would happen if authorities retrieved the murder weapon and were able to pull latents off it, but remembered what Herrera had said about evidence collection by the local police and decided it wouldn't be necessary. She'd be long gone by the time they found it.

The blood loss had left her weak. Carefully stepping over both of the dead men's guns on her way back to her vehicle she repeated the mantra, *Everything's fine, Leine. You're going to be fine.*

Close to blacking out from the searing pain in her arm and shaking from the fading adrenaline, she noted with the odd detachment of someone going into shock that at least the bleeding had slowed somewhat. With a grimace, she opened the cargo door and sat on the tailgate, bending her leg to release the knife sheathed to her calf. The sharp blade made quick work of the bottom of her shirt, which she used to fashion a tourniquet. She pulled the knot tight with her teeth above the wound. It would have to do until she located medical supplies.

In a sort of daze, she closed the back and walked to the driver's side. Before getting in, she reached into her back pocket, slid out her phone, and punched in Lou's number. Then she got in, started the engine and pulled away from what was left of Ignacio, Sidekick, the Porsche, and Josh.

The call went to Lou's voicemail again. She decided against leaving a message. She'd tell him what happened when she saw him.

That was, if she made it across the border.

She needed to address the injury before she started for home. She wasn't going to spend hours in line waiting to cross with a gunshot wound in her arm, especially without painkillers. A phone call to Herrera flitted through her mind, but his request to not make his life any harder stopped her from contacting the DEA agent. She'd just killed two local criminals. No point in stirring up more trouble.

She'd undoubtedly raise a few eyebrows if she walked into a store for bandages. Yes, she had a change of clothes, but the long-sleeved shirt in her bag would soon be soaked with blood if she wore it without a bandage. She needed to keep the fabric clean so as not to raise suspicion at the border. Another factor to consider: it wouldn't be long before someone discovered the bodies near the ravine and raised the alarm. She had to find a doctor, and soon.

There was only one other option.

I need to talk to him anyway. Resigned to her next move, she slid out the piece of paper with the map to Vista del Mar. She braced her knee against the steering wheel to keep the rental on the road and punched in Willy's phone number.

"Willy Flint."

"Willy. It's Lana Turner." She held the phone between her ear and shoulder, driving with her right hand.

Silence. Leine frowned at the windshield.

"The woman in the alley?" she prompted.

"Sorry. I'm just surprised you called." Willy's voice sounded like he was holding his breath. A moment later he exhaled. "Did you find the car? Because, you know, if you did, then you owe me. It's only fair, right?"

Leine rolled her eyes. Evidently, Willy never stopped partying. How much help would the guy be stoned?

"Yes, Willy. I did." She started to say something else, but Willy beat her to it.

"Where do you want to meet? I can be anywhere in no time. Just say the word."

"Willy, listen to me. I'm going to need a favor. A big favor." A pulse of excruciating pain rocketed up her arm and into her shoulder, taking her breath away. She glanced at the wound, which had begun to bleed again.

"Seems to me I already did you a solid. Big favors cost big money."

"I assumed that," she said, gritting her teeth to stop herself from making a sarcastic comment. The combination of pain, crashing adrenaline, and having to ask Willy Flint for a favor grated mightily on her nerves. She was in no mood to play games. *Fuck.* She hated asking the guy for anything. She knew the type. Flint was the kind of person who would make you pay dearly for a favor. And pay.

And pay.

"Okay, okay. You looking for something in particular? Drugs? Available males?" He paused. "Females?"

"No, Willy. I don't..." Leine bit her tongue, again. She was beginning to feel light headed. "I need the address of a competent doctor. Someone who doesn't ask too many questions. Preferably one who works outcall."

"Uh, well. Let me think a minute." Willy paused. "Yeah. I know someone." He lowered his voice. "Why do you need a doctor?"

"What's the address?" she asked, ignoring his question.

"How dumb do you think I am? We meet first. You pay me. Then I give it to you."

"Whatever, Willy. Meet me at the Pemex near the junction of Agua Caliente and Hermosillo Street."

"I'll be there in five."

You can do this, Leine. Just keep driving, stay conscious.

"I'll be there in fifteen," Leine replied and ended the call.

15

———————

WILLY FLINT WAS waiting for her at the station in a rusty, brown, 70s-era Pinto—more rust than brown. The interior made up for what the car lacked in exterior pizazz with a multitude of incandescent shades painted in swirls across the dash and bright, strangely clashing covers on both of the bucket seats. An acid green blanket covered the back.

You don't see that every day, Leine thought.

Which was probably a good thing.

She pulled up next to him and parked. Willy held out a bag of lime-flavored tortilla chips. Leine shook her head. The spots were getting worse. *Maintain, Leine.*

He shrugged. "Your loss. These are really good."

"What's the doctor's address?" she asked, way past caring about food, or Willy, or fucking Mexico in general. The pain from the gunshot wound had intensified to full-on agonizing while she drove. Combined with having wasted her time offing Otero's thugs, dealing with the increasingly hot afternoon, and fighting to stay conscious, the morning's events had put her in a supremely foul mood.

"You know our agreement. Ya gotta pay to play." Oblivious to Leine's disposition and avoiding eye contact, Willy Flint peered inside his bag of chips, acutely interested in its contents. She caught the acrid scent of *cannabis sativa* wafting her way from the interior of Willy's car.

Fuck it. I don't have time for this. Leine dug into her bag and counted out two hundred dollars, which she wadded up and lobbed through his window. Willy tracked the bills as they arced past him and leaned over to retrieve them from the passenger seat. A couple of seconds later he was back, head down and lips moving as he counted the money. A slow grin spread across his face. He held a slip of paper with an address out the window and tried to hand it to her.

"Tell Doctor Ramirez I sent you. He'll treat you right."

Leine glanced at the paper, memorizing the information.

"Thanks. Get in."

Startled, Willy looked up from his snack chips. "Get in?"

Leine had been tracking the two customers getting gas at the Pemex. She and Willy were parked far enough away that they weren't attracting attention.

"Get. In," she said through gritted teeth. She looked pointedly at the gun she held out of sight behind the side mirror. Willy blanched, reminding Leine of an extra from her daughter's favorite television show, *The Walking Dead*.

"Get your ass in the car. Show me where this Doctor Ramirez is and bring me in the back door. Now," she added, in case he hadn't quite gotten the message.

Willy looked back at the station attendants as though they might be able to save him from the scary woman with a gun.

"Now, Willy."

Willy Flint slowly opened his door, eyes riveted on the nine millimeter.

"And lose the chips."

Willy dropped the bag of chips onto the front seat, closed the door to the Pinto, and walked around to the passenger side of Leine's vehicle. For a second, Leine thought he might bolt, but he got in and closed the door.

"Holy shit. You've been shot," he said, staring at the blood on her arm. He leaned closer to get a better look.

Leine shifted into gear and pulled out of the parking lot. Spots continued to float in and out of her peripheral vision and she was getting lightheaded. "You're a master of deduction, Willy. Which way?"

"Left," he said, pointing east. Leine turned onto the busy boulevard. Willy sniffed at the air like a golden retriever. He turned toward her and was about to say something, but decided against it and leaned back in his seat.

"You know the smell," Leine said.

Willy cleared his throat and shrugged.

"You're the guy, aren't you?"

"I don't know what you mean."

"C'mon, Willy. It's obvious you're the one who drove the Porsche off the cliff." Leine waited for him to either accept or reject her assumption, but he stayed mute. "You're better off being straight with me now rather than later. I'm not the forgiving type."

Willy watched the scenery stream past his window while he sucked his cheeks in and out a handful of times.

"That's a really annoying habit you have, you know that?" Leine said.

"I do it when I'm nervous."

"What are you nervous about?"

"You."

"Well, you should have thought about that before you followed me into the alley." So he was scared of her. She could work with scared.

Ten minutes later they pulled up to a pleasant-looking stucco building in an older residential area. A black metal fence surrounded the perimeter of the manicured grounds with a pair of palm trees growing out of the middle of a lush yard. Leine and Willy waited until a car drove past before they got out and crossed the street, following the sidewalk to the back. Willy reached over the fence and unhooked the latch. He held it open for Leine as she walked through and closed it behind them.

"Wait here. I should probably give him a heads-up. Then I'll come and get you."

"Fine. But be quick, okay? And Willy?"

He turned.

"Keep things on the low down. No names, no stories about what I'm doing in Tijuana. Got it?"

Willy nodded. "Got it." He paused. "What should I call you, then? You have a code name or something?"

Seriously? "Anything you want, Willy. Just get the fucking doctor, will you?"

Willy nodded again and disappeared. Leine heaved a sigh of relief.

She walked unsteadily over to a wrought iron garden bench positioned beneath a large tree and dropped down onto it, grateful for the shade. Now that she had a minute to think she closed her eyes against the pain, took a deep breath, and began to sift through what she'd learned.

Elise had been inside the car as Brittany suggested, and was probably with Josh when he drove to the housing development, looking for the party. The carjacking theory had come off the table as soon as Leine located the Porsche. And, she was ninety-nine percent sure it was Josh's body in the car's trunk.

She was also fairly certain, contrary to what Willy claimed, that Willy Flint was the guy who did side jobs for the "business-men" in town and had been the one to drive the Porsche off the cliff. Which meant he knew more than he let on. Leine intended to find out what he was hiding.

What she didn't know was why Otero's thugs were so worried about her finding out about the Porsche. Worried enough to track her down and try to kill her. She wondered how they found her, unless someone tipped them off. Which suggested either Willy was playing both ends, hoping for a payout from whoever came out on top, or someone else was in the mix and knew Willy was her source. That meant Willy's life and the life of the friend on the local police force—if the so-called friend even existed—could be in danger. The press of the semiautomatic against her stomach reminded her she needed to stay alert. That meant no pain meds, at least until she was out of Mexico.

Not a pleasant thought.

Another thought kept nagging at her: the Russian guy who talked to Josh and Elise at the bar. His presence could have been an aberration—some random stoner out to party—but Leine didn't think so. Especially after Agent Herrera mentioned the rumors about increasing crime in the area not fitting the M.O. of the local crew.

Willy poked his head around the corner and motioned to Leine. She held her breath as she stood, then let it go, ignoring the nausea, and followed him through a pair of French doors into a cool, dimly lit living area. Decorated in bright, colorful fabrics, the space boasted a tile fireplace at one end and a wooden dining room set large enough to seat twelve at the other. A massive wrought iron chandelier hung from the ceiling in the middle of the room, with various matching candlesticks and candelabras throughout. Lush plants spilled from even more colorful pots placed at various intervals on the floor and book-shelves.

The cooler temperature inside was a relief from the blistering hot afternoon, and Leine felt her bad mood shift into less lethal territory. The exterior of the home hadn't suggested the comfortable and spacious interior, and Leine relaxed a bit when she saw medical books on the bookshelves they passed, as well as a framed diploma in the hallway from a well-known medical school in Mexico City.

"He's in his office," Willy said as he led her down the tiled hall past a sweeping stairway. They continued to a room at the back of the home, which turned out to be the doctor's office. Inside the room were a large desk, a floor lamp, a three-panel screen, and an examination table. A gray-haired man sat crouched over the desk.

"Doctor Ramirez," Willy said.

The man swiveled to face them. Leine pegged him to be somewhere in his seventies. His brown eyes unnaturally large behind thick lenses, the doctor wore a loose, short-sleeved shirt, a pair of pressed chinos, and a weary expression on his face. His gaze traveled to Leine's arm and back again.

"William told me you had been injured." He motioned for Leine to come forward. "Let me see."

"I'm—ah—I'm just going to go now, if that's all right..." Willy said, and started to back out of the room. Leine shot him a glance and he froze.

Doctor Ramirez studied her arm for a moment and gingerly turned it to look at the back side. "Ah," he said, probing the area surrounding the wound. Leine winced but said nothing, shutting down the pain.

"The bullet exited here," he explained, lightly touching the back of her upper arm. "It does not look as though it came into contact with bone or an artery. This is extremely fortunate. I will need to clean the wound before I bandage it." He opened a lower drawer and pulled out a pale blue, short-sleeved hospital gown. "Only remove your shirt. You may use the screen." He nodded at the three-panel divider.

Leine took the gown and walked to the other side of the screen, behind which was a door she assumed led to a bathroom. She tried the knob, but it was locked.

"You should go into the hall," Doctor Ramirez said to Willy. "This won't take long."

"You need to stay here, Willy," Leine called through the screen.

Careful not to touch the injury, Leine maneuvered the T-shirt over the wound and pulled the rest over her head. She slipped the gown on and returned to the examination table.

"Where's Willy?" Leine asked. The extortionist was nowhere to be found.

"He had to use the restroom," Ramirez replied. "He said he'd be right back."

The doctor rolled his chair to a cabinet next to the table, slid open a drawer, and retrieved a roll of gauze, antiseptic swabs, a pair of scissors, and two large bandages, which he lined up neatly on the counter. Ramirez instructed her to sit while he proceeded to tie a clean tourniquet around her arm, removing the old one and tossing it into a nearby wastebasket.

"I can give you something for the pain, if you like."

"As long as it's in a form I can take later."

Doctor Ramirez rummaged through a cupboard until he found what he was looking for, and handed her a blister pack of pills. Leine put it in her back pocket.

"Thanks."

Leine stared at the wall, trying to ignore the pain as Ramirez disinfected the entry wound and discarded the blood-soaked material. As he worked his way to the back of her arm he cocked his head to the side. "How is it that a beautiful woman comes to me with a bullet wound in her arm?" When Leine didn't answer, he frowned. "Unless this beautiful woman has been doing something she should not have been."

"That is no concern of yours, Doctor."

Doctor Ramirez sighed. "So they tell me," he said.

They? Leine narrowed her eyes. *Where was Willy? There'd been plenty of time to relieve himself.*

"Doctor Ramirez, would you mind calling Willy back inside?"

Ramirez gave her a quizzical look but nodded. "Of course. William?" he called. He continued to tend to her wound, wrapping several layers of gauze around the two pads, one at the front of her arm and one at the back. When Willy didn't respond, Leine stood up.

"But I'm not finished," the doctor protested.

Leine tucked the loose end of the gauze into the rest of the bandage to secure it. "I am." Drawing her gun, she moved toward the door and cracked it open. Muffled voices from another room floated toward her. She turned to the doctor.

"Who else is here?" she asked.

16

———

OCTOR RAMIREZ OPENED his mouth, his eyes wide as he looked at the gun.

"There is no one else. I live alone except for my housekeeper, Esmeralda, but she has the day off today."

"I'm going to ask you a question and you need to answer me truthfully," Leine said, watching the hallway from behind the door.

"Of course."

"Who do you work for?"

"It is only me. Why do you ask?"

Leine turned her head. "You misunderstand my question. Who do you *work* for?" The voices in the hall grew louder. Her heart thudded in her chest.

Ramirez glanced at the floor. Shaking his head, he raised his eyes to meet Leine's. "I assumed you knew. William told me you were one of them."

Otero. Leine eased the door closed, making sure to lock it, and strode to the window next to the desk. Vertical iron bars blocked the opening.

"Where is the nearest exit?" she asked, her body thrumming with tension.

"There are only two ways into or out of the house, unless you are on the second floor. The windows there have no bars."

Leine briefly considered holding a gun to Ramirez's head and using him to evacuate the building, but hostage-taking rarely ended well, for the hostage or the hostage-taker. If she managed to maneuver them both to the SUV, getting into the vehicle put her at high risk; one step to the left and Ramirez was out of danger, leaving her wide open.

"What about that door?" She nodded at the three-sided screen.

"It leads to a supply room with a toilet. There is a small window, but bars cover it, as well."

The doorknob jiggled, followed by knocking.

"Doctor Ramirez? It's Willy. Have you finished?"

Leine crossed the room in two strides, grabbed the doctor by the front of the shirt, and dragged him behind the screen.

"Tell them to wait."

"One minute," Ramirez called.

"Unlock the door," she said in a low voice, aiming her gun at his midsection. Ramirez reached inside his front pants pocket and produced a key ring with several keys. His hand shook as he fumbled for the correct one. Leine stepped back to give him room, fighting to remain calm.

Finally, Ramirez found the correct key, inserted it into the lock and opened the door. Leine snatched the key ring from his hand on her way into the room. She turned and held a finger to her lips as she silently closed and locked the door behind her.

The room was small, about five feet wide by eight long. A toilet stood against the back wall with a deep laundry sink beside it. A recessed window was to her right, the shadow of vertical bars visible through the glass. Stainless shelves stood next to the window. Medical paraphernalia filled the top three tiers, and cleaning supplies took up space on the two lower ones. A plastic bucket with wheels and a mop skulked in the corner.

Muffled voices floated toward her through the door. Doctor Ramirez could be heard arguing. Leine couldn't hear Willy's voice and didn't recognize the other two.

The handle rattled. "Unlock the door, now," a male voice demanded in heavily accented Spanish. Only the accent wasn't Spanish.

Doctor Ramirez responded with something unintelligible. Leine glanced at the bank of fluorescent lights above her. She slid her gun into her waistband and stepped onto the lower shelf. Grabbing hold of an upper rack with her good arm, she boosted herself high enough to latch on to the light fixture. Several shots rang out and the door handle jerked convulsively.

She climbed up one more rung and, still holding on to the light fixture, stepped across to the windowsill. Bracing herself, she let go of the light and slid her gun free. The door burst open. A spray of bullets slammed into the far wall, shattering the toilet as the lead gunman emerged.

Water gushed across the floor as Leine returned fire. Surprised by her elevated position, the gunman didn't move in time, and the bullets found their mark, shattering the right side of his face. With a scream of pain, he grabbed at his head and staggered from the room, blood pouring from the gaping hole. She continued firing through the open door as a second gunman threw himself against a wall, out of the line of fire. Ears ringing, Leine leapt to the floor and kicked the door closed. Jarred by the impact, agonizing pain coursed through the left side of her body, stealing her breath and clouding her vision. She leaned against the wall, gasping.

The broken handle quivered. Moments later, the door burst open and the body of the first man lurched through, the second gunman shooting from behind as he muscled the corpse into the room. Leine broke from behind the door and fired. The bullet burrowed into the shooter's side and he cried out, clutching his waist. Unable to handle the weight of the dead gunman, he collapsed to his knees, the corpse sagging on top of him. With a grunt, he shoved the body onto its side.

"Drop it," Leine ordered, her gun aimed at his temple.

The gunman closed his eyes and shook his head, his breath coming in short bursts. His gun wavered as though the weapon had grown too heavy. Without a word, he raised the barrel.

She fired.

Ramirez was speaking rapidly into his cell phone when Leine stepped over the two bodies and into the examination room. He placed the phone on the desk when he saw her and backed away.

"Please don't shoot. I—I have more medicine. Here—" He yanked open a drawer and ripped through its contents until he found a box of painkillers, which he held out to her. His hand trembled.

Her mind racing, Leine strode past him toward the door. Satisfied no one else was coming down the hall, she walked back to the desk and grabbed the phone to see who called. *William Flint*. She held it to her ear. Dead air. She placed it back on the desk as she turned to Ramirez, the gun aimed at his head. Sweat rolled down the side of his face. The painkillers lay scattered at the doctor's feet.

"Your shirt," she said, pointing the gun at his chest.

"What?"

"Give me your shirt," she repeated.

Ramirez quickly unbuttoned his shirt, took it off, and held it out to her.

"On the desk."

He laid it on top of the desk and stepped back.

"Bandages. Antibiotics," she managed. She was losing it. Dark spots floated in and out of her vision and her knees trembled. She had to get to the SUV.

The doctor scrambled for more bandages and gauze, placing them inside a plastic bag, which he put on the desk next to the shirt. Then he reached into a drawer for a bottle of pills, adding them to the bag. "Antibiotics," he offered.

Nodding, Leine picked up the bag and shirt and tucked them under her arm. "You never saw me," she said.

"But they will know you were here." Ramirez glanced at the two corpses lying on the floor. "What do I say when they ask what happened?"

"Whatever you tell them, lie. Give them a different hair color, ethnicity, age, different clothing, whatever. If they find me, it will be on your head." She backed toward the door and glanced into the hallway before turning to the doctor. "You don't want Esmeralda to have to look for another employer."

Ramirez blinked, licking his lips. "I understand."

"Tell Willy I'll find him," she said, and slipped out the door.

17

———

HYPERVIGILANT, SHE CROSSED the street to her car, scanning for immediate threats. A second SUV with blacked out windows was parked on the other side of the street, presumably belonging to the dead gunmen. There was no sign of anyone, including Willy Flint.

Leine climbed into her vehicle, started the engine, and calmly pulled away from the curb. There hadn't been any sirens yet, but that didn't mean the local police weren't on their way. She didn't know the neighborhood but assumed gunfire wasn't an everyday occurrence. She hooked a left onto another shade-lined street and continued to wind her way back to the rental agency.

Several blocks later she pulled to the curb, parked, and took off the bloody hospital gown. The bullet wound was seeping blood, staining the gauze crimson. Ignoring it for the time being, she slipped on the doctor's shirt. Although short-sleeved, it was large enough to cover the bandages. She checked her face in the rearview mirror and used a clean scrap of hospital gown to wipe away the obvious blood spatters.

When she was satisfied with her appearance, she pulled

away from the curb and drove toward A-1 Rentals. Her good arm felt like a lead weight. Her body screaming for rest, she fought the longing to lie down.

She had to find a grocery store where she could buy juice and cookies. The sugar would help her fight the dearth of energy that accompanied significant blood loss. *Where the fuck is an Oxxo when you need one?* The ubiquitous convenience stores could usually be found on every street corner throughout Mexico. But now? Not one in sight.

She drove down one promising street after another but still couldn't find a store. Beyond frustrated, she forced herself to head toward the rental agency before she passed out. Once she was there, she could call a taxi to take her to the border.

She turned right onto a main arterial street. On the opposite side was a small market advertising fresh fruit, soda, and cigarettes. Leine pulled in next to the curb and shifted into park. She got out and took several deep breaths as she made her way into the store. The cold blast of the air conditioner took her by surprise. She hadn't noticed how warm her skin was. She'd have to take the antibiotics soon.

"*Galletas,*" she said to the woman behind the counter. Her voice sounded weaker than she'd intended.

The clerk's eyebrows shot up as she pointed to a rack behind Leine. Leine turned, grabbed the first package of cookies she saw and ripped it open, shoving the contents into her mouth. Noticing the look on the clerk's face, Leine fished a handful of money from her pocket and threw it onto the counter.

"*Jugo,*" she said, her mouth full of cookie. The clerk pointed at the back of the store to an older, glass-front cold case. Forcing herself to walk in a straight line, Leine made it to the case and wrenched the door open. She selected two bottles of orange juice and returned to the counter. The clerk rang up her purchases, all the while politely ignoring Leine's obvious distress. Grateful she didn't have to engage, Leine paid and left.

Once inside her vehicle, she popped open the juice and drank as much of it as she could. Then she ate another cookie and washed it down with more juice. When she felt some of her strength return, she brought out her phone and glanced at the screen. Lou had called twice and left a message. She'd have to call him later. There was someone else she needed to talk to. Leine hit speed dial for Agent Herrera.

"I just made your job harder," Leine said when he answered.

"What do you mean?" His voice assumed a wary tone.

"There's more to Josh and Elise's disappearance than we thought. I found the car at the bottom of a ravine with a dead body in the trunk. I think it's Josh." She took out the bottle of antibiotics and twisted the cap off.

"Jesus. How'd you know where to look?"

"Willy Flint." Leine popped two of the pills into her mouth and followed them with a swig of juice.

"And he would know, how?"

"Apparently he was the one who drove it off the cliff." She grabbed the plastic care package from Ramirez, fished around until she found the bandages. Then she put the phone on speaker and placed it on the console. "He was playing me against the people who hired him to do it, to see who'd pay more; but I'll get to that in a minute."

"Go on."

Leine carefully removed the saturated bandages and tossed them on top of the bag. She ripped open several sterile pads and laid them out in front of her on the dash. "Someone—probably Willy—tipped off Ignacio and his sidekick, although Willy's involvement didn't occur to me at the time."

She tore off a length of surgical tape with her teeth and placed it on the dash, sticky side up. Using half of the sterile pads to cover the entry wound and half for the exit wound, she looped the gauze several times around her arm and secured the dressing with the tape.

"They knew where I was and came by to teach me a lesson. They're no longer a problem, but Ignacio got lucky and shot me in the arm. I had to find a doctor in town and instead of calling you, I contacted Willy."

"You what?"

Leine stopped what she was doing. "I took him with me, assuming I'd be able to keep an eye on him. I was wrong."

There was a pause. "Are you all right?"

"I'm fine, although two more of Otero's thugs tried to kill me while I was at the doctor's. They've been taken care of," she added. She rolled up the gauze and put everything away in the plastic sack, which she stuffed into her bag.

"Fuck, Leine. Anything else I should know?"

"Be careful. They're going to be pissed off and might take it out on you since you were with me at Vista del Mar. Although, I'm not sure Ignacio had time to tell anyone about your involvement."

"Who did you see?"

"Doctor Ramirez." She gave Herrera the address.

"Jesus. Ramirez is on Otero's payroll. You should've come to me."

"Yeah. I know." She should have gone alone to the housing development in the first place.

"Where are you calling from? I hope you got the hell across the border."

Leine glanced out the window at the rundown neighborhood. A child's rusty bicycle lay on its side in the front yard of the house next to the market. Though painted a cheery yellow, the house's façade was crumbling. The other homes on the street weren't much newer. An emaciated chicken strutted past, trailing a half-dozen baby chicks behind it.

"Don't worry. I'm headed to the rental agency right now."

"You're probably already too late. Ramirez will have reported the murders to Otero's people."

"And?"

"And Otero's got a couple of cousins who work the border. If Willy's on the payroll too, you can be damned sure he already notified them. The only thing working in your favor is that Flint's known to be unreliable. Way it sounds, you'll be lucky to get out of town alive."

"I doubt that will be a problem, but you're right. I should go."

"What rental agency are you using?"

"A-1."

"I'll meet you there in twenty."

"Really, Agent Herrera, you don't need to—"

"Yeah, I do. You've been shot. You'll be delayed at the border, if nothing else. The wait time is normally two to three hours, which would give Otero's people plenty of time to find you. I'd never forgive myself if something happened to Santa's—" Herrera paused. "What are you to him, anyway?"

"You'll have to ask him," Leine replied, bristling. Whether annoyed by his question or the implied assumption that she couldn't take care of herself, she wasn't sure. But soon her common sense kicked in, and she realized she'd have a better chance with Herrera's help—the person she should have contacted as soon as things went south. "You're under no obligation, even to Santa. I can handle it."

"Yeah, and you've handled things so well up to now." Herrera sighed. "I'm sorry. Let me rephrase that. Allow me to ensure your safe trip back for the sake of my old friend."

Give the guy a break, Leine. Take him up on the offer. You need to go home. You're in no condition to argue.

"Thank you. I'll see you there. And again, I'm sorry to have involved you."

"Makes it exciting," he muttered and disconnected.

Leine pulled away from the curb and called Lou. This time he answered.

"I'm on my way back," Leine said. "I'll be home soon, hopefully."

"Any luck?"

"I think I found Josh." She told him about the Porsche and the body. And the jagged wounds on his back. "I'll email the pictures."

Lou whistled. "Any sign of Elise?"

"No. But I have her phone."

"Have you notified anybody?"

"I'd be willing to bet the locals know by now. As for Gunderson and Nabokov, not yet." She didn't tell him about stirring up Otero's boys or her injury. Best not to worry him.

Yet.

"How'd the bait work out?"

"Great. Thanks." Leine was planning to throw the nine millimeter in the trash behind the rental place after she'd wiped it for fingerprints.

"Did you need it?"

"It was good to have."

Lou didn't press her. She said she'd talk to him when she got home and ended the call.

When she arrived at the rental place she walked behind the building and, after wiping the gun, tossed it into the garbage container. A bag containing the bloody clothes and bandages followed.

Once inside, Leine slipped into the restroom to get a better look at herself and noticed dried blood on her pant leg. The stain looked more like barbeque sauce than blood, but she cleaned it as best as she could. The heat of the day would dry the damp spot before long. She reached into her pocket, took out the blister pack of painkillers Ramirez had given her, and swallowed two.

She ran a brush through her hair and washed her face and hands, but only a hot shower and time would remove the dead-body stench. Leine couldn't tell if she still reeked or if it was just an olfactory memory of the bloated corpse. The woman at the counter either didn't notice or tactfully ignored it and checked her out with a smile. Ten minutes later, Leine was standing in front of the building wearing aviator sunglasses and a ball cap, waiting for Herrera.

While she waited, Leine considered her options. She had a light jacket with her so the bandages wouldn't be obvious, especially since the wound didn't affect her dominant arm. If Doctor Ramirez's description of her matched Willy Flint's, and Otero's people knew about the bullet wound, crossing the border would be tricky. Hopefully, Herrera had something else in mind.

Minutes later, Herrera's dark blue pickup pulled up next to the curb. Leine got in and closed the door as he maneuvered into traffic. He glanced at her left arm, which was now cradled in a makeshift sling.

"Right handed?" he asked. Leine nodded. "Lucky."

Leine reached into her pants pocket and slid out her phone and the paper with Willy Flint's map. Handing it to him, she said, "Directions to the ravine along with Willy's number. The body's pretty far gone. I took a couple of shots with my phone. Willy had the kid's watch—Josh's name was etched on the back." Leine found the photos on her phone and held them up so he could see. Herrera glanced at them.

"Take a look at his torso."

"They got his kidneys?"

"Looks like it. Probably more than that."

"Then where's the girl?"

Leine shook her head as she put her phone away. "That's the question, isn't it?"

"So can I correctly assume that Ignacio and the driver are no longer with us?"

"Yes."

"Can I also infer the other gunmen who came after you at Ramirez's have joined them?"

She nodded.

"Is there anyone else I should be aware of?"

"I think that's sufficient, don't you?"

Herrera snorted. "Yeah, that's sufficient. Christ." He shook his head and gave her a sidelong glance. "Maybe I should put you in for a stipend. You took care of some major douchebags."

Leine looked at him in surprise. "But you'll have to deal with the fallout."

"Yeah, I know, but it's worth it to be rid of all those assholes."

"The two gunmen who came after me at Ramirez's spoke Spanish with an Eastern European accent."

Herrera lifted his chin. "More evidence that we're dealing with somebody other than the homeboys."

"Or in addition to," Leine suggested.

Herrera whistled. "Organ trafficking, Russian mobsters, and Otero? Man, that's a bad combination."

Leine was thinking the same thing.

Herrera took a different route to the border—one that was invitation-only judging by the excessive security. He showed his badge to border guards at three separate checkpoints. They waved him through each time.

"Well, that was efficient," Leine said.

Herrera shrugged. "Perks of the job."

They crossed into the US and drove in silence to the overnight lot near the border where Leine had parked her car.

The meds she'd taken earlier were having an effect, and the pain in her arm had devolved to a steady throb. She could tell Herrera wanted to say something but decided not to.

"Are you all right to drive?" he asked.

"Yeah. I'll be fine. Thanks for the ride." Her hand on the door and ready to leave, she turned to him. "Is there something else you wanted to ask me?"

Herrera nodded. "I was wondering if you ever served."

"No. Why?"

"Santa wouldn't tell me much about your background, just that you could handle yourself." He shrugged. "I figured you'd been in the military or maybe one of the alphabet agencies."

Leine opened the door and got out. She leaned back inside the car.

"You're close," she said.

18

—————

LEINE DROVE UP Interstate 5 and pulled off at the first motel. She managed to check herself in and make it to her room before she collapsed onto the bed. Fast approaching blackout from exhaustion, relentless pain, and less-than-effective painkillers, she passed out the minute her head hit the pillow.

She woke up two hours later, a rancid taste in her mouth from the meds. Groggy, she made her way into the bathroom and rinsed her mouth with water. She turned on the shower and walked back into the room to lie down on the bed while she waited for the water to heat. Pulling her phone free, she hit speed dial and put it on speaker.

"Where the hell are you?" were Santa's first words. "Bob called to tell me he left you at an all-night parking lot and that you looked like shit."

Leine closed her eyes. "I'm in Chula Vista at the Traveler's Lodge just off I-5. Room 38."

"I'll be there in a few hours."

"No." Leine started to sit up but nausea hit her and she decided against it. "I just need to rest. I'll be fine."

"Bullshit. I'm coming down. Call the front desk. Tell them your husband is joining you."

She didn't have the strength to argue. "Okay," she whispered before oblivion found her again.

LEINE OPENED HER EYES, UNSURE WHERE SHE WAS. LIGHT FROM the bedside lamp illuminated a glass of water and a box of tissues along with the telephone and clock radio. Some sports channel was running replays of a soccer match on the muted television. She didn't remember turning anything on before she called Santa, although she did remember drawing the curtains closed before the shower. A narrow slice of dark could be seen through the window. She glanced at her watch. Nine thirty. She'd been out for hours.

Leine winced as she adjusted the sling. Her arm felt like it had been run over by a semi. At least she couldn't smell death on herself anymore. She turned her head as Santa emerged from the bathroom, wiping his hands on a towel.

"Hi," Leine said, her voice barely a croak. Santa's gaze snapped to hers and a look of relief washed over him. He came around the foot of the bed and sat down, facing her. She watched him, her mind a hazy mess, happy to see him.

"Glad to see you're alive," Santa said. The vein at his temple pulsed.

"You're angry," Leine said, reaching for the glass of water on the nightstand.

Santa handed it to her and abruptly rose from the bed and began to pace.

"Goddamn right I'm angry." Eyes flashing, he stopped pacing and crossed his arms. She winced, not used to being the subject of Santiago Jensen's wrath. The air crackled with electricity—and not the kind Leine preferred.

"It's only a flesh wound—" she started to say but Santa cut her off.

"Only a flesh wound? Leine, it's a *fucking gunshot* wound." Santa resumed pacing, working himself into a froth. "Bob told me you were jumped twice down there. How the hell did that happen? I thought this was supposed to be a routine visit. Research, you said." He glared at her, jaw clenched.

Leine took a deep breath before replying.

"I'm sorry I didn't call to tell you what happened. I didn't want you to worry."

"Didn't—" Santiago snapped his mouth closed and stared at her in disbelief. "Goddammit, Leine. You need to keep me in the loop on incidents like this, all right?" He crossed the distance between them and stopped, his eyes dark. "You're involved in two deadly incidents out of the country, get yourself shot, and then call me for help after the fact. Think about the position you put me in. You need medical care, and I can't even take you to the emergency room. California law requires hospitals to report gunshot wounds. What am I supposed to do?"

"I had it treated," she said quietly.

"By some bullshit, half-assed cartel quack who probably never saw the inside of an operating room."

Not knowing what else to do, she clasped his hand and pulled him to her, moving over to give him room. His body, rigid at first, relaxed in increments—his head dipped to her neck as she rose to meet him; his shoulders followed when she leaned forward to nibble his earlobe; and the rest of his body as he carefully lay down beside her. With a sigh, he released his pent-up tension and returned the embrace, immensely careful of her injury.

"Next time you go on a 'routine' trip, I'm coming with you," he murmured into her ear. He took the glass from her and set it back on the nightstand before turning his head to nuzzle her neck. This time the electricity was the right voltage, and Leine shivered at the trickle of pleasure shimmying down her spine. Santa's mouth covered hers and she gave herself over to the sensations working their way through her.

What gunshot wound?

He handled her gently but went at her with relentless focus, as though trying to obliterate his anger. His warm lips and hands moved over her, the pressure of his body against hers summoning a familiar ache. He untied her sling, dropping it to the floor, and unbuttoned her shirt, carefully avoiding the bandages. Nibbling at her collarbone, he paused briefly as he unzipped her pants and slid them off the bed and onto the floor. Their eyes locked. His hands beneath her buttocks, he slid lower, pulling her to him.

The pain receded and she gasped as Santa moved back slightly, leaving a vacuum, which Leine demanded he fill. He returned once, twice, nipping at her thighs, her knees, her hip, but retreated each time, teasing her until she was out of her mind with desire and groaned with pleasure at his slightest touch.

Santa rose to his knees and licked his way along her stomach to her chest, taking turns with her left breast, and her right. Chills surged along her spine, eliminating whatever breath remained. Beyond caring about anything except release, she moved to unbutton his jeans, but he pushed her hand away. With a frustrated growl, she tried again. He pinned her wrist so she couldn't move while he one-handed his jeans down just low enough to free himself. Greedy for him now, Leine struggled against his grip, but he wouldn't let go.

He entered her slowly. With a sigh, Leine leaned her head back and closed her eyes, reveling in the sensory overload, losing herself in the moment. The passion built steadily, and she groaned with pleasure.

His expression a mixture of fury and passion, Santa drove deeper, intensifying the thrust, obliterating the earlier tenderness. She accepted him willingly and they moved in tandem, each gasping from the building tension, their rhythmic dance rapidly escalating until together they tumbled over the edge and into the void.

The ticking clock brought her back to the present.

"Now that's an effective painkiller," she murmured and closed her eyes.

They both dozed. Leine woke first and struggled to sit up. Santa was awake an instant later, supporting her back and head with his arm, piling pillows behind her. She leaned back to watch him, trying to discern his mood.

Jeans still unbuttoned, he walked to the table and fished in her bag. He held up the blister pack of pain pills.

"You need a couple?" he asked.

Leine nodded, marveling at how quickly he could switch from anger to passion to caring for her. Hopefully she could keep him away from anger mode for a while.

"I found the car," she said.

Santa brought the pills and handed her the glass of water. "And you took a bullet for the effort. Doesn't seem like much of a trade." He watched her swallow the painkillers and took the glass from her when she was done. "Why didn't you call me as soon as it happened?"

"Because there wasn't anything you could do."

"You didn't call Herrera, either."

"I know," Leine admitted. "I shouldn't have trusted my informant. I thought I had things handled. I should have at least called Lou."

Santa's expression was a combination of hurt and irritation, and his jaw pulsed—a sure sign he was fast entering the danger zone again.

He looked pointedly at her arm. "How did it happen?"

Leine told him about Willy Flint and finding Josh in the car at the bottom of the ravine, about Ignacio and his sidekick ambushing her. She mentioned the other gunmen had Eastern European accents but glossed over the threat they represented, not wanting to fuel Santa's ire. By the end, his expression had turned from pissed off and hurt to stony acceptance.

"Flint's the key here. I'll check with Bob, find out what I can."

"I already asked Herrera. Flint's a low-level, unreliable snitch, apparently working on the side for Otero. I'd be surprised if he knew who the other gunmen were. He probably alerted Otero, who called someone else." Leine shifted her weight, trying to get comfortable. "It's pretty obvious Otero's working with the new guys on the block. He's into something bigger than a simple carjacking operation. The only angle that makes sense is organ trafficking. They took Josh's kidneys, probably more. The thing I don't know is what happened to Elise."

"You may be right about Otero branching out," Santa said, climbing back into bed. "Makes sense, if he's working with an Eastern Bloc crime syndicate. Organs are a lucrative market, especially when you don't have to pay for materials."

"Then why not do Elise the same way and leave her in the car with Josh?"

"Maybe he played the hero." Santa shrugged. "Got in the way. Could be they had to kill him and decided to trash the Porsche, make it look like a carjacking gone bad. They didn't want to lose the product, so they cut into him. Elise might have been more valuable alive."

"You mean sell her into the sex trade."

"I mean *rent* her." Santa stared at the ceiling. "They'd get more money putting her to work. If they didn't shoot her full of drugs to keep her docile, once she outlived her 'usefulness' they could sell her off in pieces."

Leine leaned her head against the pillow. "So you're saying Otero or this other group might be holding her somewhere?" A flicker of hope sprang to life inside her, accompanied by the thick, cottony fog of the medication.

"That's it. No more pain pills." She didn't have the luxury of time. The longer she delayed the search, the less chance she had of finding Elise, dead or alive.

19

―――

A KEY RATTLED the lock and the door opened. Elise sat up, knees to her chin, and waited. This time a short, stocky man walked into the room carrying a metal tray. He turned on the overhead light and set the tray next to the bed. Some kind of weird looking food sat on a green plastic plate along with a plastic fork, another glass of murky water, and a syringe.

The tribal tattoos on the man's shaved head and curling along his neck gave him a fierce appearance. He picked up the syringe and reached for her. Elise cried out and tried to wrench her arm away, but he was too quick and too strong.

"Stop it—" she shrieked, fear clouding her vision.

Tattoo backhanded her across the face. Shocked into silence, she touched her mouth. Her fingers came away bloody. Her heart was pounding so hard she thought it would jump into her throat and cut off her air. *Can a seventeen-year-old have a heart attack?*

He grasped her wrist and pulled her arm straight with one hand while holding the syringe with the other. Elise squeezed her eyes shut. Salty tears slipped down her cheeks, stinging the cut on her lip. At the prick of the needle a whimper escaped her. She opened her eyes to slits and watched her blood fill the syringe. When it was full, Tattoo removed the needle and reached in his pocket for a crumpled tissue, which he threw at her. Elise pressed it on the needle site and bent her arm to stop the bleeding.

"Eat," he said as he slid the syringe into a paper bag. Her stomach roiled at the gelatinous, oblong roll of unidentifiable food next to a pile of sauerkraut resting on the scarred plastic plate.

"Don't you have any bottled water?" she asked in a tiny voice.

The tattooed man stood with his arms crossed and stared at her. Elise quickly dropped her gaze. Ravenous, she reached for the plastic fork on the tray and cut off a slender wedge of the roll. She picked up the slice with the tips of two fingers and bit into it, holding her breath at the tangy smell of the sauerkraut.

The lukewarm blob turned out to be cooked cabbage stuffed with soggy rice and onions and some kind of questionable ground meat. There didn't seem to be much seasoning and Elise wondered why anyone would go to the trouble to make such bad food. She tried another bite but spit it out onto the plate. The stocky man continued to stare and she suppressed a shudder.

The real possibility of being raped with no one to hear her cries skated through her mind, but she quickly replaced the thought with one of him telling the person in charge to let her go since she cooperated so well. She held her breath and forced down the last of the cabbage roll, fearing it would be hours before her next meal.

Finished, she wrapped her arms around her knees, trying to make herself as small as possible. The man reached for the plate and lightly brushed her thigh. Reflexively, Elise shrank back, jerking away from his touch. A flicker of anger crossed his face.

20

"WHAT DO YOU mean, they're pulling the case?" Leine looked at Lou in disbelief, her anger rising. The bitch shot, or BS, which Leine had nicknamed the hole in her arm, was particularly active today, giving her no end of grief. The combination of the pain and the frustrating weakness in her left hand was enough to send her into orbit.

"Mrs. Bennett called this morning and they want you—us—to stop searching for Elise. She heard about your run-in with the locals in TJ, and she's worried you're out of your league."

"Out of my league? That's a good one. And who the hell told them, anyway?" Leine paced the floor of the office, trying to work off the nervous energy that had plagued her since she'd gotten back to LA. Belinda Bennett's decision was like throwing cold water on the gains she'd made in finding Elise. "Now is the time I *should* be looking for her, Lou. You know that. I'm not hamstrung by the same rules as law enforcement. And what about Josh? For god's sake, the kid's dead in a ravine with his face blown off and his kidneys hacked out."

Lou sighed and shook his head. "It's out of our hands, Leine.

To her immense relief he left, slamming the door behind him.

The key rattled in the lock and she began to breathe again.

Gunderson and Nabokov are working with the local police regarding Josh."

"Funny, I haven't seen anything on the news about the murder."

"They're keeping it quiet."

"Of course they are. Wouldn't want stories of some kid's death and missing kidneys to curtail the flow of tourists into the new and improved TJ now, would we?" Leine yanked her purse off of Lou's desk and walked to the door. She turned to look at him. "I'm not letting go of this one."

"I know," Lou said. "Watch yourself."

Leine walked to her car and got in, throwing her bag into the passenger seat with a little too much force. She intended to drive out to the Bennett's to try to convince them to allow her to continue to look for their daughter. A quick glance at the clock on the dash told her that would have to wait. First, she'd promised to meet with Santa and his new partner.

He'd been noncommittal in his assessment of the new homicide detective, insisting he wanted Leine's honest take on her. That in itself intrigued Leine. She wondered how Santa would fare working with a female partner. Granted, before he met Leine he'd been known by his fellow detectives in LAPD's Robbery/Homicide Division as "The Swinging Dick," riffing off his notorious reputation with the ladies. Apparently, all that changed when Leine showed up. She doubted the female detective would have any problems working with the new and improved Santiago Jensen.

Leine pulled into the parking lot of the Asia-Pacific Grill with five minutes to spare. She checked her face and hair in the mirror before she got out and walked into the restaurant.

The interior was cool and dark; upscale Thai meets Hollywood. Elegant, dark wood tables and chairs with an Asian motif, accented by framed photographs of visiting celebrities. Leine's mouth watered at the fragrance of basil and curry floating through the air. The hostess ushered her past a massive statue of Buddha to a table near the back. A copper fountain splashed into a colorful, glass-bottomed pool, its interior home to several overgrown koi.

Leine spotted Santa across the room. His partner—sunglasses perched atop long blonde hair—sat with her back to Leine. As she came around the front of the table, a jolt of surprise slid through her.

Santa smiled as he rose and pulled out Leine's chair. She had to force herself to sit. The woman was drop-dead, California-blond, flawlessly tanned gorgeous, with a body that would make Barbie jealous.

"Leine Basso, this is Heather Brodie. Heather, Leine."

Heather extended her perfectly manicured hand. Leine blinked several times and after a brief hesitation returned the gesture.

"It's great to finally meet you, Leine. Santiago's told me so much about you."

Interesting. Leine cocked her head and looked at Santa, wondering how long he and Brodacious had been partners. When he'd suggested lunch the evening before, it was the first she'd heard of her. Santa avoided Leine's gaze and passed her a plate of steamed edamame.

"Has he? I'm afraid I'm at a disadvantage, Heather, because I know next to nothing about you." Leine smiled sweetly at Santa as she tore into the edamame pod with her teeth.

Oblivious to the underlying tension growing between Leine and Santa, Heather grinned and bobbed her head. "Of course," she said, waving her hand at the detective. "He probably doesn't want to bother you with boring RHD stuff. There's not much to know about me, really. I was born and raised in Southern California, and

I love to surf. In my off hours you can usually find me wherever the waves are. Other than that, I'm pretty boring." Heather grinned again, her perfect white teeth like little pearls against her precious, shell-pink lips. "I understand you work with SHEN?"

Leine nodded. "I started with them about a year ago."

Heather leaned forward in her seat. "I remember watching the news when you exposed that global network of pedophiles selling movies to each other. Ugh." Heather's mouth pulled down at the corners. "I couldn't believe Stone Ellison was at the center of the whole thing. You did a great service for trafficked children everywhere."

Okay, so she's working me. I can live with that, Leine mused. On the other hand, Santa appeared to be a tad uncomfortable. *Good. I can live with that, too.*

"Yes, well, thankfully he's no longer a threat."

If Leine had her way, Stone Ellison would be singing soprano in hell. She'd had her chance, but held off killing him because he was unarmed and she'd have been brought up on yet another murder charge. At the time she'd been wrongly accused of three homicides, and the odds had not been in her favor. Thankfully, Ellison was in prison working off a very long, very unpleasant sentence and would likely die behind bars. Leine found solace in the fact that most of the prison population did not look kindly on pedophiles.

"I was just telling Santiago about my kids."

"How many do you have?" Leine asked. *She has kids? With that body?*

"Forty-two," she said.

Leine gave her a puzzled look.

"I work with at-risk youth down at a community center on La Cienega. We try to funnel them into classes they'll enjoy so they'll stay in school, maybe look at further training. So far, seven have enrolled in community colleges. Crossing fingers they go the distance."

Santa broke in. "Heather won this year's Los ANGELenos Award for the program, beating out a couple of state senators."

Heather lowered her eyes as her cheeks grew the same shade as her lipstick. "Oh, stop it. It's not like I did it all by myself, you know. I had tons of help."

Lovely, Leine thought. Not only was Heather Brodie gorgeous and athletic, but she had an altruistic side. Leine realized she had a stranglehold on her water and relaxed her hand.

"You must be proud," Leine said, and took a sip.

"It's nice to know you can make a difference, right?" Heather frowned and her eyebrows actually came together.

Shit. The woman doesn't even use Botox. Leine surreptitiously checked out her bustline, trying to determine if they were real or not. Leine opted for fake, giving herself a small measure of satisfaction.

Very small.

"So I hear you and Santiago have taken up kite surfing? Awesome, right?"

Leine sighed inwardly. The woman probably resuscitated winos. Better to just go with the flow. No sense getting jealous. It wasn't like she and Santa had ever brought up the subject of exclusivity. She had no hold on him and what or whom he did. Nevertheless, a tiny voice in the back of her brain kept comparing herself to this blonde bombshell, hoping for a tell-tale sign of insufficiency in the woman or at the very least, a nefarious case of bad breath.

She got nothing.

As the meal wore on, Heather proved to be an avid listener, an interesting and witty conversationalist, and extremely intelligent. She was also kind, compassionate, and helpful. Leine fought against the catty voices vying for dominance inside her head, countering them with a positive spin every time one appeared to be going off the rails.

She hated that she was jealous and had no idea how to rid herself of the emotion. By the end of the meal, Leine was longing for the old days when she'd receive orders to eliminate a target in some godforsaken corner of the world, allowing her to leave real life behind while she focused on doing her job.

Leine excused herself and made her way to the bathroom, hoping for a respite from Heather's never-ending happy dance. What was it with some people? Life was not one endlessly beautiful day followed by another. She found herself longing to inject sarcasm into the three-way conversation, and had to bite her tongue several times lest she come across as overly jaded and cynical.

At the sink, Leine rinsed her face in cold water and stared at her reflection in the mirror. That's what killing people for a living did to you. It made you hard. Tough. Suspicious. She tore off a paper towel and dried her face. It wasn't something she could change.

Not now.

Hell, who was she kidding? She lost her innocence as soon as she'd agreed to that first job. Jaded? Yep. Cynical? You bet. She didn't know one person that had killed someone either for God or country who wasn't. Correction: only counting the non-psychotic ones. She wondered if Brodacious had ever killed anyone.

Doubtful.

Leine tossed the paper towel and was about to go back to the table when Heather walked into the bathroom.

"I was hoping you'd still be in here," she said, smiling.

Leine plastered on a smile to match and said, "Why is that?"

She glanced behind her and then checked the stalls. "I wanted to ask you something about Santiago."

Wary, Leine kept the smile. "Ask away," she said.

"How do you deal with all the anal retentive stuff?"

"I beg your pardon?"

"You know, how he insists on lining up his equipment in the trunk exactly the same way every time he signs out a car. How he crosses himself three times when he first sees a vic. Or, how he has to have three napkins with every meal. Not one, not two. Three. One for his lap, one for his hands, and apparently one for the grand finale. He thinks no one catches it, but I do."

Leine couldn't help but smile. She found Santa's need for order endearing, and understood why he held fast to the things he did. Most cops she'd met had some kind of superstition they relied on in the field. But she also understood how it could drive the average person nuts. Having come from a background that dealt in chaos, Leine had adopted a few of those quirks herself, although they weren't nearly as ingrained as Santa's.

"I know it seems overly careful, Heather. You have to realize we all have our eccentricities. Santa's are because of his history. Obviously. I'm not going to divulge anything about his past. He'll have to do that in his own time. I will tell you this: with all he's been through it's a miracle he's not locked up somewhere, living on Thorazine and gummy bears."

"I know. I'm sorry I said anything. It's just that I'm the new kid on the block, and I'm getting a ration of crap from the guys in the department, including your boyfriend. And yeah, I know I have to suck it up, it's all part of the deal." Heather leaned against the sink and crossed her arms. "I've wanted this unit ever since I became a cop, but the reality is a little different than what I'd envisioned. I was hoping we could be friends. It's been...a difficult adjustment."

"I can imagine. Look." Leine joined her against the sink. "Don't let the guys get you down. You're gorgeous and they probably don't know how to deal with gorgeous. Rise above it. Give them back everything they shove at you and more. I'll bet sooner or later they'll leave you alone. You gotta give them time to get used to you. Believe me, I know."

Heather glanced at Leine. "What did you do before you started working for SHEN?"

"We should probably be getting back. Santa's going to wonder what happened to his dates." Leine moved off the sink and walked to the door. Taking the hint, Heather followed her out and back to their table.

Santa looked from Leine to Heather, back to Leine. "What'd I miss?" he asked, raising an eyebrow.

"Oh, nothing. Girl talk," Leine answered.

"Yeah. Right." Santa smirked, giving Leine a sidelong glance, obviously not falling for the feint. "Since when did you add 'girl talk' to your resume?"

Heather cut in. "Leave her alone. She wanted to know where I got my lipstick."

Leine laughed, knowing Santa would grill her later on, once they were home. A little uncertainty would be good for him.

21

———

EINE DROVE WEST along Sunset to North Beverly Drive and then onto Laurel Way. Downshifting with each hairpin turn, she searched the addresses for the Bennetts' home. According to the map on her phone the modern, three-story residence sat nestled among all the other massive mansions in the canyon, near the top of the ridge. Three more corners revealed the address she was looking for—copper numbers set in stone just above street level.

She turned left and drove through the open gate past the security camera, and climbed the drive. The house came into view at the top—angles of concrete and glass, huge gray and white Super Legos with massive windows, surrounded by a permeably paved drive and eco-friendly landscaping. An enormous round sculpture of polished onyx with a metal rod spiked through the center rested in a serene pond. Water flowed along the rod, collected at its base and then disappeared.

Leine parked her car and got out. The driveway continued under the house to below-grade parking. The open garage door revealed a glimpse of a red 1961 Ferrari—a 250 GT California Spyder, if she wasn't mistaken. She made her way along the walkway to the glass-enclosed entrance and pressed the doorbell.

With a solemn expression Teuta Vercuni walked toward her through an interior set of glass doors. The housekeeper opened the door and stood aside to let Leine in.

"Thank you, Teuta," Leine said as she entered. Teuta nodded and closed the door after her.

"I have broken heart that Mrs. Bennett does not allow for you to continue with your business," she said in a low voice.

Teuta led her through the entry and into a spacious living room filled with a veritable museum of Danish Modern pieces atop white marble tile. Bright swatches of Rothko-esque artwork dotted the walls, framed by floor-to-ceiling windows with a panoramic view of the Pacific Ocean on one side and the San Fernando Valley on the other.

The housekeeper's mouth pulled down at the corners. "My poor Eliseka," she murmured.

"That's why I'm here, Teuta. I want to understand why Mrs. Bennett chose to call off our investigation."

"She say only need police. In my country, police are no good," she said, spitting the words. She glanced at Leine's left arm, frowning. "Are you injured?"

"I'm fine." Leine was wearing a long-sleeved T-shirt. *I must have been favoring it*, she thought.

"Leine Basso." Dick Bennett came toward them, his voice reaching across the space, magnified by the room's angles. The skin sagged under his eyes, and his normally tan complexion was pallid, adding at least ten years to his appearance. His usual, over-the-top energy had transformed into a more thoughtful demeanor.

"Mr. Bennett," Leine said, extending her hand. He grasped it firmly.

"Horrible what happened to Josh," he said, glancing at Teuta before he turned his attention back to Leine. "I want to thank you for risking your life to find our daughter."

"It's part of the job, Mr. Bennett." Leine scanned the room for Elise's mother. "I'd like to talk to you and Mrs. Bennett about your asking SHEN to step back from the investigation."

Dick Bennett slid his hands into his pockets and stared at the floor. Shaking his head, he lifted his gaze to hers. "I'm sorry, Leine, but both Belinda and I think the risk is too great. We'd never forgive ourselves if something happened to you."

"May I ask who informed you about events in Mexico?"

"Mr. Gunderson from Immigration and Customs mentioned it."

"Listen." Leine took a deep breath and let it go. "I'm sure I can find Elise, or, at least I can find out what happened. I don't have the same...restraints as the police."

Dick Bennett's eyes shifted. The movement was slight but Leine caught the change. He wasn't telling her something. He altered his stance and glanced at his housekeeper. "Teuta, would you be so kind as to get us both some refreshments?"

"Of course, Mr. Bennett." Teuta moved toward the kitchen with surprising energy. Dick Bennett tracked her progress before he turned back to Leine.

"There's something you should know—" he said leaning toward her, his voice barely above a whisper.

"Hello, Leine." The temperature plummeted as Belinda Bennett swept into the room. Dick Bennett took a step back and clamped his lips shut.

Mrs. Bennett paused at a candy dish on a wooden credenza, selected a piece, and joined them. "You didn't need to come all this way," she said as she unwrapped a chocolate and popped it into her mouth.

"I was just explaining to your husband how I believe I can still be of use in the search effort," Leine said.

"Is that so?" Belinda Bennett's light blue eyes bored into Leine's, reminding her of a bird of prey and giving the impression she was calculating possible responses.

Jesus, the woman could freeze the Pacific with her attitude, Leine thought.

"My actions are not scrutinized as closely as law enforcement, which gives me a tactical advantage. I found Josh. I know I can find Elise."

"I'm grateful for what you've done, Leine. May I call you Leine?"

"Of course."

"As I said, I'm—we're grateful for what you've done, but we'd never forgive ourselves if anything happened to you. Please," Belinda Bennett's mask slipped, revealing something far deeper —fear? desperation?—before composure took its place again. "You need to stop."

The kidnappers have made their demands, Leine realized with a start. The Bennetts' reactions implied they were covering up something—the most likely scenario being the kidnappers had instructed them to continue to act as though there had been no ransom demand or they would kill Elise. Nabokov and Gunderson would continue to work with the cops in TJ. They'd never find her and the kidnappers knew it. Not as long as they kept her in Mexico.

If she was still there.

Teuta returned to the living room with a tray of glasses, placing it on top of a large ottoman. "I make lemonade," she said.

The Bennetts glanced at each other. A look passed between them before Dick said, "Please, sit down, Leine. The police didn't go into great detail about what you faced in Mexico—only that you had found Josh."

Leine recounted a sanitized version of events in Mexico,

skipping over the ambush at Doctor Ramirez's office, all the while watching the interaction between the Bennetts and Teuta, who had asked to stay.

The dynamics had changed from Leine's initial impression of the trio. Dick and Belinda both chose their words carefully. They obviously hadn't confided in Teuta. And why would they? She was an employee. It made sense, given the housekeeper's strong attachment to the girl. And yet, Leine sensed something else. Something in the way Teuta held herself. Defiance, perhaps? Leine assumed she wasn't happy with the Bennetts' decision to drop SHEN as part of the search team.

"I'm sorry you decided against SHEN continuing to search for your daughter," Leine said. "Won't you please reconsider? If my involvement has anything to do with it, there are several fine contractors who work with us that can take over the case."

"Thank you, Leine, but the police are investigating and believe they're close." Belinda Bennett's voice held a note of finality.

"Has anyone contacted you regarding a ransom?" Leine asked as she stood to leave.

Belinda held her gaze steady. "No."

"That seems odd, doesn't it? Forgive me, but why else do you think they kidnapped Elise?"

"I have no idea. Perhaps you could enlighten us? Since you seem to think you know the motivation of these animals." Belinda Bennett's demeanor had changed from ice-cold to hostile in a split-second, giving Leine the impression she'd hit a nerve.

She switched tactics and pulled out her business card, handing it to Belinda.

"My card. In case you misplaced the other one. Don't hesitate to call if you think of anything I can do to help."

Leine nodded at Belinda and the housekeeper and followed Dick Bennett out.

"If you want to talk, please call me," Leine murmured as she shook his hand, palming another card. He slid it from her and put it in his pocket.

"Look, I want to apologize for Belinda's behavior. The stress of the changes my company's going through combined with not being able to find Elise have taken their toll."

"That's right. You're taking your biotech firm public, right?"

Dick Bennett nodded.

"I'm sure the questions surrounding your daughter's abduction will be answered, in time. I don't suppose you can put the IPO off until her disappearance is resolved?"

"Not now. We've come too far." His face reflected a bewildering array of emotions—confusion, fear, dogged determination, hopelessness.

"Thank you for stopping by," he said, opening her car door. "Be safe."

"Why the hell shouldn't I call her?" Dick Bennett slammed his keys on the nightstand and turned to face his wife. "We're talking about our daughter, remember? Goes by the name Elise?"

"Yes, I *remember* Elise. What kind of mother do you think I am?" Belinda Bennett took a deep breath and glared at her husband. "I think we should do exactly as they instructed. Remember *them*? The men with our daughter?" The sarcasm dripped between them like acid. "They insisted there be no outsiders. They told us to call off the police or they'll kill her. *Remember?*" Her voice caught and she turned away, angrily wiping her eyes.

Dick crossed to his desk and opened his laptop, revealing the picture that had been delivered via email that morning. Elise, barefoot and chained to a bed, her dress torn, eyes swollen from crying, looking lost and alone.

And petrified.

Dick closed his eyes. "I think Leine's right. The police aren't getting anywhere."

"And that's exactly what they want, isn't it? Look, if we just pay the damned money—"

"No!" Dick slammed his fist on the nightstand. "I will not negotiate with terrorists. And believe me, these people are terrorists."

"I know it's a huge amount of cash, but darling, this is our baby we're talking about." Belinda's tone softened. She walked to where he was sitting and began to massage his shoulders. "We'll get through this. Let's talk things through."

Dick sighed again and lowered his head. "There's nothing to talk about. My gut tells me to go with Leine Basso, and my gut's never been wrong."

Belinda stopped massaging her husband's neck as though she'd been handed hot coals.

"It's wrong now," she hissed and pushed him away.

22

L EINE ZIPPED THE bag closed and carried her suitcase to the living room as the front door opened.

"Leaving?" Santa threw his keys into the bowl next to him on the hall table, all the while looking at Leine.

"I was going to—"

"You were going to leave before I got home, weren't you?" Santa brushed past her and walked into the apartment. "Easier, isn't it?"

Leine dropped her overnight case and took a deep breath. "I have to go. Trust me, I understand your concerns. But the longer I wait, the harder it will be to find Elise."

"The Bennetts took you off the case, Leine. She's not your problem anymore."

"She *is* my problem. So is every kid out there who's scared and alone, who got themselves into some kind of trouble they can't get out of." Leine raised her hands. "If not me, then who's going to look for them? I've got the skills. I've got the time." She moved near Santa and cupped his scowling face with her hand. "I love you. You know that. I'm not running from *us*. I'm running to find *her*."

"You'll get hurt."

"Welcome to my world." Leine smiled faintly.

"What's that supposed to mean?"

"How is this any different than what I get to deal with every day with your job?" she asked.

"I investigate murders. I'm not in the line of fire. You could have been killed."

"You put yourself on the line when you investigate a murder. Any one of those murderers could find out who you are, where you live. Especially the ones you put away. We both know a killer's reach can exceed his parameters."

"It's not the same," he said, his expression sullen.

"Well, then, we'll have to agree to disagree, won't we?" Leine shook her head and gave him a kiss before walking back to her case. It was like kissing an immovable object. "You're one stubborn cop, you know that?"

"Yeah." He stepped in front of her, blocking the way. Dark eyes smoldering, he leaned toward her and returned the kiss, this one more demanding than the original. When he was finished, Leine leaned back, fanning herself.

"Is it warm in here?" she asked, looking around.

"Just remember what you've got."

"Meaning?"

"Don't take unnecessary risks. Okay?"

"Okay."

Just then, the theme from *The Godfather* played from inside Leine's purse. She put her case on the floor and fished out her phone, squinting at the number. Local, but not familiar.

"Leine Basso."

"Is this same Leine Basso who receive favor from Vladimir Petrovich?"

Leine straightened at the deeply accented voice of the caller. "Yes," she answered, suppressing a groan. *Not now.*

"Good. We meet. Tomorrow, eleven o'clock."

"Actually, this isn't a good time—I'm sorry, I didn't catch your name?"

"Call me Nicholas."

"Great. Nicholas. Look, I'm on my way out of town but would be happy to connect when I get back."

"No. We meet. You will be tomorrow at IHOP near Santa Monica Pier. You know this place, yes?"

"Yes, but I—"

The line went dead.

"Shit."

Santa cocked his head. "Who's Nicholas?"

"Apparently a friend of a friend who expects me to meet with him." Sighing in frustration, she returned the phone to her purse.

"Well, you're leaving town, so call him back and make it for another day."

"Yeah. I'll give it a try on my way out." *Fat chance*, Leine thought. *Not if he's a friend of Vlad's.*

She walked to the door and turned back. "Look, I—"

Santa held his finger to her lips. "I love you. Be safe." He leaned over and kissed her again, this time gently.

"Thank you for understanding," she said, and left.

Leine put her bag in the trunk before getting into her car. She did a search on her phone, hit the call button, and waited, drumming her fingers on the steering wheel.

"Nadja Imports," said the woman on the other end of the line.

"Vladimir Petrovich. Tell him it's Leine Basso."

A few minutes later, Vlad came on the line.

"And to what good fortune do I owe this indescribable plea-sure?" Vlad's heavy Russian accent made him sound like a James Bond villain. Or possibly a character from a Rocky and Bull-winkle cartoon. It was a tough call.

"I just got off the phone with one of your buddies. Someone named Nicholas?"

"Ah, yes. Is there problem?"

"Unfortunately, I can't make good on our deal at the moment. I'm leaving town for a few days, but I will be available for whatever he needs when I get back." *And now I remember why I should never owe favors to Vladimir Petrovich,* Leine thought. Back when she was looking for the runaway, Mara, Leine had stalled in her search and needed to know the whereabouts of Vlad's nephew, Yuri. He'd delivered, but on the condition she would repay the favor to Vlad or one of his business associates when asked.

Vlad chuckled. "I should not remind a woman such as you how favor works." Vlad's amiable tone sharpened considerably. "I am calling favor. He is needing your expertise. Meet Nicholas. Do thing he asks. Then, we will be squared. This is correct term, yes?"

"Square. We'll be square." Leine rolled her eyes. Maybe what Nicholas wanted wouldn't take too long. "Do you know what he wants me to do?"

"Is much better, Leine, this attitude." The clink of glass followed by a gurgling liquid floated over the earpiece. There was a brief pause before Vlad smacked his lips and belched into the phone. "Is very simple. You go where is shipment of Nicholas, make sure is safe, then deliver to our people. No problems."

No problems. Sure. What the hell kind of shipment is this that needs babysitting?

"Can't the shipment wait?"

"*Nyet.* Is now."

"And there's no one else who can babysit?"

"Only great Leine Basso."

"May I ask what the hell is so important?"

"You may ask."

There was a long pause.

"You're not working with me here. What happens if I say no?" A field of red flags sprang up in her mind.

"How is daughter? In Paris now, yes? Is happy with boyfriend, I think."

"You're not seriously going to use my child as a bargaining chip?" Leine could feel the heat rise in her face as a surge of anger flowed through her. "That's pretty fucking low, Vlad."

"Is very important, this shipment." Vlad's amiability had left the building. His voice had taken on a deadly serious tone.

She was damned if she was going to let him use her daughter's life to blackmail her into doing his bidding. "You do remember what happened to the Frenchman's son when he used April to get to me, right?"

There was a long silence, followed by the sound of another shot being poured. Then, "My people tell me some rat fucks are looking for woman who killed two Albanian nationals south of border, in Mexico. Do you know of this?"

Checkmate.

"How would I know anything about that?" *Word travels fast on the criminal grapevine.* "Are they sure it was a woman?"

"*Da.* I doubt there is more than one Leine Basso."

Leine clenched and unclenched her fist. Vlad had her twelve ways to Sunday. Even if he wasn't sure it was Leine who shot them, he could let slip something about a former assassin living in LA who may or may not be the one they were looking for. They wouldn't care if they'd identified the right shooter or not. As long as they got rid of someone who could've killed the two gunmen, vengeance would be served. And it wouldn't take much for them to find her unless she went to ground.

She so didn't need that kind of stress in her life.

With a deep sigh, she said, "Where do I need to go, and how long is this going to take?"

"Is short trip. Shipment is in Baja. Babysit, as you say, to Los Angeles, hand over to my people. Two days, maximum."

"And who will I be working with in Baja?"

"Is associate," Vlad said, his voice trailing off.

"An associate. Right." Trying to get a straight answer from someone like Vlad was an exercise in frustration. "Vladimir Petrovich, you know I need more than that. You want me around for future projects, right? If I don't come back from this, how can I be of use to you?" *That's it, Leine. Dangle more favors in front of him. He'll bite.* Although, she sure as hell wasn't going to put herself in the same position again.

He didn't have to know that.

"*Da.* Okay." Vlad pulled in a deep breath and let it go. "The man you will be contacting is KLA shit." He practically spit the words. "But, we do what we must, yes?"

"KLA. You mean the Kosovo Liberation Army? Didn't they disband after the war?"

"Is active. Maybe use different name, but is KLA."

The KLA had been instrumental in igniting war in the mid-to-late nineties in response to ethnic cleansing by the Serbs when Slobodan Milosevic was in power. There'd been reports of KLA involvement in drug running, arms dealing, and mass murder, culminating in charges of crimes against humanity. By the end of the conflict both sides stood accused, with the rape of hundreds, possibly thousands of Muslim women a particularly egregious consequence.

"What is the KLA doing in Mexico?" Eastern European thugs in Mexico? Recent events connected in Leine's mind. Had they set their sights on Latin America because of the perceived lawlessness there?

Vlad shrugged, distaste evident in his voice. "Drugs, weapons. Who knows what is in mind of criminal?"

Leine bit her lip to keep from voicing the sarcastic remark that sprang to mind. Vlad truly didn't view himself as a criminal. More like a businessman with unorthodox methods.

"How is it they're allowed to operate in Mexico? The cartels generally don't like to share."

"KLA is involved in drug trade since before Mexicans. Think Colombia. Afghanistan."

"Is this shipment in Tijuana?"

"No, why?"

"Just curious." Tijuana was in the Baja. Maybe she could work in a side trip.

"A curious Leine Basso is not to disregard."

"Really. There's no reason."

"I see." He paused. "Then you are meeting Nicholas tomorrow, yes?"

"Yes, Vlad. I am meeting."

23

T HE NEXT MORNING Leine pulled into the IHOP parking lot and got out, locking her door behind her. The blast of the restaurant's air conditioning hit her full force and she pulled her jacket closed. It didn't take long before she spotted Nicholas sitting in a booth at the rear of the restaurant, his back to the wall.

A grossly overweight Peter Lorre instantly leapt to mind, or perhaps Jabba the Hutt from Star Wars; large, expressive dark eyes in a mottled face, thick lips and cheeks over a bullfrog chin perched atop a freezer-sized body encased in an expensive navy blue suit and tie. His crisp white shirt strained at the buttons, unable to accommodate his bulk or the meal he was in the process of shoveling into his mouth: a double stack of Belgian waffles covered in boysenberry syrup with fried chicken, side order of sausage, side of bacon, and a plate of chocolate chip pancakes with whipped cream.

"What, no hash browns?" Leine asked, walking up to the table.

Nicholas grunted and waved her into the seat across from him.

"Is coming," he replied, his mouth full. He leaned back, breathing heavily as he chewed, watching her with the interest of someone scrutinizing a wasp. *Will it come close enough to sting? Should I kill it before it does?*

Leine sat down, placing her bag next to her.

"Nicholas, I presume."

The mountainous man nodded and hoovered another forkful of waffle into the gaping chasm of his mouth. A waitress came by and briskly delivered the aforementioned hash browns, fussing over him and giving him the Best-Customer-of-the-Day smile before she disappeared into the kitchen. A scene from an old Monty Python movie flashed through her mind as Leine wondered how anyone could ingest that much food at one sitting and not explode.

Talent. Sheer talent.

"Vladimir gave me a brief rundown of what you want me to do, but I have to tell you, shepherding a shipment of unknown origin and content isn't my idea of a stress-free gig."

"Is not to worry."

"Right. Then why do you need me to babysit?"

Nicholas shrugged, washing his breakfast down with a large glass of milk.

"I do not trust people," he said, dabbing at the corners of his mouth with a napkin.

"Yeah, well, neither do I, but that doesn't tell me what I need to know." Leine leaned forward. "Vlad mentioned I'd be working with a former member of the KLA. I'm familiar with the organization, but I need to know a bit more about them. For instance, what did they do in the war?"

Nicholas frowned, his face folding onto itself as he did—evidently in an attempt to convey disgust.

"He is idiot son of diseased, dick-sucking whore—" He

stopped, an apologetic look on his face. "Forgive. Is bad person. No morals."

"I gathered that. But why? Does he steal? Cheat? Kill?"

"*Da*. All of these things." Nicholas paused, resting his fork on his plate. His gaze lost focus as he stared into the restaurant. Leine turned to see what he was looking at, but everything appeared normal.

"Is good with knife," he finally said, and jammed another forkful of waffle into his mouth.

"Is that all you're going to tell me?"

Nicholas shrugged a shoulder and continued to inhale his breakfast.

Leine sighed. It wasn't like she'd never gone into a job blind before, but common courtesy dictated she be given at least some background.

Oh, wait. What was she thinking? The words Russian mafia and common courtesy normally weren't used in the same breath, let alone the same conversation.

"I can't do the job without more information, Nicholas. I'm not suicidal. You have to give me more than that."

He wiped a meaty palm on the napkin and picked up a manila envelope from the seat beside him. He slid it across the table, narrowly missing a pool of boysenberry syrup.

Leine took the envelope and glanced inside. It contained the photograph of a man with a blond crew cut and hard eyes, clipped to a street map of Ensenada. A red circle indicated an address outside of town.

"This isn't even close to enough, Nicholas." Leine could feel her blood pressure begin to rise. *Goddamn Russians. You can never get a straight answer out of them. This is my fucking life he's playing with.*

"*Da*, I know. The rest I tell. You must memorize," he said, tapping his temple with his finger.

By the time Nicholas finished, Leine had learned the basics. She knew she was to fly to Ensenada that evening on Nicholas's private jet and meet with a man named Grigori, who would supply whatever weapons she needed. Early the next morning, she and Grigori would go to the place indicated on the map where she would meet with a man named Zamir, the former KLA member, and pick up the shipment. From there, with Grigori's help she'd accompany the shipment into the US where she was to hand it over to Nicholas's representative. He assured her there would be no problems crossing the border. When she'd pressed him as to why, he said Grigori knew a special route and had done it many times before.

Jabba was cagey about what was actually in the shipment, but he'd assured her there were no drugs, human beings, or weapons. That left an ocean of possibilities, most of which Leine didn't like.

Unfortunately, that was the plan, and she had to go along with it, or Vlad would make good on his threat to her daughter or herself. Of that she had no doubt.

The only problem being, in her world things rarely went according to plan.

24

B ELINDA BENNETT FLINCHED at the sound of the front door slamming shut. Dick Bennett's last words had a ring of finality that sent Belinda's heart rate into the stratosphere.

What am I going to do now? Her husband had been adamant that no money be paid to the animals that had their daughter. She'd presented what she thought was a clear argument for caving in to the kidnapper's demands, citing expediency as well as not having to involve law enforcement, which in turn could lead to a leak of the situation to the press. But Dick refused to budge. Where would it end, he'd countered. If they paid them the exorbitant amount they were now asking, what would stop them from extorting more?

And more importantly, there'd be no guarantee they wouldn't kill Elise.

No, Dick Bennett couldn't be persuaded, especially when he thought he was right. This tendency made him formidable in business dealings but hell to live with. There had to be another way.

She peered out the upstairs window to make sure he'd gone

before opening her laptop and signing into her video conferencing account. She pulled up an encrypted phone list, found the number she wanted and entered it into the program. It took several moments before the man she knew as Ivan appeared on the screen.

"You have news for me." Ivan's eyes glittered like icicles in harsh sunlight. As usual, the dark green wall behind him didn't give her any clues to his current location.

"I need more time," she said in a hushed voice. Belinda looked over her shoulder to make sure Teuta wasn't hovering outside in the hall. The housekeeper had been in the kitchen finishing up the lunch dishes. "He refused. He's afraid the demands for money won't stop."

"Then persuade him." Ivan's lips pulled back in a sneer. "You are good at that, remember?"

"I've tried. Perhaps if you reduced the amount—"

"No." Ivan's voice rose, his expression darkening. "This is not negotiable."

"Please, be patient." Belinda's tone softened. "I'm working on him. If he knew everything he'd go to the police or the FBI or the CIA with the information. You know I'd pay you the entire amount right now if I could, but I don't have that much at my disposal. I need access to his offshore accounts."

"You do not seem to understand the seriousness of this situation. I have no love for your daughter. To me she is a means to an end. Either you pay me the money you owe, or I recoup my loss in other ways that are not so pleasant. For her."

"She's only seventeen." Her hand shaking, Belinda brushed at the tears pooling in her eyes. Nicknamed the Ice Queen by her colleagues, the terror Belinda Bennett felt for her daughter had cracked through the rigid persona she'd developed through years of business negotiations, leaving her raw and exposed.

"You have twenty-four hours."

The screen went blank. Belinda stared at it for a long moment before rising blindly from her chair. She never believed Ivan would use her daughter as a bargaining chip, but now that he had she wondered how she could have been so sure. The man was a terrorist. It didn't take him long to find out her real name and where she lived. Anonymity on the Internet was a myth. No matter how much security she hid behind, her information was still within reach.

And that information could destroy everything.

Fighting the panic threatening to overwhelm her, she turned away from the laptop. Teuta stood in the hallway, startling her. Belinda sucked in a breath and brought her hand to her throat.

"Let me explain," Belinda started, but the housekeeper glared at her with a reproachful expression. Her hand shook as she pointed an accusing finger at her employer.

"Eliseka will *die* because of you."

THE DOOR BANGED OPEN AND THE OVERHEAD LIGHT BLINKED ON, temporarily blinding Elise. She slid to a sitting position, squinting at the two men who came through the door. One was the man with the tribal tattoos. She didn't recognize the other. The tattooed man walked over to where she sat, unfastened the chain from the leg of the bed, slapped a second cuff around her other wrist, and wrenched her onto her feet.

"Wait," Elise cried, panic scaling her throat. "Where are you taking me?"

Tattoo said nothing and jerked the chain as if she were a dog on a leash. Instinctively, Elise balked, digging her toes into the floor and throwing herself back toward the bed, but he was too strong, and the cement was too smooth, and she skidded behind him toward the door. The other man came up next to her and yanked a dark hood over her head, securing it around her neck. Terrified, Elise could only gasp. Her chest squeezed tight, and she found it hard to draw a complete breath as she fought the rising claustrophobia.

The two men led her through the building. They took several turns before they hustled her outside and into a waiting vehicle. Elise guessed from the lack of traffic noise that it was late evening, although it was possible they were somewhere in the country. The balmy weather surprised her. It was so cold in her small cement room.

Elise ran her hands around the space, stopping when her fingers closed around heavy wire. They'd thrown her into a cargo area, probably an SUV similar to the one they'd used in Tijuana.

The vehicle began to move, and Elise inched back until she could go no further. Where were they taking her? Had her parents paid the ransom? A tiny flame of hope ignited in her chest at the thought of being able to leave this nightmare behind her. She promised herself that as soon as she got back she would finish high school, immediately enroll in Stanford or wherever her parents wanted her to go, and never, ever take her life for granted again. She even went so far as to imagine setting up a non-profit in her name to benefit those less fortunate.

What started out as a smooth road soon turned to gravel. Rocks pinged the undercarriage as the vehicle hit pothole after pothole, throwing Elise around like so much baggage. She planted her feet and braced herself against the side.

Sometime later, the vehicle stopped and the door opened. The chain rattled and Elise was yanked out by the wrists. She winced at the sharp stones gouging her bare feet but remained silent, realizing during the drive that cooperation would net better results. She didn't want to make the kidnappers angry.

Whoever was holding her chain jerked her forward. She

stumbled up the steps, across a smooth surface and into a building. Someone ripped the hood from her head and she blinked at the overhead light.

They stood in a simple front room with a wood floor. Straight-backed chairs lined the walls, punctuated every so often by a small side table. A couple of rundown sofas hunched against the far end of the room, a low coffee table in front of them. Cheap prints adorned the walls, most of them depicting beautiful women in traditional Spanish clothing.

A tall man with a precisely trimmed goatee walked into the room and the man beside her stiffened. Older than the men who had abducted her, he had an air of authority Elise instantly recognized. She looked at the floor, hoping to appear submissive so he wouldn't have reason to hurt her.

"I want to see her eyes," the tall man snapped in Spanish.

The man next to her grabbed her chin and forced her head up. Elise continued to stare at the floor.

"Look at me," he commanded in heavily accented English.

Hesitantly, Elise forced her gaze to his. His eyes held a cold intensity she hadn't encountered before. Her gut clenched while he surveyed her from her feet to her face as though inspecting a piece of furniture. She quickly averted her gaze, frightened.

"Tell him I'll pay the usual," he said to the second man. "He can return in a few months for the rest."

A few months? Elise's heart beat wildly in her chest and she wobbled, her knees suddenly unsteady. She wasn't going home. Her parents didn't pay the ransom.

Tattoo kept his grip on the chain and nodded at his partner. "Start the vehicle," he said. Without a word, the second gunman left.

"What?" the tall man asked Tattoo, his tone clipped.

"He expects more for this one," Tattoo said, shrugging.

"How much more?"

"She's young, blonde, and healthy." Tattoo ran his hand along her cheek. Elise stifled the urge to scratch at his eyes. "He wants double."

The tall man laughed, the sound harsh in the low-ceilinged room.

"He should be paying me to take her off his hands. Look at her dress and the way she stands. She obviously comes from wealth. A female raised with money will be hard to train and poses a risk to my operation. Her people will have the resources to search for her."

Elise froze at his words. They were going to train her? To do what? Foreboding crawled up her spine as visions of domestic servitude, and worse, flashed through her mind. She had to escape. She cast a furtive look around her, frantically searching for a way out. A partially open window stood near one of the couches, the curtains fluttering in the evening breeze. She wondered how far they were from a town.

"Possibly, although Zamir assures me that won't be a problem. Besides, she's an American. You can charge more."

Tall Man appeared to think over what he'd said and nodded.

"An additional twenty percent. This is more than fair."

Tattoo fished in his pocket for his phone. "With your permission?" he asked, holding up his cell.

"Of course," the tall man answered.

Tattoo walked onto the porch to make a call. Tall Man sighed impatiently and turned to look behind him as though waiting for something. Elise eyed the open window.

It was now or never.

She bolted across the room. The tall man roared as he dove for the chain and yanked her backward. She lost her footing and landed hard on the floor, knocking the wind from her lungs. She rolled to one side, wheezing. His face dark with fury, Tall Man hauled on the chain, dragging her across the floor.

"Raul! Get in here," he bellowed. Whimpering, Elise shielded her head and face with her arms as he grabbed her by the waist and jerked her to her feet.

Moments later, an older man with gray hair and glasses and carrying a valise hurried into the room. The tall man shoved Elise toward him. Tattoo appeared at the door.

"This is she?" the older man asked calmly in Spanish. Tall Man nodded as he struggled to control his anger. Tattoo walked over to Tall Man and handed him a key.

"He says it's a deal," he said, nodding at the key. "For the chain," he added.

The older man walked up to Elise and squinted. His breath smelled like tequila and garlic. She swallowed several times to quell the nausea rising in her stomach.

"Open your mouth and stick out your tongue," he ordered in English. Trembling, Elise did as she was told.

He peered down her throat and felt the sides of her neck. "Turn."

Elise turned, stiffening when he slid his hand over her bottom and up her spine. He lifted each arm and jabbed at her armpits, and then took out a stethoscope, which he placed against her back.

"Breathe deeply," he instructed. Elise drew a shaky breath.

He finished examining her and put the stethoscope back in his bag. He nodded to the tall man. "Her blood work is good," he said, returning to Spanish. "There was no evidence of drugs other than alcohol, and I discerned no diseases."

His anger contained for the moment, Tall Man grunted, gesturing toward the back of the house.

"Take her. I will finish the negotiation."

With a nod, the older man picked up the chain attached to Elise's wrist.

"Be careful. She tried to escape." Tall Man handed the doctor the key.

"Yes, of course."

The older man led her down a dark hallway and through the back door of the house. They descended several steps and walked across a dirt yard, illuminated by glowing yellow lights several yards apart, each mounted on top of a tall pole.

She followed him past a yellow, two-story farmhouse with the lights on and music blaring from the upper floor. Raucous laughter echoed from inside. The building they'd just left was similar, except no lights glowed through windows other than the one in the front room. The older man led her across the rocky yard toward a large, one-story building encased in shadow. Elise bit her lip to keep from crying out as sharp stones gouged the sensitive flesh of her feet.

When they were a few yards from the entrance, a boy materialized from the shadows. He walked with an unsteady gait, his body hunched over with one arm bent at an odd angle as though someone had neglected to unfold him all the way. Elise guessed he was somewhere around twelve or thirteen, although it was hard to tell in the dark.

"*Hola,*" the boy said, beaming. His smile was the first friendly expression Elise had seen since she'd been thrown into the back of the SUV in Tijuana. She couldn't help herself—she smiled back at him. *Finally, someone nice.* She almost cried with relief.

"Good evening, Sebastian," the older man said. "This is Elise. She'll be staying with us for a while."

"Good evening, Doctor Ramirez." Sebastian looked from the older man to Elise, and, still grinning, nodded like a bobblehead doll. "Hi, Elise!" he said in Spanish, his eyes wide. "Will you be my friend?"

"Of course," she replied. Although Elise herself had never worked with special needs kids, her friend Brittany had spent an entire summer at Camp Challenge and told her about her experiences. *They just want to be treated like everyone else, Elise,* she'd told her. Not wanting this one brief moment of kindness to end, Elise took that advice to heart and held out her manacled hands. Puzzled, Sebastian looked at her, unsure what to do.

"You shake it, like this." Elise grasped his palm with both her hands and gave it a gentle squeeze. Sebastian's eyebrows shot upward in surprise. He stared at her with his mouth open, as though mesmerized.

"Move along now, Sebastian. It's time for bed," the doctor scolded, shooing him away. Sebastian shook himself as if waking from a trance.

"Bedtime for Sebastian," he said with a serious nod. He moved aside to let them pass, never taking his eyes off of Elise.

Ramirez fished out a key ring, selected a key, and unlocked the door to the building. He flipped on an overhead light and ushered Elise inside what appeared to be a foyer with a closed door at the far end. To their right was a small bathroom with a sink and a toilet but no door. He locked the door behind them and then unlocked the manacles, placing them in a large metal can nearby.

"Do you need to relieve yourself?" he asked.

She shook her head no. Even though she would have loved to wash the grime off her face, she wasn't about to pee in front of a complete stranger.

He pointed to a rack of white cotton dresses next to the bathroom. "Find one that fits and give me your clothing."

Hands shaking, Elise searched each one for a size, but they appeared to be homemade with no labels. She found one she thought would fit and, turning away from him, unzipped her ruined outfit and slipped her arms out of the sleeves. Before she let her dress drop to the floor, she quickly slid the white one over her head and pulled it down over her hips. It reached past her knees and was quite thin. She stepped out of the one she had been wearing and picked it up, handing it to the old man.

"What are you going to do with it?" she asked. If she ever got to leave, she'd like to take it with her and have it repaired. Or, at the very least recycle the crystals. It *was* her favorite dress.

"That is no longer your concern."

"What about shoes?" she asked. Her feet were raw. A trail of blood dotted the floor.

"You do not need shoes here."

Elise couldn't imagine anywhere a person wouldn't need shoes. An image of Cinderella flashed through her mind, igniting a safe memory to grab hold of. If Cinderella could survive and meet her prince, then Elise could, too.

Fairytales are based on fact, like myths, right?

He flipped off the light and opened the door in front of them. Elise peered into the darkness.

"You will find an empty bed at the far end," he whispered. Light snoring could be heard from either side of the room. "Sleep. You have a big day ahead of you."

With that, the old man left, closing the door behind him. Elise reached for the handle, but her fingertips met only a smooth surface.

She made her way slowly toward the other end of the room, waiting for her eyes to adjust to the darkness. A thin stream of moonlight shone through a tiny, barred window to her right illuminating several twin beds lined up against the wall. From what she could see, a form occupied each one, like an army barracks. Elise kept going, careful not to disturb anyone.

At the end of the row of beds she found a vacant mattress made up with sheets and a pillow. A blanket lay folded at the foot of the bed. Elise sat down and listened to the breathing of the other inhabitants. There was a different tenor to one of them and Elise strained to hear.

Someone was crying softly.

Unfolding the blanket, Elise lay on the bed and felt her own tears come.

25

———

LISE SNAPPED AWAKE and stared at the ceiling.

Where was she? Events of the previous night came back to her in dribs and drabs but skated away when she tried to concentrate. She propped herself up on her elbows, and attempted to focus on the activity around her.

Sunlight streamed through the room revealing dozens of girls of differing ages in various stages of waking up—some stood at the end of their beds with heads bowed wearing simple, knee-length dresses, their white shifts neatly folded on their freshly made beds, while others scrambled to change or hurriedly tucked sheets around mattresses. A few whispered to each other—no one spoke out loud—and some had dark circles under their eyes, as though they hadn't slept well the night before. Elise folded back her covers and sat up the rest of the way, rubbing the sleep from her eyes.

Something had been left on the end of her bed. Taking her cue from the other girls, she tucked in her sheet and blanket and then unfolded the blue fabric, revealing a plain cotton dress. She took off the white shift and, ignoring the blatant stares from several of the other girls at her expensive silk thong and pushup bra, pulled the blue one over her head. It too stopped just below her knees.

The door at the end of the room opened and everyone fell silent. Stragglers quickly took their places at the end of their cots and stood more or less at attention. Elise did the same. The concrete floor felt rough beneath her feet, and she thought longingly of the pair of Louboutins she'd worn in Tijuana. It seemed so long ago. Not that she would expect to wear heels—at this point, she'd have been happy with a pair of flip-flops.

She peered around the girl next to her to see who was at the door and snapped back in line, panic shooting through her. It was the tall man from the night before. A younger, muscular man followed behind him, restraining a dog by its collar and moving toward her down the line. Most of the girls stared at the floor as they passed.

Beads of perspiration slid down her neck to the small of her back as Elise struggled for calm. The man with the dog was the same man who'd kidnapped her from the Porsche and drugged her. He looked different in daylight, and she might not have recognized him except for the tan stray he'd coaxed into the SUV. All compact muscle, the pit bull's smaller head and scarred face was unforgettable.

The three of them stopped in front of her. Elise fixed her gaze on the floor, her breath shallow. The man let go of the dog, and it immediately trotted over to her and sniffed at her ankles. A low growl emanated from deep within its throat and Elise held her breath. She'd seen pictures of people who had been mauled by dogs. It wasn't pretty.

"Take her," the tall man ordered, and waved his hand at Elise. The man who'd been holding the dog seized her arm and shoved her toward the door. The dog followed behind, growling.

"No—where are you taking me?" she cried, trying to wrench free of his grasp.

He tightened his grip and propelled her ahead of him.

"Help me—" she pleaded with the other girls as they passed. When no one moved, tears sprang to her eyes. Most of them avoided her gaze by staring at the floor, but a few did not. Of those who watched them walk to the door, all had pity in their eyes, mixed with what could only be described as fear.

Once outside, the man forced her toward a small outbuilding Elise hadn't noticed the night before. It stood roughly four feet high and three feet across with a padlocked door and no windows.

His grip on her arm secure, the man one-handed the lock off its hasp, kicked open the door, and shoved her toward the tiny space.

Oh, my God. They're going to lock me inside. Terrified, Elise balked and threw herself backward, digging her heels into the dirt.

"Don't put me in there, please—" she begged, tears streaming down her face. The dog's growl grew in intensity, and it snapped at her heels.

Without a word, the man slipped behind her and, using his body weight, heaved her into the dark hole and slammed the door shut. The sound of the lock snapping closed landed with a dull thud in her tiny prison, leaving Elise alone in the dark.

THE DOG MAN WAS KNOWN AS CRUZ, NAMED AFTER A FAMOUS Banda musician from another century. He enjoyed the recognition on people's faces when he told them and had called the stray dog Max for *Mad Max*, an old movie Cruz had watched seventeen times. So far, none of the people at the ranch had said anything, which made him rethink his choice. Cruz had been pleased, though, to see how terrified the girls were of

Max and used it to his advantage. Even Garcia seemed intimidated.

Cruz didn't care much for Master Garcia, but he paid well and Cruz liked money. On repeated occasions he'd requested time with one of the girls, but Garcia told him he was too young and needed to wait.

He'd laughed at the reference to his age. He might have been young, but he'd proven his abilities many times over by killing whenever he was told to. Three hundred times over, by his count. Garcia was so impressed with his work that he farmed him out to other "businessmen" who needed his services.

And still he couldn't taste Garcia's whores.

Cruz made his first kill when he was eight years old. The member of a local drug gang offered what was a lot of money to Cruz at the time if he would shoot a rival gang member. Cruz did as he asked, his age and supposed innocence allowing him unprecedented access to the target. After that, Cruz made a name for himself as a vicious and talented killer and worked his way up, eventually landing with Garcia. The thrill of having so much power over someone's life never left him. That he didn't feel remorse was a plus.

Cruz slept well at night.

He enjoyed commanding the people he was about to kill to dig their own graves. He relished the look of fear on their faces, the tiny ray of hope they harbored that if they took their time digging, he'd grow bored and let them go.

Yes, Cruz enjoyed smashing hope. And why should anyone believe in hope? He was doing them a favor. Life was about survival of the fittest, taking what you could, living *la vida loca*. The crazy life.

Cruz knew how to live crazy.

When the Eastern Europeans brought in the American girl he'd helped kidnap, Cruz nearly exploded with anticipation. But she was off limits to everyone. Garcia made the excuse of waiting for blood tests to confirm she had no diseases. Cruz didn't care what he caught, as long as he was the first. As Garcia turned down each request, it dawned on him that he was saving the girl for his own pleasure. If so, Cruz would never be allowed to have her.

He would need to take her by force.

26

"HEY—ARE YOU in there?"

The whispering woke Elise. Disoriented, she opened her eyes but saw nothing. She held her hand to her face but still couldn't make anything out. The temperature had skyrocketed and she was roasting in the airless box. Struggling to breathe, she wiped the sweat from her forehead with the back of her arm.

"Do you speak Spanish?" the muffled voice asked. It sounded female and came from behind her. Elise scooted toward the voice until she couldn't go any further and leaned her ear against the wood.

"I'm here," she said as loud as she dared. The person on the other side answered with a soft knock.

"This is the first time, so it shouldn't be much longer. Recite songs in your mind or try to remember passages from books," the girl's voice suggested. "It will make the time go faster and you won't go too crazy."

"Why did they put me in here?" Elise asked. She hadn't done anything wrong. The box felt like a punishment.

"To show you what will happen if you disobey," came the reply.

"Who are you?"

"They call me Fanta, but my real name—" She stopped.

Elise strained to hear what was happening outside, but she could barely catch her words, much less distant sounds.

"I have to go." Fanta's voice trailed off.

"Wait—" Panicked, Elise banged on the wall, willing her to stay.

There was no answer.

Despair settled over her like a heavy fog and her shoulders sagged. Sweat trickled down her back and between her breasts. Something scratched feverishly a couple of feet away from where she was sitting. Alarm spiked through her and her breath caught. Elise drew her knees to her chin.

Is there something in here with me?

The scratching continued for a moment, and then quit. Elise squeezed her eyes shut and listened to her heart hammer in her chest. Although she'd never experienced a full-on anxiety attack, the stifling heat and lack of light combined with the possibility of a wild animal inside the box had Elise fighting hard to remain calm.

Fanta's words carved their way into her mind and she started singing her favorite Taylor Swift song, her voice wobbly at first. Her breathing slowed and after a few stanzas, so did her heartbeat. The scratching resumed but didn't sound any closer. Elise sang louder, trying to drown it out with her voice.

The door banged open and blazing sunlight filled the tiny space. Elise snapped her mouth shut and squinted at the silhouette.

"*Vamanos*," the man ordered, his voice gruff.

Elise crawled forward into the light, gulping in the fresh air. She didn't recognize the man who seized her by the wrist and hauled her to her feet. She glanced down at her sweat-soaked, dirt-stained dress and wondered what the rest of her looked like.

The man dragged her across the yard to the first building she'd been in the night before when the doctor examined her. She stumbled up the stairs and into the hallway at the back of the house. The man detoured into the first room on the left, and, leaving her there, walked out, closing the door behind him.

Elise found herself in a spare room with a double bed, a dresser with a mirror, a toilet, a sink, and a claw-foot bathtub. She stumbled to the toilet and sat down. She hadn't been sure how long she would be kept in the box and had stopped herself from going, not wanting to sit in her own pee.

Not sure what was expected of her, she sat on the edge of the bed when she was finished, her mind blank. She felt numb. Mistreatment, other than being ignored, hadn't been a part of Elise's life until now and she had no idea how to process what was happening. So, she didn't. She stared at the scarred wooden floor and quietly hummed another song to herself.

Soon, she heard footsteps advancing toward her down the hallway. She looked up as the door opened and the tall man with the perfectly shaped goatee walked into the room. He carried a black, leather-bound bible in one hand and a whip in the other. Elise eyed the whip with mounting anxiety and wiped her sweaty palms on her dirt-encrusted dress.

The tall man closed the door behind him with precision and turned to face her.

"You remember me?" he said in clipped English.

Elise nodded, her gaze darting from his face to the whip in his hand.

"Good. You will call me Master Garcia." He crossed the room, placed the bible on top of the dresser, and swiveled to face her, slapping the whip in his palm. Elise flinched. His mouth curved into a cruel smile, dark eyes glinting in the sunlight streaming through the barred window.

"Your name."

"Elise," she whispered.

"I can't hear you," he boomed. "What is your name?"

Elise swallowed, her mouth dry. "Elise," she said again, this time louder.

"And what is my name?"

"Garcia," she croaked.

"*Master* Garcia," he commanded. "Say it."

"Master...Garcia." Elise closed her eyes. Tears dripped to her chin.

Evidently satisfied, he paced before her, tapping the whip against his palm.

"Well, *Elise*, you have been given into my custody, and I will say from what I saw last night, we have much to do." His lips curled with a look of distaste and he took a step closer.

Elise tensed, staring at the floor. He prodded her chin with the end of the whip.

"Look at me when I speak to you."

Slowly, Elise raised her eyes to meet his. Dread weighed in her stomach like an anvil and the hairs at the back of her neck prickled. For the first time in her short life, violence mixed with indifference stared back at her. She struggled to steady her gaze.

"What did you learn in the enclosure?" He stood close enough that Elise could smell the sweat on his oily scalp. "Did you see God?" he whispered, his breath hot against her ear.

Not sure of what he wanted her to say, she decided to answer with a question. "Did I—"

He stepped back and peered down at her. "Answer me, whore," he bellowed.

Elise covered her head to ward off the sting of the whip, but it didn't come. Shaking now, she murmured, "I—I didn't see God." Her voice trailed to nothing as he strode to the dresser.

He picked up the bible and flipped it open, scanning the pages. He found what he was looking for and walked back toward her, reading in Spanish.

"*And he answered, what peace, so long as the whoredoms of thy mother Jezebel and her witchcrafts are so many?*"

He glanced up from the book with a scowl and pointed an accusing finger at Elise. "You are the embodiment of the treacherous Jezebel." His voice echoed against the walls. "You must be cleansed of your witchcraft. Only then will you be worthy in the eyes of the Lord."

Leaning his head back, he raised both arms and shouted, "Be gone, oh demons who dwell in the breast of this unclean whore. Cleanse her of her wickedness..."

The whip sliced through the air, landing with a sharp crack on Elise's shoulder. The braided leather bit through her dress and she cried out. Master Garcia brought the whip down again and again on her shoulders and back, ripping through the thin fabric of her dirt-stained shift, while reciting one passage of scripture after another. Her body swimming in hot, agonizing pain, Elise fell to the floor and curled into a ball at his feet, her arms covering her face and head in an ineffective attempt to block the blows.

After what seemed like one hundred strokes of the whip, Master Garcia stopped and, breathing heavily, stepped back, placing both the bible and the whip on top of the dresser. He bent down and seized her elbow, dragging her to her feet.

"Start the bath," he ordered.

Tears streaming down her face, Elise staggered to the tub and turned on the faucets. She looked around for a plug and realized there was already one in the drain. Master Garcia strode to where she balanced on the lip of the tub.

"Remove your dress and get in."

Legs shaking, she stood and pulled off the ruined dress. With a brief glance at the shredded and bloodstained fabric, she dropped it to the floor and stepped into the tub. Garcia grimaced when he saw her thong.

"Take off your whore's clothing. You will not wear such things here."

Elise raised trembling hands to unfasten her bra, turning away from him as she did. She heard him cross the room and glanced over her shoulder, afraid he would come back with something worse than the whip.

"Sebastian will bring fresh clothes and dress the wounds." He opened the door and paused. "Be sure this does not happen again. Most whores only need one cleansing. I pray the demons have left you and you are free."

With that, Garcia walked out and slammed the door behind him.

Elise closed her eyes and sucked in a ragged breath. Equal parts relief and despair washed through her. The water in the tub had risen to mid-calf and she carefully lowered herself to a seated position. A wave of grief followed by unshakable anger flowed through her and she hung her head. Hot tears coursed down her face. If her father knew how she'd been treated he'd raise the dead to see "Master Garcia" rot in prison. If she couldn't find a way to escape, she would do everything in her power to bring the sadistic bastard down.

No one whipped Elise Bennett.

She clung to the thought and cupped warm, stinging water over her back and shoulders, and watched the bath turn pink from her blood.

27

———

ELISE'S HEART RATE returned to normal as she soaked, grateful to be alone. The water had quickly grown tepid, and she'd kept adding warm water, not wanting the bath to end. The more she soaked, the more bearable the pain became. She leaned her head back on the lip of the tub and closed her eyes.

Moments later, someone knocked on the door. Elise snapped to and sat up, paralyzed with fear. Water lapped at the sides of the tub.

Garcia wouldn't knock. She relaxed her shoulders and grabbed a towel she'd draped over the side of the tub.

"Come in."

The door opened and Sebastian walked in carrying a small first aid kit and what looked like another blue dress, which he placed on the dresser. With a shy smile, he averted his eyes and shuffled over to the bathtub. Keeping his gaze downcast, he set the kit on the floor and turned so that his back was to her.

"I—I'm sorry you fell down and hurt yourself. Master Garcia told me to come here and help you with the bandages."

"Is that what he told you?"

"Yes, I—" At the sound of her voice, Sebastian turned toward her to answer but quickly realized his mistake. Eyes wide, his cheeks reddened and he spun back around.

"It's all right, Sebastian. Don't be embarrassed." *How sweet,* she thought. He was so different from everyone else.

Elise pulled the plug out of the drain and watched the bloody water disappear. Then she stood and wrapped the towel around herself before stepping out of the tub.

His gaze still on the floor, Sebastian edged down to pick up the first aid kit. He followed her to the bed and she sat down, lifting her hair to the side so he could clean the welts on her shoulders and back.

"You must have fallen a lot. The other girls don't usually have this many cuts," he said and opened the kit, revealing rolls of gauze and tape and antibiotic cream. He chose a bottle of rubbing alcohol and a clean cloth and gently swabbed her neck and shoulders.

"Yeah. I fell a lot." Elise squeezed her eyes closed against the stinging alcohol and thought about her father. She was sure he was going crazy, wondering where she was. At least, she hoped so. She wondered why it was taking them so long to pay the ransom. Were her parents delaying to teach her a lesson? Anger flared in her chest at the thought of her mother suggesting they wait a day or two before paying the money. *Fuck her.*

"How long have you been here, Sebastian?" she asked. So far, he was the only person who had been kind to her during the whole ordeal. Well, except for the doctor, but she didn't trust him.

"Oh, a very long time," he said, his voice earnest. "Master Garcia and Doctor Ramirez have been good to me. My job is very important."

"I'm sure it is. What else do you do besides fix the broken girls?"

"Ha. That's funny. You're not *broken*, just clumsy." He giggled as he carefully applied ointment to the cuts on her neck and back. Then he paused.

Elise turned her head. "Why did you stop?"

"I don't have a big enough bandage for your shoulder."

She smiled at the consternation on his face.

"That's okay. You can put one right next to the other one, if you want."

Sebastian's face cleared and he nodded. "Yes. That will work." He ripped open the packages of sterile bandages and gently applied them to the wounds, taking his time. His fingers brushed her skin, and she heard a sharp intake of breath. A few seconds later he resumed, securing the bandages with first aid tape, and then carefully put everything back in the kit. Elise turned to face him, her eyes searching his.

"Thank you, Sebastian. I feel much better now."

Sebastian's face turned a deep shade of pink and he nodded his head and smiled, obviously pleased.

"There is a man outside the door, waiting to take you to the doctor," he said.

"Why?" Fear returned to Elise like a starved animal, shredding the short window of calm Sebastian had brought.

"All the girls go. I'm not supposed to tell you why," he answered.

He glanced out the barred window at the brown, dusty yard and smiled. "It's a beautiful day, isn't it?"

ELISE TUCKED A STRAND OF HAIR BEHIND HER EAR AS SHE scrubbed the bathroom floor. On hands and knees with a bucket of soapy water beside her, she really did feel like Cinderella. Mindful of the bandage on her forearm, she dunked the sponge into the pail and wrung it out before attacking the next section of the floor. The rough material of her dress scraped across the abrasions on her back, fueling her anger at Garcia.

She and a girl named Celeste had been placed on bathroom duty. Slender with thick, glossy black hair, Celeste was a few years older and, from what Elise could pry out of her, had been taken from her village in Croatia. When she asked Celeste how long she'd been there, she shrugged and said she'd lost track.

Talking to any of the girls proved harder to do than Elise anticipated. They were all afraid of repercussions from either Garcia or the dog man, as he was known. When she'd asked one of the girls if she knew anyone named Fanta, she shook her head and remained silent.

Tired, Elise dropped her sponge into the bucket and absently ran her fingers over her arm. Celeste didn't look up, continuing to scrub. After Sebastian delivered Elise to the doctor she'd been given anesthesia and woke up with her arm bandaged. Under the gauze she'd found a small incision, stitched shut. Elise noticed the same-sized scar on all the other girls. She assumed he'd taken a tissue sample. It made sense, since they'd already drawn her blood.

But for what?

She cleared her throat. Celeste ignored her. She did it again.

"What do you think they're going to do to us?" she asked, keeping her voice low. Celeste paused for a second before she lowered her head and began scouring the floor with renewed ferocity. Elise sat forward, glad for the response.

"You know something, don't you?"

Celeste didn't answer, but her hand slowed.

"Nobody's going to hear you, Celeste." Elise scooted closer. "And I promise I won't say anything. What's going on here?"

Celeste stopped cleaning and stared at the floor. Seconds

passed before she glanced at Elise. The look in her eyes sent a shiver down her spine.

"Terrible things," she said, her voice barely a whisper.

Elise's heart beat faster. "What do you mean?"

She shook her head and resumed scrubbing. "I—cannot speak of these."

Elise grabbed her arm.

Celeste stared at her hand. Paused again. "They—they make you do things. With men."

"You mean sex?"

Celeste nodded, the misery obvious on her face.

There it was. Celeste's admission wasn't a huge revelation—she thought that might be what this place was—but having her suspicions confirmed filled her with urgency.

I have to get out of here.

"That is not all."

Her mind racing, Elise almost missed Celeste's last statement.

"There's more?" The muscles in her stomach tensed.

Crying softly, Celeste nodded.

"When the men who come to this place no longer ask for you, either because they are bored or you have become unattractive, the doctor cuts you open and... takes your insides."

Elise's mind blanked for a second before the information clicked. She sucked in a breath. "No."

Celeste put the sponge down and climbed to her knees. She grabbed the hem of her dress and raised it enough to reveal an angry red scar running across her lower back.

Nausea rising in her throat, Elise tried sucking in air but only managed shallow breaths. *I can't breathe.* She stared at Celeste, who was looking at her with such pity it made her want to vomit.

Elise struggled to get her emotions under control. Panicking wouldn't help her escape. "If that's true, then what happens after? They can't take both of your kidneys. You'd die."

Without a word, Celeste let the hem of her dress fall. She picked up the sponge, dipped it in her water bucket, and began to scrub the floor.

Elise had her answer.

LESS THAN HALF AN HOUR LATER, ELISE STOOD IN LINE BEHIND Celeste, waiting for lunch to be served. The incision on her forearm had bled through the dressing, but Elise was afraid to go to the doctor and ask for a new bandage. If she kept her head down, maybe they wouldn't notice her, giving her time to figure out a way to escape.

The ranch didn't appear to have a fence to keep them all in, but guards with guns walked the grounds at various intervals around the yard, and she'd seen cameras on the front of the barracks and on the main house.

The night she arrived—two nights before? Three?—the drive had been long. She wasn't even sure where she was. If she did manage to run away without alerting the guards, which way should she go? Elise knew enough about the desert to know she wasn't equipped to survive for long without water, and if she picked the wrong direction, she could be out there for days.

And what about the dog man? He'd probably trained the muscular canine to track runaways. Elise shuddered at the thought of being torn apart by the pit bull's sharp teeth.

There had to be a way to escape.

The lunch line began to move. Elise snapped back to the present and picked up a plastic plate from a stack. Plastic utensils were provided, ostensibly so no one could make a weapon from the metal kind. She glanced around her, wondering why

Garcia bothered. Many of the girls appeared despondent, resigned to their fate, and it wasn't because of drugs. When Elise spoke of her suspicions to Celeste she'd informed her that the new girls who were found to be substance abusers were forced to get clean. Otero insisted. For whatever reason, the girls didn't create any trouble.

Elise refused to give in. Her anger helped keep her defiance alive.

Lunch turned out to be the same as the day before: a flour tortilla topped with refried beans and cheese, with a couple of cherry tomatoes on the side. The drink choice was limited to milk, juice, and water.

"A can of Fanta, please," the voice behind Elise said.

Elise turned to see who had spoken. A striking redhead about her age stood behind her with a congenial smile on her face.

"The answer is still no," growled the man behind the counter. Squat and dark with a thick neck, Elise figured the man's oily hair could have easily been tapped as a natural resource.

The redhead pretended to pout, and then winked at Elise. Elise wondered if she might be the mysterious Fanta who had given her encouragement when she was locked inside the shed.

Elise selected a can of orange juice and found a seat at a table next to Celeste. The redhead walked over with her plate.

"May I join you?" she asked in Spanish.

"Sure," Elise said.

She set her plate on the table and took the chair next to Elise. She placed her napkin in her lap and said, "You're new here, aren't you?"

"Yes." Elise checked to make sure none of the guards in the room were looking their way. "Are you Fanta?" she asked, her eyes on her food.

"What do you think?" the redhead replied.

Elise glanced at her to see if she smiled. She did. Relief swam through her. Just knowing another person had tried to be helpful filled her with hope.

"We need to meet," Fanta said in a low voice.

Elise noticed a guard walking toward them and stiffened. Fanta followed her gaze.

"Where?" Elise asked, barely moving her lips.

"There's a large tree in the wash behind our building. Meet me there right before dinner, when it's dark." Fanta rolled up her tortilla and took a bite, watching the guard walk by.

Her heart fluttering in her chest, Elise did the same.

28

———

GRIGORI WAS WAITING for Leine at the airport, holding a sign that said *Basso*. Over six feet tall and powerfully built, he oozed confidence. His army green khakis and black T-shirt fit perfectly, leaving little to the imagination. A dirty-blond buzz cut and a pair of serious combat boots completed the outfit. *Add an AK-47 and a bottle of Stoli*, Leine thought, *and you've got yourself a Russian action hero.*

"You must be Grigori," Leine said, letting her pack slide from her shoulder onto the floor.

Grigori gave her a nod, scooped up her bag, and started for the entrance.

"*Da.* We go now."

So much for small talk, Leine mused. She liked that in an operative.

They walked through the parking lot to a dull-yellow Humvee. The sun had set but the asphalt still radiated heat. Leine removed her light jacket and stowed it in the back seat, next to her pack. The lightweight, long-sleeved shirt, fitted T-shirt, and cargo pants she wore turned out to be the perfect choice, although forecasts called for scorching hot the next afternoon. With any luck, she'd be on her way home by then.

They pulled out of the airport and headed for the coast, both preferring silence. The closer they got to the beach, the thicker the briny air became, bringing back memories of jobs she'd taken in France and Italy. She'd always schedule a little extra down time for "debriefing" as she called it, and the sea had worked well as a calming antidote to the violence of her job.

A short time later, Grigori pulled into a hotel parking lot, parked the Hummer, and tossed her a room key. They were booked into separate rooms at a nondescript waterfront hotel with an on-premises bar and restaurant so they wouldn't have to go into town.

"Third floor. I am second, below you," he said, pointing to a pair of balconies overlooking the bay.

"And the weapons?"

"I put in closet. I will show."

Grigori locked the Hummer and accompanied her up to her room, still silent. Leine figured his English was limited. She could have sparked a conversation in his native tongue but decided against it. That would open up a whole new narrative she didn't feel like pursuing.

They entered the hotel room, and Leine did a quick inventory as she walked in. The space was typical to tourist destinations—a mini fridge under a utilitarian desk, a wall-mounted television, a queen-sized bed next to a pair of sliding glass doors leading to the balcony.

Grigori walked to the closet, slid the door open, and pulled out a hard-sided case, which he deposited onto the bed. He stepped back, gesturing for her to open it.

Inside was an MP-5 with a 50-round ammo drum and a couple of 30-round magazines, a heavily used, 9mm pistol with extra ammunition, and a half-dozen hand grenades. Leine nodded and closed the case.

"Looks good."

Grigori appeared pleased. He stayed where he was, obviously on the verge of saying something, but Leine could tell he struggled.

With a sigh, she switched to Russian and asked, "Is there something else?"

A look of immense relief washed over his face and he nodded. "Yes. Nicholas told me you are the assassin who killed the Frenchman. I would like to know if this is true."

Several years back, the Frenchman—so-called because of a tattoo of a guillotine on his right biceps—had been the scourge of Russian arms dealers everywhere. A dealer himself, he would find out where a shipment was to be delivered through his network of spies, wait until money changed hands, and then disappear after relieving both parties of weapons, cash, and the occasional life. Tensions escalated between the Russians and their buyers, with each side blaming the other for the breach of faith. The conflict spread and soon the United States became embroiled in an arms scandal involving a Russian diplomat, which the media pursued like a coyote on the trail of wounded prey.

The agency she worked for sent her to kill him, the belief being that his death would return the world of arms dealing to normal and the media would move on to the next news cycle, allowing the US to concentrate on more pressing concerns. In the process, she'd almost lost her life and developed a deep hatred of tattoos. Years later, she'd met Vladimir Petrovich when the Frenchman's psychotic spawn blackmailed her into liberating a family heirloom from Nadja Imports, where it hung behind Vlad's desk.

"You know I can't answer that, Grigori."

Grigori's face fell.

"What do you say we check out the restaurant? I hear they make a mean *camarones al mojo de ajo*."

Grigori gave her a puzzled look.

"Garlic shrimp—like scampi."

Grigori brightened, nodding his head enthusiastically. "Oh, yes, I like garlic. And the shrimps."

Ah, Leine thought. *The language of food.*

GRIGORI HADN'T BEEN KIDDING ABOUT HIS LOVE OF GARLIC SHRIMP. He ordered the large platter and followed it up with a second. Leine watched, fascinated, as he inhaled shrimp after shrimp, washing the crustaceans down with several shots of cheap tequila.

The Russian capacity for alcohol had always intrigued her, along with the incomprehensible ability of a trained shooter to hit a target after drinking a full liter of vodka. When she mentioned this to Grigori, he laughed and said that most of his family had been weaned on vodka and trained to hit what they were shooting at no matter how much they'd been drinking.

Grigori regaled her with stories of his life growing up in a small village in Russia, and how he knew Nicholas, who was his uncle on his mother's side. Grigori had finished the second platter of *camarones* and most of a liter of tequila when he leaned toward her, a serious expression on his face.

"What is your stand on pockets?"

"I'm sorry?" Leine cocked her head to the side, wondering what the hell was going through the Russian's tequila-fueled mind.

"Pockets. What do you think of pockets? Yes? No? Will you buy clothing that does not have them?"

"I'm afraid I don't have a position on the subject, although I am quite fond of cargo pants. The side pockets are practical."

"*Da.* You see? You have position. I do not buy clothes without pockets," he declared, shaking his head. "A man must be able to carry things." He proceeded to show her the various compartments in his shirt and pants. He even had a small pouch sewn into the bottom of each sock where he kept cash and important papers. Leine wondered how far he took this obsession and if it extended to his tightie whities.

After dinner, they'd both retired to their rooms, knowing the next day would come early. Leine sat on her balcony, listening to the waves lapping the shore below her, wondering what to expect from Zamir and his group. She'd checked satellite images of the meeting place and found a dozen or so nondescript warehouses in a rundown section of Ensenada. There were two ways in and out, with the main highway a few kilometers to the north.

When an hour had passed, Leine called the front desk and requested a taxi. She took the stairs to the second floor and quietly padded to Grigori's room. Loud snores could be heard from inside. Satisfied he wouldn't be interested in following her, she continued down the stairs to the street to wait. She could have brought the big Russian with her, but he'd had too much to drink and Leine preferred to work alone.

Ten minutes later, the cab pulled up. She got in and gave the driver the address to the warehouse, instructing him to drive by slowly.

"But señora, this is only an industrial area. There are no clubs or restaurants."

"That's fine. Just circle the block. My husband is considering purchasing one of the properties, and he asked me to take a look for him."

The cab driver shrugged and did as she asked.

After a drive by, Leine instructed him to wait for her at the end of the block while she investigated further. The cab driver objected, going on about the crime rate in that section of town until Leine gave him some money to shut him up.

She crept behind the warehouses, keeping to the shadows until she reached the address indicated on the map Nicholas had given her. Situated halfway down one of the rows of warehouses, the building had definitely seen better days. Constructed primarily of crumbling block, it boasted a rusty, corrugated steel door secured with a shiny new padlock. Graffiti decorated the walls and the area smelled like stale beer and piss.

Charming.

Leine scanned the roof. On the satellite map, she'd noticed three box-shaped images on the side of the building. She saw now that they were individual air conditioners spaced a few feet apart, probably leading to second-floor offices.

She spotted a pipe running up the building and cursed her injury. There was no way she'd be able to climb onto the roof quickly. Leine continued around to the front of the warehouse, taking note of the condition of the street, where the lights were, and the proximity of other businesses. The other warehouses looked empty, with most of the doors unsecured.

The cabbie gave her a brief honk from where he had parked at the end of the street and Leine waved, indicating she'd be there in a minute. She started to head back to the car when something glittery in the middle of the pavement caught her eye. She crouched down to get a better look.

It was a tiny, pear-shaped crystal.

29

ELISE SLIPPED AROUND the back of the barracks and picked her way down the slope to the lone tree growing in a gulley. Fanta was already there.

"You weren't followed?" Fanta asked.

Elise checked behind her and shook her head. "I don't think so."

"Good." Fanta nodded. "I wanted to talk to you before Garcia decides to put you to work other than as a maid."

"I wondered why he hadn't yet."

"I think it has to do with when they get the tests back."

"But they took my blood days ago. The doctor told Garcia he didn't find any diseases. That I was clean."

Fanta pointed at the bandage on her arm. "They just did that, right?"

Elise nodded. She glanced at Fanta's arm. She wore a smaller bandage. "When did you get yours?"

"A few days ago." Fanta paused. "Do you know what they do with the girls who are no longer useful?"

"Yes."

"You're American, right? What's your name?"

"Elise. What's yours?"

"Julia."

"Why do you want to know if I'm American?"

"I want to escape to America." Julia inhaled deeply. "You will help me. We will help each other."

"Then you're going to take me with you," Elise said.

"Of course."

"But how? Do you know where we are? I mean, we're still in Mexico, right?"

"I believe we are no more than one hundred kilometers from the United States. Once we are far enough away from here we can hitchhike to the border where you will vouch for me. Tell your government I am fleeing a dangerous situation. They will believe you because you are a wealthy American girl."

"Why do you think I'm wealthy?" Instantly on alert, Elise studied her newfound ally.

Julia shrugged. "Because when you first arrived you wore expensive-looking underclothes—much finer than any of the other girls. And because of the way you act. You are used to telling others what to do. Only rich girls from America have been raised this way."

Elise unclenched her fingers, relaxing a bit. "Has anyone else tried to escape?"

Julia nodded. "Three nights ago, a girl I have spoken with disappeared. When they called her name, no one could find her. She was still very popular in the yellow house, so I know they didn't..." She paused. "I *know* she escaped. We have to try."

"Do you know which road to take? What about the guards?"

"That's another reason I need you. You know Sebastian?"

"What's he got to do with this?"

"Sebastian is allowed to go everywhere on the ranch. He knows where the guards are. The other girl said he showed her, although she was sure he didn't know he was helping her plan her escape. And, he goes into town with Master Garcia every week, so he knows the roads."

"Why do you need me for that?"

"I've seen the way he looks at you." Julia gave her a coy smile. "He would do anything you asked."

30

———

A LIGHT RAIN had fallen during the night, leaving cloudy, oil-streaked puddles in the low spots to match the cloying, humid air. After a quick breakfast, Leine and Grigori drove to the meet. The Russian didn't display any ill effects from the ample amount of tequila he'd ingested the evening before, and acted chipper and raring to go. He suggested they leave early in order to check the location.

"Turn left," Leine told him, reading from the map as though she was traveling the route for the first time. Grigori followed her instructions and parked the Hummer a short distance from the warehouse.

Leine slipped her 9mm into an ankle band while the Russian shrugged on a shoulder holster and pocketed the grenades. Grigori would keep the MP-5 with him, and Leine would take the money, locked inside a case. They both wore lightweight Kevlar vests under their clothes.

She grabbed the case and proceeded to the warehouse. Grigori skirted the alley, remaining out of sight in case things went sideways. Zamir didn't expect him, which worked in their favor.

The rusty metal door was open, and Leine walked into the cavernous building. The overhead lights cast stark shadows on the rough concrete floor. A shiver spiraled up her spine from the unexpected coolness.

A black GMC Yukon was parked on the left. To her right a metal stairway led to a door one floor up, and on the back wall was what looked like the door to a walk-in cooler. A man resembling Rutger Hauer wearing a buzz cut and a bad attitude rose from behind a table and drew his weapon, leveling a .45 at her. Leine raised her hands and scanned the warehouse for additional gunmen. There were none.

Leine tensed, calculating the distance between them.

"Take it easy, Rutger," she said. "I'm expected. Nicholas sent me."

The man frowned at the reference.

Apparently not much for watching TV or the movies, she thought.

"What is your name?"

"Leine Basso," she replied. "And you are?"

Buzz Cut relaxed his grip on the .45.

"Zamir. You have the money?" he asked in accented English.

Leine lowered her hands and set the case on the floor.

"Right here," she answered.

Zamir pointed at the case with his gun.

"Open it."

"As soon as I see the shipment."

Zamir grunted. "Wait here."

He strode to the back of the warehouse and opened the door, disappearing through a wall of plastic strips meant to keep the warm air out. A few moments later he returned carrying a blue and white hard-sided cooler, which he set on the floor between them.

"I need to see the contents," she said, foreboding stippling her spine.

Zamir bent down and removed the cover. He reached inside and pulled a piece of Styrofoam off the top, revealing a plastic bag of red-tinged liquid underneath. Zamir lifted the bag out of the cooler and held it so she could see the contents. Inside were two brownish-pink kidneys. Appalled, she choked back the bile rising in her throat.

Fucking Vlad. When neither Russian would describe the contents of the mystery shipment, she'd assumed it would be illegal.

She hadn't counted on brutal.

She stiffened, acid burning the back of her throat. She could feel Zamir's eyes on her, and she consciously relaxed her hands, forcing herself to breathe normally.

Something the waiter said in Tijuana jogged her memory. When describing the Russian man at the bar with Josh, he mentioned white hair and light blue eyes and that he looked similar to an actor he'd seen before. This guy resembled a young Rutger Hauer—an older actor with white hair and light blue eyes. Although Zamir was Albanian, not Russian, an outsider unfamiliar with the two languages wouldn't necessarily know the difference.

Leine kept her expression impassive as events tumbled into place. Eastern Europeans in Tijuana. Josh, dead in his car with jagged gashes where his kidneys should have been. The shipment in the cooler. She smoothed her hand over her front pocket, feeling the small crystal bead she'd found in the street outside of the warehouse the night before.

Elise.

A loud commotion erupted behind Leine and she turned. Zamir looked up sharply as two men dressed in camouflage dragged Grigori through the door. The Russian lifted his head, revealing a bruised and bloody face with one eye partially swollen shut. Bloodstains marred his T-shirt and his holster was empty. One of the gunmen carried the MP-5, which he handed to Zamir.

"Who is this?" Zamir asked.

"We found him on the roof," the taller gunman said. "He had a pocket filled with grenades and this." He presented Grigori's side arm.

"He's with me." Leine said, unchecked anger bubbling to the surface. *Calm down, Leine. Focus.* "What the hell did you do to him?"

Zamir waved her question away and narrowed his eyes, his expression cold.

"Again I ask, who is this?" His voice dropped an octave.

"He was making sure you didn't ambush me and steal the money." Leine nodded at Grigori. "Nicholas assured me that my associate would accompany me across the border with the shipment. If that isn't what you were told, then I suggest we call our respective bosses and straighten this out, because I'm not doing this alone."

"You will not be alone." Zamir turned toward the metal stairway leading to the second-floor landing and whistled. The door at the top of the stairs opened and two men dressed in fatigues with AK-47s slung over their shoulders filed out. They took the stairs to the ground floor and walked over to join him.

"Hold on a minute," Leine said, eyeing the gunmen. "No one said anything about company."

"And I was under the impression you would be alone." Zamir shrugged. "Plans change."

Leine and Grigori exchanged glances. Nicholas hadn't mentioned any of this to either of them. Which told her they meant to go as far as the border crossing, probably hijack the shipment, and kill them both.

Why would Zamir and his gunmen go to all this trouble for just two kidneys? The amount he might gain wasn't enough to warrant damaging his reputation in the criminal world. At most, one would fetch an additional twenty or thirty thousand above what Nicholas paid.

Unless the recipient had a rare blood type.

"Look. I realize Grigori wasn't part of the deal, but Nicholas sent him to keep me and the shipment safe," Leine continued. It wasn't exactly the truth, but it didn't hurt to make them think Nicholas wanted her alive, too. "Since I'm expected to go along on this little joyride, wouldn't you feel better if you had another professional backing us up if things went sideways?"

Zamir appeared to think over what she'd said. Leine noticed he didn't seek agreement from the others, pegging him as the leader. She studied his body language, trying to get a read on him. Two against five wasn't great odds, but doable if she could acquire a weapon. She was damned sure going to have words with Vlad when she got back.

If she got back.

"Is not healthy to make Nicholas angry," Grigori said, his voice hoarse.

Zamir raised the .45 and pointed it at Grigori's head. "Is not healthy to make me angry, either."

He's going to kill him. "Wait—" Leine said, trying to stall for time.

One of the gunmen stepped forward and murmured in his ear. Zamir raised his chin.

"Good point, Andre. This one will be worth top dollar on the open market," he said, lowering his gun. "Search them both."

Andre handed his weapon to another gunman and walked up to Leine. He looked strong as did the other three. Deep scars crisscrossed his face and neck, marking him as a fighter. She glanced at Grigori. The look on his face told her he was working the odds, too.

Andre pushed her arms out to the side and kicked her feet apart. Leine kept a neutral expression, trying not to wince. Though the gunshot wound was healing, it still hurt like a bitch.

The guy was thorough. When he discovered the bandage on her upper arm, he lifted her sleeve. He motioned to Zamir, who was on the phone. Zamir ended the call and came over to investigate.

"How did you get this?" Zamir asked, his expression unreadable.

"It's nothing. A dog bite."

Zamir studied her for a long moment. Leine kept her gaze steady. He muttered something and Andre resumed frisking her.

Relief flowed through her. Zamir hadn't ripped the bandage off to reveal the gunshot wound. Catching her in a lie this early would compromise them even more than they were. Although, the pat-down didn't exactly give her the warm fuzzies.

Andre found her phone, threw it to the floor, and stomped on it, breaking the case. When he started working his way to her feet, she said, "There's a nine millimeter pistol attached to my ankle." Grigori frowned. Leine shrugged. "Professional courtesy."

Andre nodded and lifted her pant leg. He slid the gun free and handed it to Zamir. One of the other gunmen approached from behind and yanked her arms back before she could react, lassoing her hands behind her with a zip tie.

"This wasn't part of the deal, Zamir," Leine said, gritting her teeth.

Grigori strained against the two gunmen holding him. The shorter one rammed a pistol against his head.

Zamir frowned. "You're right. I will have to call Nicholas and raise the amount he owes me, now that I have two of his people."

Andre stepped behind Grigori and, with the help of the

other two, cinched his wrists. The gunman behind Leine did the same to her ankles.

That'll make things a bit more challenging, she thought.

Zamir studied Leine's pistol before he slid it into his waistband. "Russian made? I would have expected Swiss or Austrian."

"Why is that?"

Zamir smiled. "Because of your reputation."

"What are you talking about?" The sinking feeling in her chest told her that this was something other than a simple shakedown. Had Vladimir already betrayed her? Short-sighted, even for Vlad. He would have waited until Nicholas received the shipment before he set the Albanians loose on her. What the hell was going on?

"I could kill you now, but you are worth so much more alive." Zamir leveled his gaze at her. "You would be surprised who is looking for you. Did you know that your picture is readily available on the Internet?"

When she didn't respond, he smiled. "It is true. Your photograph has been posted in a certain chat room that I frequent. Although, I will say it is not a good likeness." He shook his head. "So many ways to make money in the digital world. But you must know where to look, yes? I could not believe my luck when you appeared."

Zamir was talking about the deep web. The invisible Internet most people weren't aware of where criminals used message boards and set up chat rooms to do business under the radar. Drug deals, child pornography, arms dealing, human trafficking, murder for hire, you name it, the deep web was a one-stop shopping Mecca for black-market goods. Leine had trolled for leads when working cases for SHEN and exploited it extensively as an assassin. The irony that it had been used to track her wasn't lost on Leine.

"I hate to tell you this, Zamir, but you've got the wrong gal."

"If either of us dies," Grigori added, "you will know the unimaginable fury of my family."

Zamir snorted. "I am shaking with fear." The other gunmen joined in the laughter.

The sound of a vehicle approaching outside echoed through the building. A white box truck with a refrigeration unit mounted above the cab pulled into the warehouse and backed up to the cooler door. Zamir and his men leaped into action. Two of the gunmen stayed behind, their weapons trained on Leine and Gregori.

Zamir opened the back of the truck while Andre and another gunman extended the ramp. The two men and the driver disappeared through the strip door into the cooler and reappeared pushing a shrink-wrapped pallet on wheels, stacked ten high with bundles of currency. Two more pallets followed before they replaced the ramp and closed the back of the truck.

Zamir said something to the driver and handed him a stack of money. Smiling, the driver turned to leave. Zamir raised his gun and fired. The sharp report echoed through the warehouse. The man fell forward, onto the cold concrete. Zamir motioned to Andre.

"Put him in the cooler."

Andre and the other guard each took an arm and dragged the driver through the PVC strips, streaking a path of blood across the floor.

"We go now." Zamir slid on a pair of expensive sunglasses and motioned to the two guards. "Bring them."

And then it hit Leine.

Without the clean shave and the expensive suit she hadn't recognized him. Zamir resembled the man standing next to the Bulgarian target in the picture accompanying the French news article. Z. Ristani. *Zamir Ristani.*

Dick Bennett's former business partner.

31

IT WAS AFTER ten o'clock Thursday morning when Santiago Jensen's phone rang.

"Detective Jensen, this is Lou over at SHEN. I need to speak with you about Leine."

"Is she all right?" Santa leaned forward in his chair.

"That's what I want to talk to you about. I've been trying to reach her since early this morning. She's not answering her phone."

"She was on her way back to Tijuana last I saw her."

"I'm aware of that. I've been monitoring her location through a locator we installed on her phone. For some reason she ended up in Ensenada. That wouldn't have been a red flag in and of itself. She could have gone there to check out a lead."

"But?"

"But the program quit logging her location a few hours ago."

"So either her phone died or it's been disabled."

"It's a distinct possibility."

Santa clenched his jaw as unease morphed into worry. Leine never let her phone die. Charging the battery was the one thing she made sure she did every night before she went to bed, and she took a solar charger with her everywhere.

"Where's the last location you have her?"

"A rundown warehouse on the outskirts of town."

"I'll call my guy in TJ, have him check on it for us."

"That would be very helpful. Thank you, Detective."

"Call me Santa."

Bob Herrera agreed to drive to the warehouse in Ensenada right away to see if Leine was there. Santa paced a groove into the carpeting next to his desk while he waited to hear back from the DEA agent.

Heather stopped in to check on him and asked if he wanted some takeout, but he declined. There was no way he could eat, not when Leine might be in trouble. Heather gave him a sympathetic look and left for lunch. Santa didn't notice her leave.

Goddamn that woman, he thought. He'd never worried about another human being as much as he worried about Leine Basso. Yeah, she could take care of herself, and yes, once upon a time she'd killed people for a living, but that didn't lessen his fear for her safety. Santa didn't view things in stark black and white. He'd learned that in his line of work there were several shades of gray.

Like his feelings for a former assassin.

Two hours later, his phone rang. The screen read Robert Herrera. He answered on the first ring.

"No trace of her, Santa," Bob said. "The neighborhood's pretty sketchy, mostly a bunch of abandoned warehouses. There's a Hummer parked down the street with the windows bashed in. I checked the glove box and found a rental agreement issued to a Nicholas Romanov."

"Leine had a phone call from someone named Nicholas before she left. Said it involved a favor for a friend. I suggested she turn him down, do the favor after TJ if he still needed her."

"Looks like she didn't take your advice."

"Guess not. Anything else?"

"One of the warehouses had fresh tire tracks coming out of it. Maybe a panel van or something bigger."

"Did you get inside?"

"Yeah." Herrera paused.

"And?"

"There was blood on the floor in the back by a walk-in cooler. Somebody dumped a body inside."

Santa closed his eyes. *Shit.* "I'm coming down."

"Figured you were. Text me your ETA. I'll meet you in Tijuana."

"Thanks, Bob."

Santa hung up the phone and rubbed the back of his neck, trying to ease the tension lodged there. He emailed the sergeant to get clearance for comp time that afternoon and the next day, which happened to be Friday. He'd have a little more than three days to search for Leine.

What the hell have you gotten yourself into this time, Basso?

32

O NE OF ZAMIR'S men drove the refrigerated truck and Andre rode shotgun. They followed Zamir, Leine, Grigori, and the two other gunmen in the Yukon. Zamir had ordered his men to place Leine in the second row next to him and secure her wrists to the grab handle. The taller gunman took the seat behind them, and they strapped Grigori into the front passenger side. Both vehicles were now on a secondary road, headed north.

"Nicholas will wonder what happened to us if we don't check in," Leine said to Zamir. That much was true. Either she or Grigori was supposed to call in a progress report every few hours. A shipment delay was unacceptable.

"You will contact him soon enough," he replied.

Kidneys could be held outside of the body if they were properly packaged and delivered within twenty-four hours. The time dropped to under twelve hours for a pancreas or a liver, with less than six for a heart. Leine wondered how long it had been since the kidneys had been removed from the donor, whoever it was. She took a deep breath and let it out slowly in an attempt to rein in the adrenaline. She assumed they were keeping Grigori alive because they had to line up a buyer. And because they weren't in a place conducive to removing his organs.

There was no way the shipment in the blue cooler had been taken from a willing donor. Not with what she suspected were two matching kidneys in the bag. She glanced in the rear side mirror at the refrigerated truck, her anger growing.

Zamir leaned toward her, breaking through her thoughts. He gestured at her bandaged arm.

"That must have been some dog, eh?" He smiled as though they were having a friendly conversation. "For a woman, you are very tall. How did this dog jump so high to bite your arm?"

"We were playing. He got a little excited and before I knew it, he'd bitten off a chunk."

"What kind of dog was it?"

"A big damned German Shepherd."

Zamir studied her face for a moment before he nodded and leaned back in his seat. It looked like her story worked. For now.

She wondered how much the contract payout was for. It had to be lucrative enough that Zamir believed it was worth more than killing her for revenge. Leine doubted any of Zamir's gunmen knew who she was or she'd be dead by now, price on her head or not. Emotions generally ran high when it came to the death of fellow members of an organization like the KLA.

Leine glanced out the window at the saddle-brown land-scape. They'd left Ensenada behind over three hours ago and were now driving along a pockmarked dirt road in the middle of nowhere. The occasional tree or shrub broke through the monotony of the desert landscape, but for the most part the terrain boasted a mixture of dust, dirt, and bright colored food wrappers.

Not a great place to fight off armed gunmen, Leine thought. Then again, what place was? She wished Grigori had been more forthcoming about the location of the border crossing. At least then she'd have some idea what to expect. Going into a situation blind and in restraints was never good.

After the question about the dog bite, Zamir didn't attempt any more small talk, giving Leine a chance to mull over what she'd learned, hoping to latch onto new information that would lead her to Elise.

If Elise was still alive.

Although a long shot, it was possible the two kidneys belonged to the missing girl. They weren't Josh's—too much time had lapsed since his death.

"Turn here," Grigori said.

The SUV slowed and turned onto a smaller dirt track, heading farther into the desert along a deeply rutted road. The box truck followed, precariously teetering back and forth. Leine found it interesting they were using a refrigerated truck to transport money. The kidneys would survive in the hard-sided cooler. The only thing that made sense was that Zamir intended to use the vehicle to transport organs. She assumed the money was for startup costs, among other things.

What a waste of life, she thought. Memories of the many targets she'd eliminated as an assassin crowded her mind. She'd considered what she did a service, albeit a violent one. Yes, she had killed people, but every one of them except for Carlos had been responsible for heinous acts of their own, and her guilt wasn't as crushing as it might have been.

Carlos was another story.

Leine would bet her life that if Zamir succeeded in transporting the truck across the border without detection, every healthy organ he could find would be snapped up by desperate transplant recipients in the US. Wait times were notoriously long across the globe, and many died before a match became available.

Half an hour later, they came to a makeshift gate with

barbed wire on either side and stopped. Zamir got out to open it, and returned to the SUV. The vehicles continued through.

A short time later, they rounded a bend and slowed to a stop in front of a sprawling Quonset hut. Two sliding doors hung from a long track running a third of the width of the structure. Grigori exited the vehicle, followed by the gunman who'd been sitting behind Leine. Inside the SUV, Zamir covered Leine with his .45 while the other two walked up to the doors. Zamir's gunman banged on the rusty metal with the barrel of his AK.

The door slid open and a dark-haired man Leine hadn't seen before walked out to greet them. He motioned angrily at Zamir's gunman and said something to Grigori, obviously unhappy. Zamir's thug raised his gun and shot him, point-blank. The dark-haired man dropped to the ground. Throughout the exchange, Grigori's expression remained impassive. The gunman shoved the dead man to the side, and prodded the Russian forward with the barrel of his gun.

Several shots rang out from inside the Quonset hut. A moment later, Zamir's gunman reappeared at the open door and whistled. The refrigerated truck drove around the SUV and continued inside. Zamir motioned for his driver to follow them into the structure. They parked near the refrigerated truck, and the driver and Zamir got out, leaving Leine attached to the grab bar of the SUV.

Inside was a cavernous space with a dirt floor. A dozen cots had been stacked three high against one wall, with half-empty shelves lining another. Several gas cans stood on a shelf along the back wall, sharing space with an assortment of tools.

An older-model dump truck was parked on top of a rectangular piece of sheet metal in the center of the structure. Two bodies lay next to a makeshift table with a shortwave radio and what was left of a bag of tortilla chips, a *coguama* of Tecate, and two Pacificos.

Zamir barked commands at his men, keeping an eye on both captives while his driver climbed into the dump truck. The engine turned over once, twice, followed by a loud backfire and belching smoke as the diesel motor chugged to life. The gunman shifted into gear and drove the hulking machine forward until it cleared the metal plate underneath. Then he killed the engine and hopped out. Andre covered Grigori while the driver and the other gunman dragged the metal plate sideways, revealing a concrete ramp leading underground.

Leine craned her neck for a better view. The ramp led to a reinforced tunnel large enough to drive a truck through. With everyone momentarily distracted by the ramp, she grasped the end of one of her hair pins by the tips of her fingers and worked it loose.

The passageway was most certainly compliments of one of the more powerful cartels. In the last few years, the drug cartels had discovered high-end industrial drills, enhancing their ability to dig large tunnels. Access would have been easy with the amount of cash these criminal organizations had at their disposal. Leine had never heard of one this large, though. Most were pipelines several inches across drilled under strata a few hundred feet from the border. The DEA had recently discovered a tunnel five feet wide near Calexico, but nothing this large.

With Zamir and the other gunmen's attention still on the tunnel, Leine shoved the bobby pin into the female end of the zip tie they'd used to attach her to the grab bar, working to bypass the tie's small teeth. It took a few tries before she was able to loosen the plastic enough to pull her bound hands free.

Careful to keep her arms above her head to give the impression that she was still tied to the grab bar, Leine transferred her efforts to the tie around her wrists. Zamir turned to look straight at her, and she stilled her hands. Apparently satisfied his prisoner was still secure, he returned his attention to the tunnel.

Punctuated by utility lanterns, the passageway was reinforced with wood framing and rebar. A small generator on a wooden platform sat near the entrance. The SUV driver trotted down the ramp to the machine and fiddled with the controls. After several futile attempts at starting the machine, he stepped back and gestured to the other gunman to try.

Leine loosened the second tie enough to slip one hand free, while keeping the other on the grab bar to give the illusion of still being attached. Watching Zamir out of the corner of her eye, she worked the bobby pin into the tie around her ankles with her free hand. Seconds later, she shook off the plastic tie. She slid the pin back into her hair, held onto the bar above her head with both hands, and waited.

Neither gunman could get the generator to work. Clearly frustrated, the driver motioned for Grigori, but Grigori balked.

Andre shoved the barrel of the AK-47 into his back and pushed him forward onto the ramp.

"Go," he growled. Grigori relented and walked down the ramp to join the other men. Andre remained several yards behind him.

Grigori turned his back and presented his bound wrists. With a nod from Zamir, the smaller gunman used his pocketknife to cut him free.

While the rest of them looked on, Grigori made a great show of trying to start the generator but failed each time. Leine lowered her arm to the handle and eased the door open, watching him closely. She dropped into a low crouch and edged around the back of the Yukon. Leine estimated the distance between Zamir and the SUV at five feet.

Grigori bent over the pull cord and muttered something. The two gunmen leaned in to see what he was talking about. Grigori spun and there was a flash of metal as he slammed a knife into the closest guard's gut, burying the blade. The man grunted and doubled over as Grigori head-butted the other guard and grabbed the AK. Using the guard as a shield, Grigori swiveled, strafing the air with bullets. Andre dove for cover.

Zamir started for the ramp. Leine crossed the gap between them and snapped her foot up, delivering a savage kick to the Albanian's hand and sending the .45 spinning through the air. Zamir spun toward her and she pivoted, swinging her leg in a roundhouse kick that connected with the side of his knee. Zamir collapsed with a grunt but at the last second rolled toward the gun.

Leine covered the distance in two strides, threw her weight onto her back foot, and using the momentum, thrust her other leg up, feeling a satisfying thud as her heel connected with his jaw. His head snapped back and Zamir fell to the ground, stunned. He rolled onto his elbow and shook his head.

At the same time, Andre darted from behind the dump truck and fired at Grigori. Still holding the unconscious guard, Grigori pivoted and returned fire, the automatic spraying bullets. Hit in the thigh, Andre lurched backward, dragging himself behind the truck. Gregori let go of the gunman he'd been using as a shield and advanced up the ramp toward Andre.

A popping sound split the air as a burst of automatic gunfire exploded behind him. Grigori stumbled. Leine turned in time to see the barrel of the MP-5 swing toward her from behind the hood of the refrigerated truck.

Adrenaline hammering through her, Leine dove to the ground and rolled, chunks of dirt exploding around her.

"Don't let her get away," Zamir screamed, trying to rise. Focused on Leine, the driver stepped around the truck and took aim.

Shots rang out from Leine's right. The driver doubled over, gripping his stomach, and dropped the submachine gun. He raised a blood-covered hand, disbelief filtering across his face as he collapsed.

Grigori hobbled into view. Blood stained the tan material of his fatigues. He leveled his gun at Zamir.

"Grigori, don't—"

Grigori shook his head, his eyes on the Albanian. "I am going to enjoy killing this asshole."

"He may have information I need," Leine said, gritting her teeth against the searing pain in her arm. Blood soaked her left sleeve.

"Where'd that come from?" she asked, nodding at the blood-smeared knife Grigori was wiping on his fatigues.

He smiled, a mischievous glint in his eye. "They didn't find all of my pockets."

Grigori covered Zamir while Leine patted him down. She found a cell phone, which she handed to Grigori, and a wad of bills, which she pocketed.

"Don't shoot him. Yet," Leine said to Grigori.

She walked to the Yukon and climbed inside the cab. There, she found a handful of zip ties in the console, along with several of the grenades and a book of matches, and brought them back to Grigori. She pocketed two of the grenades and the matches, and walked over to where the .45 lay. Picking up the firearm, she moved behind Zamir, kicked him behind the knees to force him down, and secured his wrists and ankles.

"Don't take your eyes off him, Grigori," she said, and started for the refrigerated truck, stopping to pick up the MP-5 next to the mortally wounded driver.

"We don't have much time," Grigori called.

She glanced at her watch. He was right. Nicholas would be expecting the shipment in the next couple of hours. Since the donor had surely given up his or her life to provide the kidneys, she couldn't allow them to go to waste. She turned back.

"Call Nicholas. Tell him what happened. How long will it take to get through the tunnel?"

"With no problems, maybe twenty minutes."

She reached the truck, climbed onto the tailgate, and yanked open the door.

33

———

ELISE WALKED OUT of the doctor's office in the main house and headed for the barracks. Ramirez had changed the dressing on the incision to a smaller bandage, similar to Julia's. Time was running out. She feared she would soon be offered to the men who visited the ranch. The evening before, two men had come to the cafeteria and taken Julia away. She didn't return to the barracks until late, after everyone had gone to sleep. The next morning, when Elise asked her if she was okay, Julia replied that they had to leave that night.

The early afternoon sun filtered through filmy clouds, sparing Elise the scorching heat she had come to expect during the day. She barely registered the rocky terrain, having gotten used to it—which was the only good thing about not having shoes. She hoped it would make the trek through the desert easier.

Elise checked to make sure no one was watching before she edged around the barracks and walked down the slope to the lone tree at the bottom of the gulley. Not seeing anyone at first, relief flowed through her when Sebastian poked his head around the trunk, a big grin on his face. Elise smiled.

"I didn't think you were coming," Sebastian said, staring shyly at the ground.

"Of course I came, Sebastian. You're the only nice person I've met here." She picked a piece of lint off his shirt and flicked it away.

Sebastian bobbed his head, his cheeks growing a deep shade of pink.

"I have something for you." He reached into his pocket and brought out a shiny metal bracelet, which he eagerly handed to her. "It's a magic bracelet."

"How sweet." Elise smiled, touched by his generosity. The copper bracelet was made of little metal flowers and leaves woven into links. "Would you put it on for me?"

Sebastian grinned as he looped the bracelet over her wrist and snapped the clasp closed.

She held it up for him to see. "Why do you say this bracelet is magic?"

"That's what the man told me when I bought it. That it was a magic bracelet."

Tears sprang to her eyes at his earnest expression. It seemed like such a long time since anyone showed her kindness. Whenever she saw Sebastian she made a special effort to talk to him and find out how his day was going. Now that she and Julia planned to escape, her relationship with Sebastian took on a new urgency. She just hoped he wouldn't get in trouble for what she was about to ask him.

"Sebastian," she began. "Someone told me that you get to go lots of places, not just here on the property. Is that right?"

He nodded enthusiastically. "Yes. Sometimes Master Garcia takes me into town. I help him carry the supplies to the car."

"I miss going into town so much. How far away is it?"

Sebastian looked skyward for a moment and then frowned. "It's longer than I can walk." He fell silent for a minute, thinking, before another grin split his face. "Do you want me to ask Master Garcia if he'll take you?"

"No. No, that's all right, Sebastian. When you go with Master Garcia, which way does he drive, usually?"

Sebastian pointed past Elise to her right and then at a ninety-degree angle. "We go on two roads. The second one is really long."

At least now we know which way to go, Elise thought. She stepped closer to Sebastian and put her arms around him, giving him a squeeze. He froze for a moment, but then his body melted into hers and a small sigh escaped his lips. Elise patted his back like she would a newborn. A warm feeling flowed through her. She couldn't remember the last time she felt even the slightest bit nurturing. It felt good.

She took a step back and raised her arm, holding up the bracelet. "Thank you, Sebastian. I'll keep the magic bracelet with me, always."

ELISE JUMPED AT THE SHRILL WHISTLE COMING FROM THE YARD. The heat returned later that afternoon with the intensity of a forest fire. Elise and another girl had just finished cleaning the bathrooms in the stifling yellow house. Celeste was no longer assigned as Elise's cleaning partner. In fact, she hadn't seen the dark-haired girl anywhere. When Elise asked about her, she was told to go back to work.

An anxious look passed between Elise and the other girl before they picked up their buckets and made their way outside.

Master Garcia and the dog man stood in front of the main house with a girl Elise had never seen before. Her dress was filthy and torn and there was dried blood and scratches on her legs. Manacles encased her ankles. She stared at the ground while the rest of the girls gathered around them, leaving a wide space in front.

Elise searched the crowd for Julia and found her a few yards away. She inched over to stand beside her.

"Who's that?" she asked.

"The girl who escaped," Julia said, her voice flat. She was staring at the dog. Its ears lay flat against its head and a low growl emanated from deep within its muscular chest.

A spike of anxiety shot through Elise. "What do you think they're going to do to her?"

"I don't know," Julia whispered.

The doctor and another guard joined Garcia, the doctor carrying a coiled bullwhip. The rest of the guards stood at various intervals around the crowd's perimeter.

"Let this be a lesson to all of you here," Master Garcia's voice boomed. He grabbed the girl's chin and jerked it up so everyone could see her face. Her body trembled and there was terror in her eyes.

"This Jezebel left under cover of night. Walked into the desert alone. She had no water, no food." Garcia dropped her chin and placed his hand on her shoulder. "She is lucky we found her. So many terrible things could have happened."

The girl closed her eyes and licked her dry, scorched lips. Tears coursed down her cheeks, streaking through the dirt on her face. Elise wondered if anyone had given her water, or if they were just going to let her suffer.

The answer came soon enough.

"I am *displeased*," Garcia roared.

Fear in both the girl and the crowd was palpable. Elise's heart skipped in her chest.

What if Julia and I get caught? This girl was out there for four nights and they still found her.

"Hold her," Garcia commanded.

Dog Man and another guard gripped the girl's wrists and pulled until her arms were fully extended. Garcia seized her shift and in one movement ripped the back open to her waist. He then turned to the doctor, who handed him the bullwhip.

Garcia walked into the crowd, and they quickly parted to give him room.

"They're going to use that?" Elise couldn't believe he needed that big of a whip, not when she could still feel the sting of the smaller one he'd used on her when she first arrived.

"He's going to kill her."

Julia's voice almost didn't register. She'd said the words so quietly that Elise wasn't even sure she'd heard her correctly.

"But—he can't, can he? I mean, what about the police? Aren't there laws?"

Julia ignored Elise and watched, stone-faced, as Garcia snaked the whip through the air, testing it. The girl flinched with each loud snap.

With a grim expression, Garcia brought the whip back and Elise turned away. There was a sharp *crack!* and the girl screamed.

Another blow split the air. The screams turned to sobs.

And again.

Elise put her hands over her ears and ran from the crowd, fury at Garcia and the doctor burning in her chest.

She didn't care if Julia backed out or not. She would escape.

Tonight.

34

L EINE SCANNED THE interior of the back of the truck. Nicholas's shipment was secured to one wall with a bungee cord. The pallets were held in place with floor locks.

There was another door at the far end. Expecting more organs, Leine threaded her way toward it and yanked the door open.

A dozen pair of eyes blinked at the influx of light like owls on a tree branch. Leine's breath caught in her throat at the sight of twelve children—none of them could have been older than twelve—wrapped in ratty blankets and sitting on the filth-encrusted floor of the cooler.

"*Mamá!*" a little girl cried. Another girl shushed her, jabbing her in the side with her elbow.

"I—it's all right," Leine said in English, her throat tight. She remembered where she was and switched to Spanish. "It's safe to come out now. You all must be very cold."

One by one, each child made his and her tentative way out of the cooler toward Leine. Many of them glanced at her as they walked past, curiosity filling their dark eyes. As soon as they had found their way to the back of the truck, Leine climbed down and began to lift them out.

Grigori joined her, his eyes widening as he took in the scene.

"They were going to—" he whispered, staring at the children.

Leine nodded, her lips pressed into a hard line. He clenched his jaw and turned away. He'd tied his T-shirt around his upper thigh to stem the bleeding, leaving him bare-chested. His back had several scars—a few resembled bullet wounds that had healed, but one extended from his shoulder across his back to below his kidney.

She glanced to where he'd been holding Zamir at gunpoint. The Albanian wasn't in sight.

"Where's Zamir?" she asked, alarm sweeping through her.

"Do not worry. I will handle Zamir." He spoke his name as though he'd tasted poison. "I found this on the driver." Grigori handed her the man's cell phone before he disappeared around the back of the truck. Sliding the phone into her pants pocket, Leine glanced at the next child in line—a girl of about eight in a pretty green dress—and smiled.

"Stay there. I'll be right back to help you down, okay?"

"Okay," she answered in a tiny voice.

Leine hurried around the end of the truck, hoping she wasn't too late. She needed to interrogate Zamir, not bury him.

Yet.

His face a deep shade of red and breathing heavily, Grigori loomed over the Albanian with the AK-47 shoved against his forehead. He had tied Zamir by the wrists to the back of the dump truck with zip ties.

"You bastard," he said in Russian. "You were going to use those children like—like they were your own fucking body parts supply store?"

"Don't kill him just yet, Grigori," Leine said.

A vein pulsed in the Russian's temple. "Why not?"

"I need to find out if he knows anything about a case I'm working on."

Rage plain on his face, Grigori continued to stare daggers at Zamir. Leine waited while the Russian got himself under control. Little by little, like a boiling teapot that had its burner turned to low, the tension in his body lessened. He took a deep breath and stepped back, lowering the gun. Leine inserted herself between the two men, facing Zamir.

"Where do these children belong?"

Zamir turned away. Grigori stepped forward, his fists clenched.

"You son of a whore—"

Leine gave him a look that said *back off*. He hesitated but stood down.

"I'm only going to ask once more. Where did these children come from?"

Zamir's stony gaze focused behind Leine and she turned. Several curious children had drifted from behind the truck into the main area. A little girl walked next to the wounded driver. He moved his arm, startling her, and she began to cry. Leine glanced at Grigori.

"Would you make sure they stay behind the truck? And ask them where home is," she said.

Grigori nodded stiffly and hobbled over to retrieve the little girl and corral the rest of the kids. Leine turned her attention back to Zamir.

"Now, I can make this easier for you or I can let Grigori have at it when we're finished. If you answer my questions truthfully, I promise you won't suffer. If you refuse to answer, I'm sure Grigori would love to have a few moments alone with you."

Zamir sneered. "Why do you think I would tell Nicholas's bitch anything?"

Leine smiled and shoved the barrel of the .45 into his crotch. Zamir's eyes narrowed, fear reflected in their depths. Beads of sweat appeared above his lip.

He remained silent. Tired of playing games, Leine stepped back, aimed the .45 at his leg, and shot him. Zamir screamed and tried to fold himself into a fetal position.

"This isn't helping, Zamir."

Groaning, Zamir squeezed his eyes closed and clamped his lips together. Sweat rolled down the side of his face.

She reached inside her pocket and slid out a copy of Elise's picture. "Do you recognize this girl?" she asked, holding it in front of him.

He refused to look. Leine grabbed him by the hair and forced his head up. "Open your eyes."

With an insolent glare he glanced at the picture. Dawning comprehension lit his face, and he glowered at Leine, fury evident in his eyes.

"I knew it was you who killed my men," he said, his voice dripping venom.

"So you do know where she is."

"I know you will die soon." He spit at her feet.

Leine put the picture back in her pocket. He'd just confirmed he was connected to Elise's disappearance, at least by association, thereby sealing his fate. She was pretty sure Grigori wouldn't have a problem with that.

Clearly, it would take too much effort to extract the information she needed from Zamir, and she was running out of time. Leine made her way over to the dying driver. Wariness on his face, he gazed up at her through pain-filled eyes. Blood had pooled in the dirt below him. She checked to make sure none of the children were watching.

She hunkered down and showed him the gun. Misery and resignation swam in his eyes.

"You think you can intimidate me," he gasped, his voice weak. "You are nothing, an ant."

"And you're in pretty bad shape," she said, surveying his wound. "I will help you if you help me. All you need to do is tell me where this girl is." She showed him the picture of Elise.

When he didn't respond, she pressed the gun to the side of his head. The driver flinched, his breath coming faster.

"Zamir should have killed you when he had the chance," he wheezed. "Like Ivan should have done to that bitch's mother when she betrayed him."

What is he talking about?

"Like I said," she continued, "you're in pretty bad shape. I'd say you'll bleed out in a matter of minutes unless someone does something. I can make things easy or a whole lot more painful for you. What'll it be?"

The driver drew in a shallow breath as tears leaked from the corners of his eyes. *He's close,* she thought.

"One more time. Where's Elise? And, for the bonus round, tell me what 'the bitch's mother' did to betray Ivan."

He clamped his lips closed. She lowered the gun to his crotch. Sweat ran in rivulets along the side of his face.

Leine lowered her voice. "If you don't tell me what I need to know, I will make your last few minutes a living hell."

The driver closed his eyes and bowed his head. His shoulders sagged.

"When the mother... did not pay money she owed Ivan, he sold daughter."

"What money? And who did Ivan sell her to?"

He didn't respond. Leine applied more pressure.

He pulled in a ragged breath. "She betrayed him, I don't know how. He lost money and took her daughter to make her pay him."

Belinda Bennett's responsible for this? "The daughter is still alive?"

The driver nodded.

"Who has her?"

He closed his eyes, opening them an obvious strain. "His name is Felix Garcia Otero. He runs many businesses in Tijuana."

Otero. "Elise is in Tijuana?"

"No. There is a place several kilometers outside of town—a ranch where Otero supplies the men who work for him with young women." He coughed and blood bubbled between his lips. "Ivan will receive a percentage of what she earns there."

He must have her at the whorehouse Herrera mentioned, Leine thought. "Do you mean the one where he keeps the girls to service his 'messengers of Christ?'"

The driver nodded. "Yes. I show you."

"No. You're going to tell me."

With a little more encouragement the directions came. Leine looked the location up on his phone. From the satellite imagery she identified three buildings and a couple of smaller structures on the property—maybe sheds or a well house—and nothing but desert for miles in any direction.

The driver died not long after that. Leine walked behind the truck where Grigori had arranged the cots as seating for the children. They were watching Grigori pantomime a story. A few giggled as he grimaced in pain. She glanced at his bloody pant leg. *Probably not acting out that one,* she thought.

"Can anyone tell me where home is?" she asked with a smile.

"La Paz," the girl in the green dress replied, her voice small. The other children looked at her with solemn expressions. Leine turned to Grigori.

"Did you call Nicholas?" she asked in a low voice.

"*Da.* His people wait for us at other end. He refuses to come to Mexico." Grigori shrugged. "An old problem, I think."

"You take the shipment and the money. I'll stay here. Someone needs to get these kids back." Nicholas was going to be one happy Russian when he saw the pallets of money.

Grigori shook his head. "You must wait. I will come with you after I deliver to Nicholas the shipment."

"Your leg needs medical attention, Grigori. No offense, but you would be of no use to me in your condition. Get the wound tended to. I'll be fine."

"But your arm—"

Leine glanced at her blood-soaked shirtsleeve. "I'll fix it. I'm sure there's a first aid kit of some sort in the Yukon."

Grigori sighed and shook his head. "You are very stubborn, you know this?"

"So I've been told." She paused. "Before I leave, for my own peace of mind—who are the kidneys for?"

"I thought you knew," he said, surprise evident on his face. "They are for Vladimir's wife. She has rare blood type and will die soon if she does not receive transplant."

"Of course. I should have known." No wonder Vlad sounded more stressed than usual. It didn't make it right, but at least now Leine had an answer. She turned and faced the kids. "Are you ready to go home?"

Her words were met with shy smiles and enthusiastic nods.

"Come with me." She gestured for them to follow her. "I left Zamir for you," she whispered to Grigori. He nodded.

"Thank you, Leine Basso."

The children, all of whom were eerily quiet, followed her to the SUV. Leine's heart squeezed tight at the thought of these innocent children being terrified into silence. They were supposed to be rambunctious and happy.

Not inventory in a body market for criminals.

The keys were still in the ignition. Leine opened the doors and helped the kids pile inside, making sure everyone was accounted for. Then she got in and turned the key. The engine roared to life, and she backed out of the Quonset hut and shifted into park, nose out.

A crack of a single gunshot reverberated through the air. A few moments later, the refrigerated truck's engine caught and idled for a moment, echoing in the silence before fading underground.

Zamir would no longer be a problem.

Leine turned to look at the kids. Two sat beside her in the front passenger seat, four sat in the middle, three were in the back seat, and three peered at her from the cargo area.

"I need to do one more thing before we go. While I'm inside the building I want you to put your seatbelts on."

"But there are not enough for all of us," one of the older boys said.

"I know. You're going to have to share. The bigger kids can hold the smaller ones on their laps, okay? You three in the back, I want you to come up front and get in on the action too."

The kids began moving around, trying to figure out how to get each other belted in. Leine got out and walked back inside the now silent metal building. She grabbed two of the gas cans and a length of jute rope, and walked over to Andre where she cut off a section of his shirt with the knife attached to his belt. She paused where Zamir slumped against the dump truck, a bullet hole in his forehead. She felt his carotid, just to be sure he was dead. Then she followed the ramp down to the first section of the tunnel and set everything on the ground. A few trips later, and she'd transferred all six of the gas cans to the tunnel entrance.

Leine stood the cans next to each other and removed the grenades from her pockets. After tying one end of the rope to the strip of shirt, she stuffed the material into the mouth of one gas can and poured fuel over the rest of the rope with another, leaving the last few inches dry. Next, she balanced the grenades between two of the cans and let out the rest of the rope behind her as she moved up to ground level. The jute ran out a yard past the top of the ramp.

She waited a few minutes longer, thinking about Grigori and whether he'd be through the tunnel yet.

With one last look around the Quonset hut, Leine slid the book of matches from her pocket and bent one of them up and away from the others. She lit it and tucked the burning matchbook underneath the dry section of twine. The end would burn once the matchbook caught. Then she left the building.

She walked quickly to the SUV, got in, and was halfway to the main road when there was a *whoompf!* and the ground shuddered. Leine and the kids turned toward the sound at the same time. Dust streamed through the open door of the Quonset hut.

It would take whoever owned the tunnel a long time to excavate.

***

Leine continued driving as she slid the gunman's cell phone out of her pocket and punched in Santa's number. It went to voicemail. She left a message, telling him to call Bob Herrera. Then she called the DEA agent.

"Herrera," he answered.

"Bob. It's Leine."

"Where the hell are you?" Herrera told someone nearby she was on the line. "Hold on. There's somebody here who wants to talk to you."

Leine waited while he handed the phone over.

"Leine? It's Santa."

"Hey," Leine answered. "What are you doing with Bob? And where are you?"

"I was just going to ask you the same question. Thank God you're all right."

The sound of traffic *whooshed* by in the background.

"Lou was worried about you and called me," Santa continued. "The software on your phone stopped tracking you this morning in Ensenada, so I called Bob and asked him to take a look. He didn't like what he found and I drove down."

You always have my back, don't you, Santa? Leine allowed herself a small smile.

"I'm currently about an hour northeast of Tijuana with a dozen kidnapped kids who belong in La Paz. You might want to let Bob know I just destroyed the entrance to a tunnel running under the border. A big one. It's about three kilometers north of me."

"What's your position?"

Leine read him coordinates on the GPS display.

Santa relayed the information to Bob. There was another pause and Bob came on the line.

"There's a feeder road that leads to the main highway seven kilometers southwest of you. Meet us at the *carne asada* place in TJ. I'll make sure the kids get back to La Paz. Now what the hell's this about you blowing a tunnel?"

Leine gave him a rundown of the tunnel and the Quonset hut, leaving out Grigori, the refrigerated truck, and the money.

Bob whistled. "As soon as I report this, there'll be a posse of Mexican Marines, DEA and ICE agents headed your way—part of a joint task force. I'd rather not be present—I'm already on the local cartel's shit list and this would just make it harder to do my job. Santa certainly can't be, since he's not here in an official capacity."

"I should be there in about an hour. If I'm going to be late, I'll call you."

Leine ended the call and checked the rearview mirror to make sure they weren't being followed. The road was deserted. She glanced over her shoulder at her passengers.

"You guys were very brave and did really, really well. We're almost home, okay?"

The children were mostly silent, although a few sniffles could be heard. One young girl appeared to be sleeping. Leine caught the attention of the boy sitting next to her.

"Is she all right?"

The boy nodded, his eyes huge in the fading afternoon light.

Amazing what kids will do under stress, Leine thought. She'd like the ability to fall asleep when she was scared.

Now that her favor for Vlad had been repaid, she'd make sure the kids were safe and then she'd be free to find Elise.

If she wasn't too late.

35

ELISE PAUSED AT the top of the rise to wait for Julia. She leaned forward and put her hands on her knees, breathing heavily. The adrenaline pumping through her veins added to the urgency she felt.

"Come on, Julia," she called, anxiety spiking through her at the delay. They needed to travel as far as they could as fast as they could before Garcia discovered their escape. Sebastian had led them past the guards and to the point of no return—the place in the desert where he warned them not to pass—but she and Julia had hugged him goodbye and kept going.

"I'm coming." Winded, Julia clambered up the hill and stopped to catch her breath. "I don't think we need to worry—it's really dark out here, you know?"

Elise glanced at the lights, tiny in the distance, and shook her head.

"As long as we can see the ranch, I don't think we're safe. They could have night vision equipment." Josh had been crazy about action movies, and Elise went to a few, at first to humor him. Surprisingly, she'd ended up enjoying them as much or more than he had. Along with the dope guys playing the leads, the girls were usually bad asses and wore awesome clothes. Most of the time the characters would have scopes on their rifles or somebody would pull out a pair of night vision goggles, or NVGs.

She wished she had a pair of them now.

Her heart skipped at the thought of someone sighting on them through a scope, and she focused on the ranch's lights again. The tiny dot of a vehicle moved away from the main building. Elise willed the person behind the wheel to continue down the drive. The headlights did as she wished, and she was about to say something to Julia when the vehicle veered off into the desert, the headlights aimed straight toward them. Elise sucked in a breath and spun around.

"We have to go, NOW," she said, and took off down the back of the hill at a dead run.

———

CRUZ GLANCED AT THE DOG, MAX, WHO SAT IN THE PASSENGER seat staring out the windshield, waiting for his command. Training the pit bull to intimidate and attack had been easy, and Cruz felt a deep kinship with the fiercely loyal animal. Tonight would be a test of all the time he had invested, would show Cruz how best to use this living weapon.

The dog man's heart raced as though he had guzzled a thousand Red Bulls. When he realized the American girl had run, he couldn't contain his excitement. He alone would be the first to have her, out in the desert among the cactus and rattlesnakes, the rocks ripping the sensitive flesh of her back. He kicked himself for leaving the monitoring room to eat dinner. He'd missed the warning signal and lost precious time.

The last runaway had been such a disappointment. She

hadn't fought back at all, just lay on the ground and whimpered like a mewling, helpless kitten. Unable to get it up, Cruz would have killed her for being so weak, but Garcia refused to pay if he delivered any of the whores dead. Once, when Cruz had no recourse but to kill one of them, Garcia had even suggested he pay him for lost earnings or some other nonsense. When Cruz explained what he would do to him in his sleep, Garcia reconsidered.

The American girl would fight him—of that he was certain. She acted like she was better than the other girls and Cruz couldn't wait to take the bitch down.

A green dot blipped on the tracking device mounted on the dash of the SUV, representing one of the girls. Cruz wondered if the two of them had split up, since there was only one indicator, but when he scanned the surrounding area there was no answering ping from a second transmitter.

Then another dot appeared, blinked twice, and vanished.

The tracking device must be faulty, he thought and mentally shrugged. At least one signal was strong.

It was all he needed.

Cruz licked his lips in anticipation. Once he'd found them, he'd make the American girl watch as he took his time with the redhead, and then, depending on what kind of shape they were in, he would inflict additional injuries without Garcia's infuriating interrogation.

He smiled, looking forward to capturing the girls. The terror in their eyes when they realized what he was going to do to them would be the icing on the cake. He'd threaten them with torture if they said anything to Garcia, and would set up a schedule with the American whore, just like he'd done with the other one before she ran.

His frustration grew when Garcia chose to make an example of her in front of the other girls. Cruz had barely gotten her to agree to sneak him into the yellow house on the nights she worked before she escaped. He'd have to start over with the American. Although, thinking of how he would intimidate the arrogant bitch into submission gave him endless pleasure.

Cruz turned on the CD player. He smiled as the first bars of Patti Page's, "How Much is that Doggie in the Window?" floated through the cab of the SUV. Max whined in answer to the bark in the song, adding his own and pacing in his seat until the next stanza played.

The dog man continued further into the desert, humming along with the tune and following the blinking dot on the monitor.

"How could they know so fast?" Julia asked, breathless from their rush to put distance between themselves and the headlights. They'd run a zigzag course intended to throw off their pursuers.

"I don't know." Fear fluttered in Elise's chest. She'd bet on having at least two hours' lead time. The doctor usually came by the barracks once the girls who weren't working were locked in but rarely did a full head count. Even so, she and Julia had made lumpy dummies of themselves underneath their blankets. The other girls' ambivalence should have worked in their favor. No one cared enough to look.

It was as if Garcia couldn't imagine anyone trying to run away. Not after he'd practically whipped that poor girl to death in front of them all. Elise had been relieved to find out the doctor and the other gunman dragged her off toward the main house, but Julia burst that small flicker of hope.

"Remember when I told you that the girls who have been

here a long time go into the main house to see the doctor and don't come back?" she'd asked. "It's the same with runaways."

"But that could mean they sent them away," Elise had argued.

"They send them away, all right," Julia had answered. "In a body bag."

The thought of being whipped again or even killed spurred Elise on, pain from the sharp rocks and spiky plants scarcely registering. Tunnel vision blanked out all else as she ran, her focus entirely on cresting the next rise, taking them further from their trackers.

If we can just make it to the border, she thought. *Then everything will be fine.*

Julia was sure that when they got to the busy, well-lit traffic jam of the Mexican-American border, that they'd be safe from Garcia's thugs. No one would stand for two young girls to be held against their will and used as sex slaves. She was certain they would be especially horrified when they told them about the others having their organs removed.

Elise stopped to catch her breath. She could barely make out the lights identifying the three buildings on the ranch. She scanned the dark terrain, searching for headlights, but didn't see any. Julia joined her and they rested, waiting for their breathing to return to normal.

"I don't see lights anywhere, do you?" she asked, her voice tinged with hope.

"No," Elise replied, still watching, not yet daring to believe. "Let's wait a minute to make sure, okay?"

"Okay." Julia sighed and wiped the perspiration from her forehead with her arm. "The first thing I'm going to do when I get to America is call my mother in El Salvador and tell her I am living in America now, and that she should come."

"Do you have anyone there? I think you need someone to

vouch for you, like an employer or a relative." At least, that's what Teuta had told her.

Julia turned toward Elise. "You have rich parents. Can't they tell Immigration that I am to work for them?"

"Maybe." Elise didn't want to disappoint Julia by explaining that her parents weren't exactly generous. Her mother had hired Teuta because she'd showed up at their house one day, looking for work, and told them she would take a lot less than the other housekeepers in the neighborhood. Maybe Elise could talk her father into helping Julia, although he was as tight as her mother when it came to money.

Something moved in the darkness, catching Elise's attention. She blinked, trying to clear her vision, and realized she was looking at a pair of headlights that were too close.

"We have to split up," Elise said, her breath catching. "You go that way and then curve to your right." She pointed toward the west. "I think then you'll be heading north. I'll walk the opposite direction and curve left. Keep going until you get to the first town. Find a safe place to sleep and we can find each other in the morning. That should confuse them. They won't know which one of us to follow."

Julia shook her head. "*No.* I don't want to lose you, Elise." Her voice cracked, as though she was on the verge of tears.

Elise glanced at the approaching headlights and her heart skipped.

"It's the only way. Here, let's make a pact." She held out her hand and Julia gripped it with hers. "If we don't find each other at the first town, leave me a message in Tijuana at a place called The Blue Manatee. I'll check there before I cross, okay?"

Julia nodded, once. "Okay. The Blue Manatee."

Elise threw her arms around the redhead, choking back a sob. Julia buried her head in Elise's neck.

"God, Elise, I'm so scared."

"I know. Me too."

The two girls broke apart and wiped at their tears.

"See you." Elise said.

"Yes, see you," Julia answered. Then she turned and ran.

The darkness swallowed her whole.

36

L EINE PULLED INTO the parking lot of the Happy Cow an hour and twenty minutes after her call to Santa and Herrera. The DEA agent's truck was parked under the sign. Herrera, Santa, and two other men Leine didn't recognize stood next to it. Two other vehicles were parked nearby. When they saw her pull in, they walked over to the SUV.

Santa leaned through the window and peered into the back seat.

"*Hola,*" he said to the children.

"*Hola,*" came several quiet replies.

He turned to Leine. "You're bleeding."

Leine followed his gaze. The bloodstain on her sleeve had grown. She'd put pressure near the wound and had stanched the flow temporarily, but it hadn't been enough.

"Bob's got a first aid kit in his truck," he said.

Herrera opened the passenger door to count heads. The other two men stood a short distance away.

"Yep. Twelve. Just like the report says," he said to them.

"Report?" Leine asked.

"I checked to see if there had been any reports of missing kids out of La Paz, and bingo—two days ago, twelve kids on a field trip went missing." He leaned against the seat. "I called the mayor to let him know we found them. He's sending the parents on a school bus to pick them up."

He turned to the kids. "Did you hear that?" he said. "The mayor himself is sending a bus to bring you all home." Cheers erupted from the backseat.

Leine glanced in the rearview mirror. Several of them gazed longingly at the man behind the *carne asada* counter, carving up what was left of a pig. The smell of seared meat wafted through the window, reminding Leine how hungry she was, let alone twelve kids who'd been kidnapped two days before.

She gave Santa a meaningful look. "I'll bet they're starved after what they've been through," she said. Santa smiled.

"Who wants a taco?"

It had grown dark by the time Santa changed the bandage on her arm and Leine and the children had eaten. Herrera introduced the two men with him as fellow DEA agents.

"I have reason to believe Elise Bennett is being held against her will at Felix Otero's whorehouse," Leine said. She relayed the information from Zamir's gunman to Herrera and the other two agents.

"That's the place," Herrera confirmed. "We'll make sure the right people know."

"I'm willing to do reconnaissance," Leine continued, "if you'll wait to contact your people until I report back. I'm worried what might happen to Elise in the raid."

Herrera considered her offer. "I'll hold off for a few hours," he said, glancing at his watch. "I assume you're going with her?" he asked Santa.

"Yes."

"Just remember, you're not here. Keep your ass under the radar."

With Herrera's blessing, she and Santa said goodbye to the kids and left in Herrera's truck. Bob and the other agents would stay with the children until the bus showed up to take them home. Then they'd comb through Zamir's SUV.

They followed the main highway south and then west, driving past empty, half-finished houses and stores, the occasional steer, and billboards to now-defunct hotels and restaurants.

The warm evening air flowed through the window, the smell of Baja del Norte redolent with dust and asphalt, the faint, briny scent of the sea, the weight of life's many detours—some good, some not. Leine's memories of the country were tinged with blood—a byproduct of her former life and, apparently, the life she led now.

She glanced at Santa and her face warmed. He always managed to be there when she needed him.

Besides April, this man is the best part of my life.

Leine mentally shook off the unfamiliar sentiment and focused.

"The driver said Belinda Bennett betrayed the man who kidnapped Elise." She leaned back and watched the play of headlights on the shadowy desert terrain.

Santa glanced at her. "You don't think he meant the ransom?"

"No. He said a man named Ivan was using Elise to force Belinda Bennett to pay up. When she didn't come through with the money, he sold her to Otero to recoup his losses. Apparently he has a deal where Otero pays him a percentage of earnings."

"What earnings? I thought Bob said Otero kept these girls as a kind of perk for his employees."

"It's possible he charges other men who aren't in his organization to use them." She hoped they weren't too late.

Several kilometers later, a sign above a metal gate materialized to their left that read *El Rancho del Maestro*. Santa slowed to a stop.

"The ranch of the master?" Santa shook his head. "This guy's got a serious case of egomania."

"I think it might refer to God, although it could be all about Otero. He's known to be a religious zealot."

"I wonder how he justifies prostituting young women against their will."

"Or running a criminal enterprise." Leine scanned the darkness beyond the gate, focusing on a speck of light in the distance. "Looks like the ranch is a couple of kilometers that way."

Santa put the truck in gear and continued past the entrance to the ranch. They drove up a slight rise and then back down the other side. At the bottom he headed off-road, following a wash into the desert, paralleling the ranch. When the wash petered out Santa cut the lights. He climbed up another rise and parked. After rummaging around in the console, he handed her a pair of night vision binoculars and a handheld radio.

They walked to the crest of the next hill and stopped. Santa had gotten close enough to the ranch to give them a good visual of the three main buildings. Several lights burned from the windows of one of the two farmhouse-like structures. Snippets of raucous laughter, music, and the occasional slam of a screen door floated toward them through the still desert air.

In contrast, a solitary light had been left on in a room on the first floor of the main farmhouse and one on the porch. The structure was oddly silent. The dark upper level matched the single story building at the back of the property. Two guards with machine guns patrolled the grounds facing the road, and another walked the perimeter. There didn't appear to be any other security.

"We need to approach from different angles," Santa said. "I'll take north, you come in from the west."

"Sounds like a plan." She switched on both radios and keyed the mic. "Once for copy that, twice for what the hell did you say?"

Santa nodded. "Meet you back here in thirty minutes."

Leine checked her watch—seven thirty. She secured her radio to a belt loop and headed for the back of the compound.

She'd made it to within a hundred yards of the dark, one-story building when Santa's voice came over the radio.

"Motion cameras."

Leine keyed the mic and scanned the roofline. It didn't take her long to spot the video camera mounted on the front of the building. Otero wanted the girls to know he was watching.

She checked to make sure there was no one nearby and then sprinted to the side of the building, keeping to the shadows. Her back to the wall, she inched her way toward the front, staying out of camera range. She reached the end and glanced at the angle of the lens, and determined that if she remained flat against the wall, she could continue undetected.

She peered around the corner and figured she was about three meters from the door. Leine slipped past the camera and reached for the handle.

"*Hola.*"

Leine froze, her hand halfway to the doorknob. She turned slowly. A rail-thin boy of about twelve or thirteen stood behind her, his arm held close to his side.

"Who are you?" he asked in Spanish, cocking his head.

Better just run with it, she thought.

"My name is Lana. What's yours?"

The boy's face split into a grin and he nodded. His head and neck moved as though loosely attached, like a bobblehead doll.

"My name is Sebastian and I live here. Where do you live?"

Leine started to breathe again. He wasn't concerned about her being there. She glanced behind them in case anyone else wanted to join the party, but there wasn't a soul nearby. It would only be a matter of time before someone showed up. She ushered him around the side of the building.

"I live north of here." She smiled back at him. "Maybe you can help me. I'm looking for this girl." She slid Elise's picture out of her back pocket and, using a penlight for illumination, showed it to him.

He squinted at the photo and nodded enthusiastically. Leine's heart beat faster.

"That's Elise. She's very nice," he said, lowering his gaze.

"Yes, she is nice. Do you know where she is? I have something important to give her."

Sebastian shook his head, his eyes glistening with tears. He opened his mouth several times to speak but couldn't, apparently overwhelmed with emotion.

Leine's breath caught in her throat. *Oh, God. I'm too late,* she thought. The crushing guilt of not finding Elise in time gripped her like a dead weight.

"What happened? Is she all right?" Leine asked.

Tears streaked down his cheeks. He wiped his nose on his sleeve.

"I—I don't know. Nobody can find her. I think she's lost."

She's still alive, Leine thought with a jolt. *Maybe.*

"Do you think something happened to her?"

Sebastian shrugged, misery obvious on his face.

"It wasn't my fault, I promise. I told Master Garcia and he got mad."

"Why was Master Garcia mad?"

"Because I made her lost."

Sebastian broke down sobbing. Afraid his crying might attract attention, Leine put an arm around his shoulders and pulled him further from the front of the building. He willingly followed.

"Shh, Sebastian. It's okay. I'm sure Master Garcia doesn't think you lost Elise."

Sebastian grew quiet but the tears continued.

"Yes, he does. He told me."

"When's the last time you saw her?"

Sebastian gulped in air and wiped his eyes. "After dinner. I usually help with the dishes and then I have an hour to play. She asked me to show her and Julia how big the ranch is, so I did." His face fell. "But when I said we had to go back, they kept walking."

Leine took him gently by the shoulders and looked him in the eyes. Working to keep her voice calm, she said, "Who is Julia?"

"She lives here. She's got red hair, and she's nice, too."

They're both trying to escape. "What time is dinner?"

"Six thirty and seven o'clock. We eat at different times so it doesn't take so long to get our food."

"What time did Elise and her friend find you? Six thirty or seven?"

Sebastian thought for a moment. "It was during the first time."

Six thirty. "Can you show me where? Maybe I can find them both."

The tears slowed and he gazed back at Leine, his expression

grave. "Master Garcia already sent Max to find them. If he can't find them, no one can."

"Max must be very good at finding people. Did he take a car?"

Sebastian smiled through his tears. "Max can't drive," he said, as though she'd just said the funniest thing he'd ever heard. "He's a dog."

37

WITHOUT MUCH PROMPTING, Sebastian led her to the place where he'd told the girls they couldn't go any farther. Leine waited until the perimeter guard passed by before they left. They walked north, into the desert for about twenty minutes before they stopped next to an old *palo verde* with a thick trunk. Leine called Santa on the radio.

"Elise escaped. Meet me two clicks north of the compound." She read him the coordinates from the phone. "I'm next to a big *palo verde*."

Santa keyed the mic once, indicating he copied.

"This is the place you can't cross." Sebastian rotated in a circle, his arm outstretched. "There's an invisible line all the way around the ranch, and we aren't allowed to go beyond it."

"What happens if you do?"

"Master Garcia gets very angry and sends Max and Cruz out here to find you."

Leine fished the small flashlight from her pocket and directed the beam at the ground. She made a few passes along where he'd indicated but saw nothing. Then she checked the tree. A small solar-powered box was attached. She shined the light in front of her and walked a straight line to another tree about five yards away, where she found a second box.

"Sebastian, do the girls have to wear anything they can't take off, like an ankle band?"

He frowned and shook his head. "No."

"How about an arm band or maybe a necklace?"

"No. Master Garcia doesn't like them to wear jewelry. Except…"

"Except what?"

The whites of Sebastian's eyes glowed in the darkness. "I—I gave her a magic bracelet. Do you think she'll get in trouble?" Panic filled his voice.

"I'm sure what you did was fine," Leine soothed. "Magic bracelets are usually a good thing, right?"

Sebastian sighed. "Yes. That's what the man told me. Do you know what time it is?"

Leine glanced at her watch. "Eight fifteen."

His eyes grew wide and a panicked look crossed his face. "Eight o'clock is my bedtime. Master Garcia will be angry with me if I'm not there."

The raid was still hours away and Leine didn't want to arouse suspicion. Keeping him there would probably be the worst thing she could do.

"Are you sure you can find your way back okay?" she asked.

"Yes. I do it all the time."

"Will you promise me one thing?"

"Yes."

"Will you promise you won't tell anyone about me? I want to find Elise, but I need it to be a surprise, okay?"

"Okay. I promise." Sebastian smiled and dipped his head up and down. "I hope you find her. She's nice." He turned and faced the ranch, lights twinkling in the distance. "It was good to meet you," he said, and headed back toward the lights of the ranch.

Leine watched him until he disappeared into the shadows before slipping behind the tree to wait for Santa. A short time later, she heard rocks skitter to her left.

"Leine?" Santa's low voice carried in the stillness.

"Here," she said, stepping from behind the tree.

"Elise escaped?"

"I just had a conversation with a boy named Sebastian who works at the ranch. Turns out, he unwittingly showed her which way to go. She and another girl took off almost two hours ago. Otero's using a dog to track them."

"Where's Sebastian now?"

"I had to let him go. He's a special needs kid, and it sounds like Otero keeps close track of him. I made him promise not to tell anyone about me." Leine smiled at the alarm on Santa's face. "It's the best I could do. We're going to have to trust him."

"Since when did you trust anyone?" Santa asked, pulling out his phone.

"Tonight." She glanced at the cell. "Texting Herrera?"

He nodded. The screen lit the contours of his face as his thumbs flew over the keys.

She turned on her flashlight and walked over to the *palo verde.* "I figured out why the ranch isn't heavily guarded. Otero installed electronic monitoring." She shined the light on the sensor attached to the tree trunk. "I assume the girls all wear some kind of tracking device that trips the sensor when they go where they're not supposed to."

"Otherwise it would trip each time a rabbit passed by."

"Right. Which means Otero's guy will lead us directly to them."

"Then we'd better get going," Santa said. They hurried back to the truck and climbed inside.

Santa slipped on a pair of night vision goggles from the console and drove through the desert with the lights off, methodically working a grid pattern moving them north in increments. Leine scanned the area with the binoculars, looking for any indication of the girls' location. At one point, she thought she saw a flash of headlights, but when they crested the next rise there was nothing but black terrain capped with glimmering stars.

Half an hour in, Santa stopped the vehicle and turned to Leine.

"You know," he said, "it's more than likely Otero's guys have night vision capabilities. We may not see anything unless we're right on top of them."

"I'm not giving up. We can go back the way we came if we don't find them."

"I didn't suggest stopping. Just wanted you to be aware of the possibility."

"Got it." Her words came out clipped.

Santa sighed and shifted into gear.

Elise ran as fast as the rough terrain would allow, ignoring the sharp branches that scraped against her legs. She stumbled and her bare foot landed on a section of cholla. She cried out as the spines embedded themselves in the soles of her feet. Her lungs bursting, she hopped away from the cactus on one foot and carefully lowered herself to the ground. She crossed her leg, bringing her foot up onto her thigh and began to pick out the spines. The barbed hooks didn't want to come easily, and she grimaced as she yanked them out. After the last one she rubbed the holes where they'd been and looked in the direction Julia had gone, hoping her friend had covered more ground than she had.

A pair of headlights headed in the same direction she'd run.

How could they know where Julia was? Her heart slammed in her chest. *It's pitch black out here.* They had to have night vision goggles. She scrambled to her feet.

They'll come for me next.

"THERE—" LEINE POINTED TO A FLASH OF HEADLIGHTS IN THE distance.

Santa drove toward them, steering around cactus and creosote bush. Leine leaned through the open window. The pair of headlights turned and headed east, bouncing like they were highlighting lyrics at a karaoke bar. She searched through the binoculars until she had the SUV in sight. She caught a glimpse of a dog's head through the passenger window.

"It's him," Leine said.

CRUZ GLANCED AT THE BLINKING DOT ON HIS MONITOR AND turned east.

Then it vanished.

"*¡Cabrone!*" He slammed his fist on the steering wheel in frustration. Max whined and paced in his seat. The transmitter was faulty. That could be the only explanation. He smacked the monitor but received no answering blip.

A low moan came from the cargo area. The redhead was waking up. He hadn't hit her hard enough.

"Shut up, *puta,* or you will die, now."

The moaning stopped.

He glared through the windshield, willing the American girl to materialize. He'd called in the redhead's capture to keep

Garcia from sending more trackers, but that didn't give him a lot of time to find her and do what he wanted to them both.

He drove toward the last location on the monitor, but then stopped the SUV, cut the lights, and shifted into park. Rifle in hand, Cruz exited the vehicle and looked east through the night vision scope, scanning the desert.

The landscape glowed from ambient starlight, the bushes and cactus dark, amorphous shadows. A coyote darted between the chaparral and slipped back into the night. The wind picked up, rustling through the sparse vegetation. Still, he saw no one.

White-hot anger boiled through him, and he had to consciously relax his grip on the rifle. Breathing heavily, Cruz glanced through the window at the monitor. Two dots.

The transmitter was working.

ELISE RAN BLINDLY THROUGH THE DESERT, THE SOUND OF A vehicle approaching from behind spurring her forward. She tripped again and fell to her hands and knees. A sob escaped her as she clambered to her feet.

I will not let them take me again, she said to herself, pushing through the pain. *Just keep going, Elise. One foot in front of the other. You'll be fine.*

"How much is that doggie..." The faint strain of music floating toward her was familiar and she glanced over her shoulder, confused by the innocuous song. Too late she turned back, stumbling as her foot hit air. Elise fell over the edge of the arroyo, hitting the loose dirt with her forearm and knees and skidding down, down, down, grasping at the spiky vegetation and roots, ripping them free until she hit bottom with a sickening thud.

Dazed and unable to pull in a breath, she rolled to one side and raised herself onto her elbow, placing her other hand on the ground for support. At the same time, she registered something hard and smooth beneath her.

That's when the stench hit.

Gagging, she recoiled and snatched her hand back from something wriggling, and scrambled to her feet, blood roaring in her ears.

A vehicle pulled up behind her, the headlights spilling past, illuminating the ground. Elise blanched at the sight of writhing maggots crawling where her hand had just been. She recognized the shredded blue dress and froze.

"Oh my God," she whispered.

The runaway's corpse lay face up, staring at the desert sky. Her dress had been ripped in two down the front, leaving her body exposed. A jagged gash formed a dark river of blood from her ribcage to her navel, and her intestines stretched across the sandy riverbed, dragged from her abdomen by a scavenger and partially consumed. Dozens of gleaming skulls wearing macabre smiles lay scattered across the wash around her, perched atop piles of bones picked clean. The tattered remnants of their blue shifts hung across bleached white ribcages, and hips, and femurs.

Elise's breath caught when she recognized another victim, face down in the pile of death, her scalp half gone, the familiar black hair a mat of dried blood.

Celeste.

A low growl erupted behind her. Elise slowly turned, nausea building in her chest.

Backlit by the lights of the SUV, Cruz stood in front of the vehicle, a rifle in his hand. A few feet from her the angry pit bull stood coiled and ready, lips curled back in a snarl and ears flat against its head.

Elise's body began to shake and she closed her eyes, unable to stem the tears rolling down her face.

"No, no, no," she whispered.

The dog's growls grew louder and more menacing.

"You'll just have to wait, Max," Cruz murmured, standing next to the canine. "You can have your time with the American bitch. I promise." He stepped forward and grabbed Elise by the hair, yanking her back toward the truck.

"Stop. Please," she cried. "I'll do whatever you want."

He jerked her head back, and her scalp burned with pain. The dog man dragged her to his vehicle and released his grip, dropping her next to the front tire. The dog shadowed her, standing guard. Cruz walked to the back of the SUV and opened the tailgate. Julia spilled onto the ground in an immobile heap. Elise gaped at her friend, willing her to move.

She didn't.

"What have you done?" Elise screamed. "You killed her, didn't you?" She struggled to stand, her rage spurring her on. Cruz watched her with amusement. With a deep growl Max charged her, snapping at her legs, coming within a hairs breadth of her skin. Elise froze, folding in on herself, her gaze to the ground.

A large rock rested near her foot.

Something inside her snapped. She stooped to pick up the rock and hurled it at the dog's head. It slammed home with a thud and the pit bull yelped and ran, shaking off the pain. Redhot rage welled up inside of Elise, blotting out everything else as she glared at the dog man. Seething with anger, she pressed forward, her chest rising and falling with each breath.

Cruz brought the rifle up, taking a step back as she advanced. "Stop now or you will die."

"Then shoot me." She ground out the words.

A flash of anger traced through his eyes. He raised the barrel of the gun and looked through the sight, his finger on the trigger.

"Stop!"

Cruz spun in place, swinging his rifle toward the voice. A sharp *crack* came from behind him and his head snapped forward, the side of his skull exploding in bits of bone and flesh.

38

———

ELISE STARED AT the dog man's inert body, visibly trembling. Leine stepped into the headlights and walked slowly toward her.

"It's all right, Elise. It's over," Leine said.

Elise's gaze shifted from the man on the ground to Leine to the gun in her hand, fear flickering in her eyes. Leine leaned the MP-5 against the front of the SUV and continued her careful approach.

"How much is that dog—"

Santa emerged from the left and Elise's attention snapped to him. She tracked him as he walked to the passenger side of the SUV and reached through the open window. Mercifully, the song stopped.

"There's a monitor in here." He opened the door and slid into the passenger seat.

Leine scanned Elise, looking for anything that might be transmitting their position. She wasn't wearing shoes, and her thin clothing didn't have buttons. *No rings or a necklace.* "Can I see your bracelet?"

Elise looked at her wrist as though she'd never seen it before. She held out her arm, and Leine unfastened the piece.

"Sebastian gave it to me. He said it was magic."

"It's magnetic," Leine said, studying the back.

"I've got two blinking dots," Santa called. He exited the cab and walked behind the SUV to see to Julia.

Leine nodded toward Elise's arm. "What happened to you?"

Elise glanced at the bandage and frowned. "I think they took a skin sample to check how healthy I was."

"May I?" Leine asked, reaching for her arm. Elise nodded. Leine peeled back the bandage and gently probed the skin around the incision. "There's a hard lump under your skin."

"I thought it was scabbing up."

"I think a transmitter has been implanted in your arm." She handed Elise the bracelet. "Put this back on and keep it near the bandage. The magnets must interfere with the signal."

Elise attached the bracelet. Her gaze skated toward the girl lying on the ground behind the SUV. "My friend—is she—"

"I've got a pulse," Santa called.

Its head down, the pit bull crawled into view, sliding on its belly toward Cruz. Blood dripped from its ear. Whimpering, it snuffled at what was left of his master's head and nosed his shoulder, trying to get him to move.

Elise's knees wobbled. Leine grabbed her by the elbow and wrapped her arm around her shoulders.

"Come and sit down," she said, leading her away from the mass grave to the back of the SUV. Julia lay on her side in the cargo area and Santa was in the process of checking her vitals. Leine eased Elise into a sitting position. "I'll be right back," she said and started to walk away. Elise's eyes widened and she grabbed Leine's hand.

"Don't leave me," she said, her voice cracking.

Leine's heart squeezed tight and she stopped, waiting for Elise to relax her grip.

"It's all right, Elise. I'm coming right back." She nodded at Santa. "That's Santa. He's one of the good guys, I promise."

Elise studied the detective, who was now rubbing Julia's legs and feet, trying to restore circulation.

"I'm going to get water for you and a blanket for your friend, okay?"

"Okay," she whispered, releasing Leine's arm.

When Leine returned with the pickup, Elise's complexion didn't appear as colorless as it had before, although she had a long way to go before she normalized. *She's crashing,* Leine thought. She handed a blanket from Herrera's truck to Santa and her own jacket and a bottle of water to Elise.

"How many girls does Garcia keep at the ranch?" Leine asked, checking the cuts on Elise's legs and feet.

Elise took a sip of water and wiped her mouth.

"All of them, I think. I'm not sure." She stared into the dark night.

Leine cleared her throat and she refocused.

"There were close to thirty girls in the room where I slept," she said. "There might be more, I don't know."

"Thank you, Elise. Sit tight. We'll be on our way in a couple of minutes."

Leine motioned for Santa to follow her. He finished wrapping Julia in the blanket and walked around to the side.

"The mass grave has to be Otero's handiwork," she said, indicating the arroyo in front of them.

They walked closer to the bodies, shining flashlights on the gruesome scene before them.

"They've been gutted," Santa remarked.

"The clothing is similar to what Elise and her friend are wearing." Leine closed her eyes as a curtain of weariness descended over her. "Looks like this is where they dumped the bodies of the girls who were no longer useful."

"Jesus," Santa breathed. He shook his head and slid his phone out of his pocket. "This is the end of Garcia and *El Rancho del Maestro.*"

Leine studied the grisly scene before her, taking it in, letting it settle deep in her bones.

I'm sorry I didn't find you sooner.

39

HERRERA WAS ABLE to expedite Leine's and Elise's trip back to Los Angeles, while Julia formally requested asylum. Gunderson and Nabokov were on their way to the federal detention center where she was being held to secure her release. Santa drove back to Los Angeles early the next day.

Elise was immediately put under protective custody at an undisclosed private hospital. Dick Bennett rushed to Elise's side as soon as he learned of her rescue. Belinda Bennett couldn't be reached.

The lacerations on her back and feet were healing, and Elise insisted she was ready to go home but soon learned that the transmitter would need to be surgically removed from her arm before her release.

Leine arrived at the hospital about an hour after Elise's father. Dick Bennett appeared gaunt with dark circles under his eyes. His clothes looked as though he'd slept in them for a week. When Leine asked how he was doing, he shook his head.

"The stress is unbelievable. The IPO's happening tomorrow, ready or not. I'm just relieved you found her."

"Where's Mom?" Elise asked.

Dick smiled and reached for her hand. "She'll be here soon, baby. Promise."

When the nurse came in to check her vitals, Leine and Dick Bennett walked out to the hallway to allow them privacy. He leaned against the wall and sighed. The policeman assigned to security stepped a discreet distance away.

"Where is Mrs. Bennett?" Leine asked.

Dick Bennett shrugged. "I honestly can't tell you. I've been at the office working around the clock. I tried her cell, but she's not picking up. I left a message, so I'm sure she'll be here soon."

"I'm sure she will," Leine replied.

He spoke of how he was going to take the time to be a better father, really listen to Elise, get involved in the high school and all her activities. Leine wondered how that would be possible, now that he was obligated to investors.

Not your problem, Leine. She remained silent, allowing him his moment, hoping he meant what he said.

When the nurse was finished, Leine said her goodbyes to Elise and Dick and went out to her car.

It was time to confront Belinda Bennett.

Leine drove the last mile up the curving canyon road and parked in the shade beneath a tree near the Bennetts' driveway. Careful to avoid the camera, she slipped through the open gate. The green light she'd noticed on her first visit now glowed orange.

The gate combined with the security camera's orange indicator light gave her pause and she drew her gun. The entrance to the Bennetts' driveway had been open on her prior visit because they'd been expecting her, but at that time the green light indicated the security camera's normal operation. An orange light generally meant there'd either been a technical failure or a manual override.

Either whoever was inside the house had taken the security system off line, or Belinda had been expecting someone and didn't want a record of the visit. Neither of which boded well.

As she neared the top of the drive, she recognized Belinda's black Mercedes parked next to the '61 Ferrari she'd seen the last time. Both vehicles were near the entrance. Like before, the garage door leading to the lower level under the home was open.

An unfamiliar SUV took up residence at the other end of the drive. At first she didn't see anyone nearby. As she drew level with the Mercedes, a tattooed man with a shaved head wearing a gray T-shirt appeared at the garage entrance and started up the driveway toward her. Leine dropped to a crouch behind the car.

A slight breeze kicked up and she glanced behind her. The leaves shading her car danced in the wind, the sunlight glinting off the windshield.

Can he see that? She turned back.

There was no sign of him, but the front door of the SUV was open.

Shit. Where the hell did he go? Leine quickly slid the suppressor from her side pocket and screwed it on as she scanned the area. Something flashed in the Mercedes' outside mirror and she turned. The man was coming up behind her in a crouch, his gun out.

Leine pivoted, tracking his approach in the mirror. When he drew level with the back window, she fired.

The bullet carved into his forehead and he staggered, crumpling to the ground. Sprawled on his back, his sightless eyes stared at the brilliant California sky.

It was the same man she'd seen in the photograph with Zamir.

Leine waited a moment to be sure no one else had heard the discharge and then evaluated her options. Gaining entry was her first priority.

She followed the walk to the entrance and tried the front door. It was locked. She considered using the burglar tools in her pocket but decided instead to try an alternative. Skirting the dead gunman she followed the driveway into the garage under the home.

As she suspected, a stairway as well as a small elevator led to the upper level from the garage. Leine sprinted silently up the stairs and tried the door leading into the house. It was open. She eased into the hallway.

Listening to the rhythm of the air conditioning and other typical house noises, Leine eased past a laundry room and small bathroom, and paused near the entrance to the kitchen.

Satisfied she was alone, Leine proceeded through the living area and slipped down a long corridor that led to the back of the house. Angry voices floated toward her from a room at the end of the hall. She edged closer, her footsteps silent against the marble tile.

"You've run out of options, Belinda," offered the cool voice. The man's accent pegged him as one of Zamir's associates. "Now that your daughter is safe, I have no recourse but to extract my payment from you and your husband."

"You must do as he says, Mrs. Bennett, or he will kill us both." Teuta's desperation came through loud and clear.

"It can't be undone," Belinda Bennett's voice cracked. "They already have the information. After tomorrow, Zorbane will control the company."

"I don't care about your husband's fucking IPO. I care about the formula, and you have access."

"No, I don't. Dick keeps the password for the system on an encrypted website. His partner has the second password, and you need them both. If anyone attempts to obtain the information without the two-step verification process, the files will disappear. You have to believe me, Ivan."

"He will do anything you tell him to do. Your death is too high a price for his silence. Call him."

"Mrs. Bennett, *please…*" Teuta sounded on the verge of tears.

"Take the Ferrari, Ivan. It's worth millions," Belinda pleaded. "I'll pay you the rest, I promise."

"Your promises are worthless." Ivan scoffed. "The car would not even be a down payment."

Leine inched her way toward the open door. A crescent-shaped steel desk was visible to her left. The reflection from a glass-fronted painting on the far wall showed Ivan with his back to the door.

"We will see how you feel when your body struggles for air."

"No—stop! What are you—"

The sound of tape ripping told her Ivan had grown tired of talking. Belinda's muffled protests were soon drowned out by rustling plastic.

Leine went low and moved silently through the doorway into the room. Belinda sat at the far end, her wrists and ankles duct taped to a chair with her back to a gas fireplace. Ivan was in the process of securing a dry cleaner bag over her head. With each shallow breath the thin plastic shrank in size, conforming to the contours of her face, revealing her distorted, panicked features, and billowed out with each exhale.

Teuta had been taped to another chair next to her employer. She watched Ivan, her expression a mixture of fear and anger. The housekeeper's eyes widened in surprise as Leine stood up and sighted on the back of Ivan's skull. Alerted by Teuta's sharp intake of breath, he turned.

Ivan dropped to the floor as Leine pulled the trigger. The bullet pierced the wall above the fireplace. Leine tracked him, firing as he dove for cover behind a nearby sofa. He grunted and his gun clattered to the floor.

She crouched down and peered under the sofa. Ivan lay lengthwise on the marble tile, stretching for his gun. Leine emptied her magazine into him.

"Mrs. Bennett! She is dying," Teuta cried, straining at the tape around her wrists.

Leine closed the distance between them and ripped the bag open. Belinda gasped, sucking in gulps of air.

"Thank God you're here," Belinda wheezed. "He was going to kill me."

"What the hell did you think would happen?" Leine asked. She stepped behind the sofa to make sure Ivan was dead. There was no pulse. Leine returned to the two women and slid her knife from the sheath attached to her leg.

"Ivan was a friend of Dick's business partner—"

Leine bent to cut through Teuta's restraints. "Zamir Ristani? You need to choose better associates, Belinda."

"I'll have you know, Zamir has connections worldwide."

"Had, you mean."

Leine felt Teuta stiffen. She glanced sharply at the house-keeper. "You knew Zamir?"

Teuta relaxed and shook her head. "Only from Bennetts. They say he is-was good man."

"Yeah. Not so much." Leine finished cutting through Teuta's restraints and straightened.

"Aren't you going to free me?" Belinda asked, frowning.

"Are you aware that your daughter has checked into a private hospital?" Leine asked her.

"Where is she?" Belinda Bennett struggled against the tape. "Let me go. I need to see her."

Teuta rose from the chair, her movements stiff, and crossed to the sofa to look at Ivan's dead body.

"I'm sure you'll get to see her soon." Leine brought out her phone. "But first, I'm going to call a friend of mine and see what they want to do with you. Can't have you leaving the country now, can we?"

There was a flash of movement in her periphery and she turned.

Teuta held Ivan's gun in her hand. Leine dove behind the chair. Bullets sliced through the air, the rounds shredding the room around her. Ears ringing, Leine rolled onto her side and rose to one knee, her knife in her hand.

Teuta ducked behind the sofa, moving too quickly for Leine to hit her.

What the hell? Why is Teuta trying to kill me?

"It's over, Teuta. Ivan's dead." She reached above her to see if Belinda had a pulse. Her hand came away slick with blood. *Correction. Why is Teuta trying to kill Belinda?*

"He was vicious man. You have done favor for world."

"Ivan was your boss, is that it?" Leine asked, peering around the side of the chair to get a bead on the housekeeper. *Teuta must have been spying on Elise for Ivan. That's how he knew she was in Tijuana.* A slice of shadow on the wall indicated she was using Ivan's body for cover.

"I have no boss," she said, her voice dripping disdain. "He was employee who did not follow instructions."

"You mean when he kidnapped Elise?" Leine scanned the room for better cover. A coffee table with a marble top stood a couple of feet behind her.

"When he sold her. It was then I knew he make irreversible mistake. Otero will never give her up. We lost bargaining power."

"So your concern for Elise was an act?" Leine asked.

"A spoiled child," she said, contempt littering her words. "Just like her mother."

Leine wiped the perspiration from her forehead with the back of her hand and slid her pistol from her waistband. She ejected the spent mag and snapped in fresh ammunition from the side pocket of her cargo pants. Her old rib injury throbbed and blood from the gunshot wound stained her shirtsleeve. Again.

Goddammit. When this is over, I'm taking a month off.

"Well, Teuta, it looks like we're at an impasse. What do you want to do?"

There was the sound of shuffling, followed by a pause. "I do not wish to kill you, Leine Basso."

"That's awfully kind of you, but I'm sure you can understand that's a little hard to believe at the moment."

Another pause. "We are two of a kind, you and I. You work for me, yes? I pay very, very well."

Seriously? Leine thought. *What is this, a fucking job interview?* Leine eyed the coffee table and calculated how long she'd be exposed if she turned it over to use for cover. If she could keep the housekeeper off balance, she thought she might make it without becoming target practice.

Depending on how good a shot Teuta was.

"I'm flattered, Teuta. But I'm afraid I've already got a job." Working for her was right up there with being on North Korean leader Kim Jong-un's payroll. Leine popped from behind the chair and squeezed the trigger, peppering the sofa with bullets. Return fire zinged past her from the right.

Leine lunged behind the table, pushing it onto its side.

The shots hadn't come from where she'd expected. The housekeeper had moved.

You're losing it, Leine. When the hell did she change position?

She scanned the room, searching for shadows. Something caught her eye and she backtracked. *There. Next to the door.*

Leine maneuvered herself into position on the other side of the upended coffee table and waited.

The housekeeper's shadow wavered on the wall as Teuta fired from behind the door. The bullets chipped at the marble tile and pinged off the corner of the table. Leine tracked her as she moved. She caught a glimpse of sleeve and fired.

The sharp intake of breath told her she'd hit the mark. Leine leaped to her feet and rushed Teuta's position, firing as she ran. The housekeeper burst from behind the door, gun in her left hand, hugging her right arm by her side.

Leine feinted right as a lamp exploded beside her, recovered and fired, hitting Teuta in the shoulder. Teuta cried out and gripped the wound. The gun clattered to the floor, skipping across the tile. Leine kicked the nine millimeter out of her reach and at the same time grabbed her wrist, twisting it behind her.

With a screech of pain, Teuta went slack and pivoted, but Leine pinned her other hand and wrenched it up between her shoulder blades.

"You're strong for your age," Leine said through gritted teeth. Despite being shot twice, Teuta raised her knee and brought the heel of her sensible shoe down, narrowly missing the delicate bones of Leine's foot.

Leine dragged her toward the sofa and seized a nearby lamp, yanking the cord from the wall socket. Teuta moaned as Leine wrapped it around her wrists and pushed her onto her knees.

Breathing heavily with one hand on her throbbing rib Leine gasped, "Stop it. Just stop, okay? It's over."

Teuta scowled at her and spit on the floor near her feet.

"What is it with you guys and spitting?" Leine asked, her irritation flaring. "I get it. You're pissed."

"You will regret this, Leine Basso. I swear on my mother's grave."

"I've never heard that one before," she said, the sarcasm thick in her voice. "How about something a little more original?"

Unwilling to let go of the feisty older woman, Leine dragged her across the floor toward the fireplace. Ivan had left the roll of duct tape on the mantel. Though the blood loss and trauma from the gunshot wounds was significant, the older woman gave no indication of distress other than ragged breathing, and her struggles made it supremely difficult for Leine to tape her ankles.

Tough woman, Leine thought. She found herself wondering about Teuta's training.

With the housekeeper suitably restrained, Leine hurried back to Belinda to see if she was still alive. Blood poured down the side of her face and torso. A reedy pulse beat weakly against Leine's fingers.

Leine found her phone and dialed 9-1-1.

40

S ANTA BROKE AWAY from the embrace first and picked up her bag. Leine's stomach growled at the aroma of garlic and spices floating toward her from inside the apartment. "That smells incredible. What is it?"

"Dinner," Santa said over his shoulder.

Leine followed him through the living room and into the kitchen, taking note of the glass vase filled with a variety of multi-colored tulips—her favorite flower—as well as several lit candles on a table set for two. An open bottle of red wine and two glasses had been placed nearby.

Santa grabbed two hot pads off the counter and opened the oven, waving away the heat as he slid out a deep pan covered in banana leaves and set it on top of the stove. He dropped the pads and, using a fork, lifted one corner. Steam filled the air, and the mouthwatering smell of roasted meat, citrus, and pepper followed.

"*Cochinita Pibil,*" Santa said and stepped aside so Leine could see what was in the pan. She leaned over and inhaled the heady bouquet of the traditional, slow-roasted pork. The orange-red sauce bubbled in the pan.

"Mmm. What's the occasion? Leine asked. Santa had mentioned how his mother made the *pibil* days ahead by wrapping it in banana leaves and burying it in the ground, allowing the pork to cook slowly, giving the meat its famous, melt-in-your-mouth quality.

Santa shrugged. "I wanted to show you I'm more than just a pretty face."

Leine leaned over and gave him a proper kiss. "I already knew that."

"And, I wanted you to feel welcome in your new home."

Leine smiled. "My new home," she repeated. It sounded right. Ever since she'd finally decided to take the plunge and move in with Santa, she'd felt more settled. Calm.

Weird.

Two months had passed since they'd rescued Elise. The early morning raid by the Mexican Marines on *El Rancho del Maestro* made headlines across the Baja and mainland Mexico, as did the safe return of the twelve schoolchildren from La Paz. The disruption of Otero's operation was lauded as a significant victory in the war on human and organ trafficking. Both Felix Otero and Doctor Raul Ramirez were taken into custody by the marines, and many of the young women being kept at the ranch were released to their grateful families. Those with no friends or relatives in Mexico were taken to a holding facility and given access to a phone and email. The Catholic Church offered to help locate the families of the girls who had no contact information. The church also offered to provide a home for Sebastian and the dog, Max, in exchange for help with serving meals and other chores.

Belinda Bennett had survived her gunshot wounds, but had been in a coma since the shooting. The prognosis wasn't good. Dick Bennett had made good on his promise to be more involved in his daughter's life and, as a result, Elise was now researching medical schools to attend. When Leine met with her for coffee the week before, she'd marveled at the change in the young woman's priorities. Elise had confided that when she went back to hanging out with her old friends she realized Brittany was the only person with whom she had anything left in common. She even changed her blog from *Beverly Hills Blonde—Rich and Loving It!* to *Beverly Hills Backers*—an online community of young adult angel investors based in the Beverly Hills area who were interested in backing socially responsible startups.

Leine had called Vlad to make sure Grigori and his shipment arrived in time and intact, and to inquire about his wife's health. He assured her all was well and that they were now "square," but that he'd keep her contact information in his database for future jobs. Immediately after their conversation Leine bought a new phone and changed her number.

Yeah, that is so not going to happen.

She watched as Santa dished up the *cochinita pibil*, her gaze wandering from his hands to his handsome face, to the way his jeans caressed his hips, and sighed contentedly. For the first time in a long time, Leine Basso had found a home.

Ready for more heart-stopping action? Start reading *Cargo*, the next page-turning thriller in the Leine Basso thriller series!

ACKNOWLEDGMENTS

I'd like to thank the following people for their amazing help and support in writing *The Body Market*: Mark Lindstrom—your mind is incredibly devious, and I love every twisted brain cell in it; my editor, Laurie Boris—without your talents and super-human attention to detail the book wouldn't be nearly as good, not to mention as error-free; Al Kunz, for much the same; my stalwart writing group: Ali Mosa, Jenni Conner, Darlene Panzera, Sharon Kleve—you guys are the best writing partners a girl could have, and keep me from writing plot holes the size of planets; The Bodacious Betas: Ruth M. Ross-Saucier, Michelle Yelland, Brian Yelland, Bev Van Berkom, Larry Van Berkom, TSODA134—your early input and exacting standards make the stories I write so much better; Linton Robinson for all the great information on Tijuana; Richard Buffington for the welding tutorial; Carly McElwee for putting up with my inane questions about texting and verbiage; Vicki Adams for some great plot ideas; and, last but not least, the ARC team: Barbara Rauch, Jen Blood, Sherry Fundin, Al Kunz, Carol Wyer, Cathy Speight, Trudy Brandenburg, Waynita Keeth-Suica, Garren Tooker, Sheli Story, Bill McElwee, Sonia Malingen, Kitty Wiemelt, and Charlie Ray. You guys ROCK.

ABOUT THE AUTHOR

DV Berkom is the USA Today bestselling author of riveting action-adventure and crime thrillers. Known for creating resilient, kick-ass female characters and page-turning plots, her love of the genre stems from a lifelong addiction to reading spy novels, thrillers, and action/adventure stories.

A restless soul and adventurer at heart, she spent years moving around the US and traveling to exotic locations before she wrote her first novel and was hooked. More than twenty books later, she now makes her home in the Pacific Northwest with her husband, Mark, and several imaginary characters who like to tell her what to do.

Her most recent books include Claire Whitcomb Westerns *Legend, Gunslinger,* and *Retribution,* and the Leine Basso thrillers *Terminal Threat, Fatal Objective, A Plague of Traitors,* and *Shadow of the Jaguar.* DV's currently hard at work on her next book.

For more information, visit her website at www.dvberkom.com. To be the first to hear about new releases and subscriber-only offers, go to: bit.ly/DVB_RL

ALSO BY D.V. BERKOM

Leine Basso Crime Thriller Series:

A Killing Truth

Serial Date

Bad Traffick

The Body Market

Cargo

The Last Deception

Dark Return

Absolution

Dakota Burn

Shadow of the Jaguar

A Plague of Traitors

Fatal Objective

Terminal Threat

Final Encounter (2024)

Kate Jones Adventure Thriller Series:

Kate Jones Thriller Series Vol. 1

Cruising for Death

Yucatán Dead

A One Way Ticket to Dead

Vigilante Dead

Claire Whitcomb Westerns:

Retribution

Gunslinger

Legend